PRAISE FOR THE NOVELS OF DANIELLE STEEL

"One of the things that keeps Danielle Steel fresh is her bent for timely storylines. . . . The combination of Steel's comprehensive research and her skill at creating credible characters makes for a gripping read."
—*Newark Star-Ledger*

"Danielle Steel has again uplifted her readers while skillfully communicating some of life's bittersweet verities. Who could ask for a finer gift than that?"
—*The Philadelphia Inquirer*

"A literary phenomenon . . . and not to be pigeonholed as one who produces a predictable kind of book."
—*The Detroit News*

"Steel knows how to wring the emotion out of the briefest scene." —*People*

"The world's most popular author tells a good, well-paced story and explores some important issues. . . . Steel affirm[s] life while admitting its turbulence, melodramas, and misfiring passions." —*Booklist*

"Steel is one of the best!" —*Los Angeles Times*

"Steel pulls out all the emotional stops. . . . She delivers." —*Publishers Weekly*

"Magical." —*Library Journal*

"What counts for the reader is the ring of authenticity."
—*San Francisco Chronicle*

"Danielle Steel writes boldly and with practiced vividness about tragedy—both national and personal . . . with insight and power." —*Nashville Banner*

By Danielle Steel

NEVER TOO LATE • UPSIDE DOWN • THE BALL AT VERSAILLES
SECOND ACT • HAPPINESS • PALAZZO • THE WEDDING PLANNER
WORTHY OPPONENTS • WITHOUT A TRACE • THE WHITTIERS
THE HIGH NOTES • THE CHALLENGE • SUSPECTS • BEAUTIFUL
HIGH STAKES • INVISIBLE • FLYING ANGELS • THE BUTLER
COMPLICATIONS • NINE LIVES • FINDING ASHLEY • THE AFFAIR
NEIGHBORS • ALL THAT GLITTERS • ROYAL • DADDY'S GIRLS
THE WEDDING DRESS • THE NUMBERS GAME • MORAL COMPASS
SPY • CHILD'S PLAY • THE DARK SIDE • LOST AND FOUND
BLESSING IN DISGUISE • SILENT NIGHT • TURNING POINT
BEAUCHAMP HALL • IN HIS FATHER'S FOOTSTEPS • THE GOOD FIGHT
THE CAST • ACCIDENTAL HEROES • FALL FROM GRACE
PAST PERFECT • FAIRYTALE • THE RIGHT TIME • THE DUCHESS
AGAINST ALL ODDS • DANGEROUS GAMES • THE MISTRESS
THE AWARD • RUSHING WATERS • MAGIC • THE APARTMENT
PROPERTY OF A NOBLEWOMAN • BLUE • PRECIOUS GIFTS
UNDERCOVER • COUNTRY • PRODIGAL SON • PEGASUS
A PERFECT LIFE • POWER PLAY • WINNERS • FIRST SIGHT
UNTIL THE END OF TIME • THE SINS OF THE MOTHER
FRIENDS FOREVER • BETRAYAL • HOTEL VENDÔME
HAPPY BIRTHDAY • 44 CHARLES STREET • LEGACY • FAMILY TIES
BIG GIRL • SOUTHERN LIGHTS • MATTERS OF THE HEART
ONE DAY AT A TIME • A GOOD WOMAN • ROGUE • HONOR THYSELF
AMAZING GRACE • BUNGALOW 2 • SISTERS • H.R.H. • COMING OUT
THE HOUSE • TOXIC BACHELORS • MIRACLE • IMPOSSIBLE
ECHOES • SECOND CHANCE • RANSOM • SAFE HARBOUR
JOHNNY ANGEL • DATING GAME • ANSWERED PRAYERS
SUNSET IN ST. TROPEZ • THE COTTAGE • THE KISS • LEAP OF FAITH
LONE EAGLE • JOURNEY • THE HOUSE ON HOPE STREET
THE WEDDING • IRRESISTIBLE FORCES • GRANNY DAN
BITTERSWEET • MIRROR IMAGE • THE KLONE AND I
THE LONG ROAD HOME • THE GHOST • SPECIAL DELIVERY
THE RANCH • SILENT HONOR • MALICE • FIVE DAYS IN PARIS
LIGHTNING • WINGS • THE GIFT • ACCIDENT • VANISHED
MIXED BLESSINGS • JEWELS • NO GREATER LOVE • HEARTBEAT
MESSAGE FROM NAM • DADDY • STAR • ZOYA • KALEIDOSCOPE
FINE THINGS • WANDERLUST • SECRETS • FAMILY ALBUM
FULL CIRCLE • CHANGES • THURSTON HOUSE • CROSSINGS
ONCE IN A LIFETIME • A PERFECT STRANGER • REMEMBRANCE
PALOMINO • LOVE: *POEMS* • THE RING • LOVING • TO LOVE AGAIN
SUMMER'S END • SEASON OF PASSION • THE PROMISE
NOW AND FOREVER • PASSION'S PROMISE • GOING HOME

Nonfiction
EXPECT A MIRACLE: *Quotations to Live and Love By*
PURE JOY: *The Dogs We Love*
A GIFT OF HOPE: *Helping the Homeless*
HIS BRIGHT LIGHT: *The Story of Nick Traina*

For Children
PRETTY MINNIE IN PARIS
PRETTY MINNIE IN HOLLYWOOD

Palazzo

DANIELLE STEEL

Palazzo

A Novel

Dell
New York

Palazzo is a work of fiction. Names, characters,
places, and incidents are the products of the author's
imagination or are used fictitiously. Any resemblance
to actual events, locales, or persons, living or dead,
is entirely coincidental.

2024 Dell Mass Market Edition

Copyright © 2023 by Danielle Steel
Excerpt from *Only the Brave* by Danielle Steel copyright
© 2024 by Danielle Steel

Published in the United States by Dell,
an imprint of Random House, a division of
Penguin Random House LLC, New York.

DELL and the D colophon are registered trademarks of
Penguin Random House LLC.

Originally published in hardcover in the United States by
Delacorte Press, an imprint of Random House, a division
of Penguin Random House LLC, in 2023.

This book contains an excerpt from the forthcoming
book *Only the Brave* by Danielle Steel. This excerpt has
been set for this edition only and may not reflect the
final content of the forthcoming edition.

ISBN 978-1-9848-2191-1
Ebook ISBN 978-1-9848-2190-4

Cover design: Derek Walls
Cover images: © Yodchai Prominn/Shutterstock (sky),
© DEEPOL by plainpicture/Frederic Cirou (buildings
and boats on the Grand Canal)

Printed in the United States of America

randomhousebooks.com

2 4 6 8 9 7 5 3 1

Dell mass market edition: April 2024

To my beloved children,
Beatie, Trevor, Todd, Nick, Samantha,
Victoria, Vanessa, Maxx, and Zara,

May your histories and your memories
be forever blessed by angels,
and cherished by each of you,
linked to each other by your memories,
kindness, compassion, forgiveness, love,
and gratitude for all that we have shared.

I love you with all my heart.
Mom/d.s.

Palazzo

Chapter 1

Cosima Saverio sat on the terrace of her penthouse apartment in Rome, looking out over the familiar monuments and rooftops of the city as the sun came up. In the distance, she could see Saint Peter's Basilica and Vatican City, the dome of the San Carlo al Corso Basilica, and to the north, the Villa Medici and the Borghese Gardens. It was a view she never tired of. It was her favorite time of day, before the city sprang to life. It was already warm and would be hot by midmorning. As she stood at the rail of the balcony a few minutes later, she could see below the Piazza di Spagna, the Spanish Steps, the Fontana della Barcaccia, and the Trinità dei Monti church.

The apartment was conveniently located on the top floor of the store, which was her family business. The Saverios made the finest leather goods in all of

Italy, or all of Europe, rivaled only by Hermès, which was a worldwide enterprise. Saverio leathers were sold only in their two stores, one in Venice, the other in Rome.

Like all of her ancestors, Cosima had been born in Venice, to an illustrious family that traced its history back to the fifteenth century. The Palazzo Saverio in Venice still belonged to them, although her father had moved the family to Rome shortly after her younger sister, Allegra, was born, and Cosima had lived in the same apartment with her parents and brother and sister on the top floor over the store almost all her life. Her younger brother, Luca, had his own villa now on the Via Appia Antica, and her sister lived in a smaller apartment on the floor below her, with a design studio. It was more convenient for Allegra because it had an elevator, which didn't go to the top floor. Cosima lived in solitary splendor in the same apartment she had grown up in. She reached the penthouse apartment by a narrow staircase, and the terrace gave her a three-hundred-and-sixty-degree view of the city she considered her home. Venice was their history, but Rome was where she lived and worked, and ran the family business she had inherited fifteen years before, at twenty-three.

As a young girl, it had never been her plan to run the business or even work there. When they were children, her father intended to have her younger brother, Luca, run it one day, and step into his shoes. Luca had never shown any interest in it, even as a boy. His friends had been the spoiled, indulged sons of other Italian noblemen, and he had a passion for fast cars and beautiful women at an early age. He didn't have his father's interest in business, or his grandfather's talent for creating beauty as a remarkable artisan. Ottavio Saverio had designed each piece for his shop in Venice, whether a saddle or an alligator handbag or an exquisite pair of custom-made shoes. People who were familiar with the finest of everything could recognize a piece created by Saverio anywhere.

Ottavio Saverio had been the eighth child and only son of a respected banker in Venice. He had inherited the palazzo in Venice by default when each of his sisters married and moved away to Florence, Rome, and other cities in Europe. None of them wished to be burdened by the palazzo where they'd grown up. It was four centuries old and troublesome and expensive to maintain. Ottavio had used his inheritance to buy all of his sisters' shares of the palazzo. He had used what was left to establish the store in one of the narrow streets off the Piazza San Marco where he created his magnificent leather pieces, and gained a reputation throughout Italy, and eventually Europe, for the exquisite work he did. Each piece was a masterpiece of beauty and luxury, made of the finest leathers and exotic skins. Every creation was unique at first. He filled the orders quickly and the business grew into an astonishing success in less than a decade. For all the years that he ran it, he was the master craftsman and genius behind the name. Saverio products were sold only at the store in Venice. Women waited a year or even two for their orders to be filled and were never disappointed by the results. Ottavio's list of clients included royals, famous women, movie stars, and wealthy people from all over the world.

His son and only child, Alberto, never became a craftsman like his father, although Ottavio made him study as an apprentice for two years so he would understand the products they were selling and how they were made. But Alberto was more interested in the business side of the store. Once he inherited the company, Alberto maintained his father's tradition that Saverio products were sold only in their own store and nowhere else.

When his father died, Alberto kept the store in Venice, and moved his wife, Tizianna, and their three children to Rome. He bought the building that still housed their store, and built the apartment that had previously been home to their whole family and where Cosima lived alone now on the top floor. She had designed Allegra's apartment on the floor below, when she was old enough to live alone, so they each had privacy. Luca had already moved out by then, when he turned twenty-one and Allegra was still only seventeen.

When their father opened the store in Rome, it

was spectacular and increased the business exponentially. Alberto had groomed his son to run the business ever since he was a little boy, but he had never succeeded in capturing Luca's interest. Luca neither understood nor cared about the magic of what they made.

What Alberto had wanted was to have their business grow without giving up any of his father's traditions. It was a fine line between the two, and Alberto had grandiose plans that were always just slightly more expensive to implement than he'd anticipated, so the business wasn't as profitable as it should have been. He had a flawless eye for quality and beauty and was an extremely elegant man himself. He and Tizianna were among the social leaders of both Venice and Rome and exuded an aura of elegance and style.

Cosima inherited some of that, but she had a more retiring nature than her parents and loved her studies. She'd always been relieved that she would never have to run the business. She worked at the store in Rome for a month every summer to please her father. She was a dutiful daughter. Luca managed to escape that because he was five years younger than Cosima, and Allegra was still a child.

In July and August the family went to their other home in Sardinia. They spent two months on the family's boats and entertaining the friends they invited to stay with them. Invitations to their home were greatly sought after. Alberto and Tizianna were fabulous hosts, and were invited everywhere in return, or by new friends in the hopes of being invited to stay in their home. They were generous with their hospitality and lavish with their guests. Cosima still remembered the extravagant parties her parents gave, both in their apartment in Rome and at the palazzo in Venice, where they held grand balls.

After lengthy discussions with her father, Cosima had chosen a career in the law. She went to university in Rome and lived at home. She loved her years at university, her studies, and the friends she made. Her father teased her that she would be the attorney for the business one day. He never expected her to practice law, but he thought it would be useful for her in business, if she didn't marry first. Her mother had never worked, and he didn't expect his daughters to.

Allegra, the youngest of the three children, had inherited her grandfather's talent and had a passion for design. She was always sketching a dress or a bag or a shoe on a scrap of paper. She had a bright, happy nature and enjoyed living on the fringe of her parents' busy social life even when she was very young. They would let her stay at their parties for a short time, and she always wished she could stay for the entire evening. Cosima was less interested in their parties but always had a flock of suitors among the sons of their friends, even though Allegra was far more flirtatious than her older sister by nature. Cosima always had a more serious, studious side, much more so than her younger brother and sister.

Luca was five years younger than Cosima and Allegra was nine years younger than her older sister, four years younger than Luca, and hated being treated like a baby. She couldn't wait to grow up and discover a broader world. Luca hated spending time with his family and preferred to be with his own friends. He had a wild side in his teens. His parents struggled to curb it with little success.

At twenty-three, Cosima had one year of law school in Rome left to complete. She arrived at the family home in Sardinia after working at the store for a month during her school holiday, as she always did. She worked in the administrative offices, not with the customers, and won high praise every year for her efficiency. She had the precise mind of a future lawyer, and also her mother's blond beauty. Allegra and Luca had their father's dark hair, and Cosima and Allegra both had their mother's deep blue eyes. Tizianna was from Florence, and Cosima had her typically Florentine fine-featured beauty. Luca and his father had classic aristocratic faces that belonged on a Roman coin.

The summer before Cosima's final year in law school, she arrived in Sardinia just as her parents were about to leave for a weekend in Portofino with friends who had a home there and had just bought a new speedboat. Luca was supposed to go with them, but a party in Porto Rotondo given by friends of his changed his mind at the last minute and he decided to stay in Sardinia. Cosima stayed in Sardinia with him. She was tired after having worked six days a week at the store for the last month. So her parents left for the weekend and took fourteen-year-old Allegra with them, since their hosts had a daughter the same age. They had a son close to Luca's age too, but Luca found him dull and was happy to escape the weekend in Portofino. Even the lure of the new speedboat didn't sway him.

The house was quiet after they left. Luca disappeared immediately with his friends, and Cosima relaxed and lay in the sun and was happy to have some time alone. She knew they were expecting a house full of guests the following weekend and her parents would expect her to help entertain them, so she was happy to have time to read and take it easy before they came back.

The weekend in Portofino ended in disaster. The hosts allowed their exuberant, reckless nineteen-year-old son to drive them all in the new speedboat. He collided with another boat at full speed, going dangerously fast in the new boat he wasn't familiar with. The two boats crashed and exploded in midair. Both sets of parents were killed instantly, as were the hosts' son, who had been driving the boat, and daughter. The only survivor was Allegra, badly burned on much of her body and with a spinal cord injury so severe that she had to be airlifted to Rome for surgery.

Cosima got the call on Saturday afternoon. She came into the house from the pool to answer the phone. Twenty minutes later, she was dressed and waiting for a cab to take her to the airport to fly to Rome to be with Allegra. Her parents were dead, and she was in shock, unable to believe what had happened. She was torn between grief for her parents and terror for her sister after the accident. Everything rested on her now, and the responsibility for her brother too. She was suddenly faced with adult decisions. She couldn't reach Luca, who was on the family's boat in Porto Rotondo, before she left. She had to leave him a note with the terrible news. He called her crying when she got to Rome and they sobbed together about their parents and Allegra.

Cosima spent the next weeks at her sister's side as Allegra recovered from surgery and was kept in a medical coma while she healed from the burns. It gave Cosima much time to think and grieve for her parents. After the surgery, the doctors told Cosima that Allegra would never walk again. Her spinal cord had been severed. It was yet another terrible blow after losing their parents.

Cosima left Allegra only long enough to plan and attend her parents' funeral in Venice and returned to her sister at the hospital in Rome as quickly as she could. She let Luca return to Sardinia after the funeral, as he wished, since she had no time to spend with him while Allegra was in the hospital, and he didn't want to spend the rest of the summer in Rome.

Luca was greatly subdued and in deep grief over his parents at first. But as he began to feel better, he returned to his old ways and by the end of the summer was going wild with his friends, who came from all over Italy to visit him with no supervision. Cosima was in Rome, couldn't control her brother, and didn't want to leave Allegra alone. She was struggling with the loss of her parents too, and the use of her legs. Cosima left her only for very brief periods of time to go to her father's office and attempt to understand what she needed to know. Her father's assistant and the family attorney, Gian Battista di San Martino, were both very helpful, trying to impart as much information as they could in a short time. They brought papers to the hospital almost daily for Cosima to sign. And Gian Battista was a constant presence and strong support for Cosima to rely on. He took her out to dinner sometimes just so she would get a change of scene from the hospital.

It was two months later, in September, when she got Luca back into some semblance of control, and back to Rome. He refused to return to the university where he'd been studying, and insisted he needed time to "mourn" their parents, which in his case meant going to every party in the city, being out every night, and consuming large amounts of alcohol. But he was back at their apartment, and she got him to check in with her several times a day, so she at least knew where he was, although he often stayed out all night and came home in the morning. She suggested that he work at the store, which he refused to do, and with no set activity, he did whatever he wanted. He stayed out late, slept half the day. She didn't have time to force the issue with him. She was busy with Allegra. And Luca became harder and harder to control. He was enjoying having no parental supervision at eighteen, and paid little attention to Cosima and her rules.

Allegra's progress was slow but steady. She'd had several skin grafts and painful surgeries, but she was surprisingly brave, and philosophical about her injuries. She was quieter than before, after the loss of her parents. But unlike her older brother, she was back in school by Christmas, with a remarkably positive attitude. She would be in a wheelchair forever, but Cosima nursed her as lovingly as any mother, and without parents, the two sisters were even closer than before. Cosima had hired a man to carry Allegra up the staircase to their apartment. Luca was almost never there to help them.

Within six months, Cosima was more serious than ever, still mourning their parents, and had been catapulted into full adulthood. She was running the business, learning as she went. It was the hardest year of her life, and once Allegra was out of the hospital, Cosima went to Venice as often as she could to oversee the store there. Sometimes Gian Battista went with her when he had the time. When he didn't, the palazzo in Venice, where they had spent holidays and family time, seemed achingly empty. It was painful to remember how vibrant it had been when her parents were alive, and how sad it seemed now. Cosima had no time to see her friends or do anything except work at the stores and take care of her sister. Gian Battista was the only source of support in her life.

Allegra was determined to be as independent as she could be once she came home from the hospital. She still talked about designing for the store one day, as though to confirm she had an active future ahead of her. Their longtime housekeeper, Flavia, helped Allegra when Cosima was at work. When she wasn't working or with Allegra, Cosima was chasing Luca down and trying to help him find a sense of direction. He took full advantage of the lack of parental control and fought Cosima on every point.

Their parents' estate was divided equally among them, and Cosima rapidly discovered that her father had spent more than the business had made, on their lifestyle, constant entertaining, several homes, luxurious boats and cars, and extravagant improvements to the store. She was constantly trying to rein in expenses, to pay the bills and her parents' debts, and fighting to keep the business afloat.

She couldn't let it go under. She wanted to honor her father, which was a mammoth task for a girl then twenty-four. Her own studies fell by the wayside. She had more important tasks at hand while running the business, taking care of Allegra, and trying to keep Luca in control.

Her father had bought another, bigger building in Rome before he died, on the Via Condotti. He was hoping to enlarge the store into something even more grand. Cosima sold it as soon as she was able to, before construction was started. She sold it at a loss, but they needed the money, and she poured it back into the business. Their production was so meticulous and so slow that she wasn't able to increase their income immediately, and had to find money from other sources, just to keep the business going and meet their expenses and payroll.

They had a huge staff, particularly in Rome, of very fine and well-paid artisans, and a large sales staff with a limited amount to sell. Many of the long-term employees resented her ownership at her age, and the direction she was taking, with her constant concern about cutting costs. She kept a much more watchful eye on their cash flow than her father had. It didn't sit well with the employees, so she had a battle on her hands getting them to follow the new guidelines, directions, and boundaries she gave them. It was an intolerably hard time for her, with life-and-death struggles every day that made her miss her parents all the more, although she was aware now that some of their financial struggles were her father's fault.

A year after her parents' deaths, Cosima put the house in Sardinia on the market. Luca objected strenuously, but she told him point-blank that they were short of money, and since he had no solutions to offer, and didn't want to work himself, he finally gave her his permission to sell their summer home. She was able to sell it at the end of August at a fair price, along with their boats, and the sale gave her much-needed cash to pay her parents' remaining debts and use for the business, and for the family personally. When she gave Luca his share, he spent it within months on new cars, and on the entourage of unsavory people he had collected around him, who preyed on him for money and what he could provide for them. She couldn't stop him, although she tried valiantly to convince him to be more prudent and more selective about his friends. He laughed at her.

She was forced to concentrate on the business, so she could pull it out of the slump her father had created and keep it running. It took another year of dedicated hard work and focus, but she finally increased their profits, and within another year, she could breathe again.

Five years after her parents' deaths, business was booming in both stores, Rome and Venice. Cosima had increased their production speed by adding more artisans and trimming off the fat elsewhere, despite grumbling from the old-timers, which she steadfastly ignored. Allegra was attending design school by then, and very efficient at leading her life from her wheelchair. Luca had taken a showy apartment in Milan and was dating models. He was twenty-three years old and had become a well-known playboy in Rome and Milan, and constantly asked Cosima for money. He had blown through most of his inheritance by then, and had developed a penchant for gambling, in Venice, San Remo, and Monte Carlo. Cosima had done nothing but work for the last five years, but it had borne fruit, and the business was safe for now.

It had now been fifteen years since her parents' deaths, as she watched the sun come up over Rome from her terrace. She no longer took two months of vacation in the summer, only a few weeks with Allegra, while remaining in frequent contact with her office. The days of extravagance and extreme luxury were over. She had worked hard for the last fifteen years and now Allegra did too. She took Allegra to more modestly priced beach resorts for their holidays, places where they could manage her wheelchair. Allegra was very independent and confident. She had finished design school and Cosima allowed her to introduce small leather items of her own design. Allegra dreamed of designing handbags for the store one day, with a more youthful look, but Cosima had stuck with their traditional models and didn't want to risk losing business with extreme innovations or excessively modern designs. They had their set, ultrareliable, loyal client base, and Cosima didn't want to lose that, so she kept Allegra on a very tight leash as to what she would allow her to design, none of which used her talent or challenged her, which was frustrating for Allegra. Cosima took no risks with the business and stuck with what had always worked.

Allegra rarely went to Venice now. The palazzo was too complicated for her in her wheelchair, and so was the city. Luca stayed at the palazzo occasionally and gave wild parties there, which Cosima scolded him for, and he always reminded her that he was part owner of the palazzo and the business, his share was equal to hers, and she couldn't tell him what to do. They had two old caretakers to watch over the palazzo. And all she could do now was coexist with Luca, knowing that she would wind up picking up the pieces of his messes later, and lending him money. He acted like the son of a rich man, with unlimited funds at his disposal, all of it provided by Cosima to keep the peace and keep him out of trouble. She paid him a substantial allowance every month, which seemed like more than he deserved, since he always wasted it and gambled more than he admitted. He spent as little time as possible with her and told everyone that his older sister was a tyrant and a bore who didn't want him to have a good time and drove him crazy. Cosima felt as though she spent her life cleaning up after him and keeping him from spending as much as he wanted. As a result, he avoided her whenever possible, and tried to poison Allegra against her. He was painfully transparent in his manipulations, and called Cosima shamelessly for money, which she wouldn't give him. He even borrowed money from Allegra at times. She was far more careful with her money than he was, and always had some stashed away. He was totally without conscience or embarrassment about who he borrowed money from. He hadn't become someone Cosima was proud of. He was one of the burdens she managed and endured. She attempted to limit the damage as much as possible, which was all she could do. He couldn't be stopped, only reined in a little, like a wild young stallion.

But as the day dawned over Rome, for once she wasn't worrying about the business, or thinking about her brother, or even Allegra's future, which she worried about too. She was simply enjoying the view from her terrace of the elegant shops on the Via Condotti, the familiar area around the Piazza di Spagna, and the irresistible beauty and magic of Rome before she got swept up in the day and the decisions she would have to make all day at her desk.

She had recently rented out the Palazzo Saverio in Venice. She was determined never to sell it, and to preserve the family history. But renting it was one way to stop Luca from abusing the privilege of owning it. Renting it saved them money, since she hardly used it, and Allegra not at all now because it was on so many levels and had no elevator for her chair, which made it impossible for her without construction for accommodations. For the past six months, since renting the palazzo, Cosima had stayed in a small hotel when she was in Venice, which she was becoming accustomed to. She had rented the palazzo to an enormously wealthy American couple who owned a chain of department stores.

The Johnsons, Bill and Sally, were Texans, very pleasant people who would have loved to carry Saverio leather goods in their stores, but Cosima had explained it wasn't possible. It was against the family philosophy of keeping their goods exclusive to their own stores, a tradition she had upheld to honor her grandfather. Sally and Bill were gracious about it, and had brought in a decorator to transform the palazzo into Texan luxury. Cosima had agreed to it provided the Johnsons made no permanent structural alterations.

They were giving a housewarming party that weekend, which Cosima had agreed to attend, although she never went to big parties. She thought it would be rude not to accept the invitation, and she was curious to see what they'd done to the palazzo. But she was apprehensive too. She was sure it would be vulgar and nothing like the interior during her parents' lifetime, but she had to be practical now.

She had rented the palazzo for an enormous amount, so she wouldn't have to sell it. And the Johnsons had agreed to the price without hesitating or complaining. They loved Venice, spent two months there every year, and were thrilled to have the palazzo. Sally had told Cosima that people would be flying in from all over the States and Europe for their party.

Despite how effusive the Johnsons were, and how larger than life, Cosima liked them. They had grown children she'd never met, and interesting taste, and it was always possible that they had done the palazzo beautifully, although the famous decorator they'd used had a reputation for over-the-top excess. He'd done a château in France, and Cosima had cringed when she saw the photographs. She hoped that the Johnsons hadn't gone too overboard in their décor at Palazzo Saverio, even though it was more than likely they had. But they hadn't bought it, and how far could they go in a rented house? She was about to find out.

She had important meetings that week before the party. She had the entire new fall line of designs to approve, and she worked closely with the designers. They'd added a line of silk and cashmere clothes for men and women five years before. It was doing extremely well and had turned out to be a real moneymaker. They had also added a line of hunting clothes for men. They were very popular, along with their other equestrian items, which had been inspired by the saddles her grandfather had made.

Saverio's only real competition was Hermès, and even her grandfather had said that there was room in the world for both of them. Each house had its own distinctive style, and their clients were loyal. Both houses followed many of the same old-fashioned rules to protect their exclusivity and brand. Many of the Saverio customers loved having to come to Italy to buy from them.

Cosima entertained her biggest customers when they came to Rome, and invited them to dinner at her apartment, or their favorite restaurants, and even let them wander peacefully through the store after hours, noticing items they might not have seen otherwise, and she had her selling staff bring them some of the very latest items directly from their workrooms. Their signature handbag, the Tizianna, named after her mother, had been made famous by Sophia Loren. Grace Kelly had ordered three of them when they came out and wore them alternately with her Hermès Kellys. There was even a smaller one, for evening, named the Adria bag, which her grandfather had named for her grandmother when he created it. Cosima had the Tizianna in every color and wore them daily. It was a perfect work bag.

Luca objected vehemently to the signature bags, and said they were just one more old-fashioned element that kept them out of step with the modern world. He thought everything about Saverio was antiquated, and he had no respect for tradition. Allegra had designed a bag she named the Cosima, which she was dying to have made, but Cosima wouldn't let the workroom produce it. She thought it was too avant-garde and fashion-forward for their line. She insisted that Saverio wasn't dictated by passing fashion trends. It was about timeless elegance and style. Their products were classic. At twenty-nine, Allegra was hungry to move forward as a young designer, but Cosima kept her within the boundaries of their brand and history.

Luca was bored by all of it, except that their profits paid his bills. He was more interested in buying fast horses and gambling, or in almost anything for a quick profit. Whatever brought in fast, easy money, Luca liked. He considered their own products ancient history and predicted that one day Saverio would be viewed as the dinosaur of the industry. He dismissed his sister's success at keeping their stores relevant and alive as one of the most respected brands in the world, no matter how limited their distribution. That was part of the magic of Saverio products. Being hard to get created a high level of demand for them, none of which Luca understood or appreciated. History was of no interest to him, only easy money, which he was able to spend even faster than they could make it.

Cosima left the terrace to shower and dress, and she would stop for a cup of coffee with Allegra before she went to her office. She liked to be at her desk by eight o'clock. She would have a slew of emails to answer from suppliers and important customers, people who appreciated Saverio and couldn't get enough of them, many with famous names, and new customers begging to own one. The business was already far more successful than it had been in her father's day. It was still a struggle at times, but she had big dreams, and maybe one day she'd no longer have to worry about money. Until then, she was honoring the name, and carrying on the traditions, just as her grandfather and father would have wanted. It had been a long, hard climb for fifteen years to grow the business, selling only in the two cities her father and grandfather approved of, and she respected their wishes.

At thirty-eight, she felt as though she had only just started. They still had far to go, but she was sure that they would get there. She was thinking of opening a pop-up store for two weeks for Fashion Week in Milan, trying to keep the brand current and in full view in another city at a busy time, which would attract attention. She still had new ideas for the brand. Considering where she had started at twenty-three, unprepared to run the business, she had done a very good job. And there was always so much more to do. Every day there were new challenges for her to face. She could hardly wait to get to her desk each morning. She loved the business and all it represented. It was the epitome of elegance and style.

It was a new day, and a beautiful morning. She brushed her long blond hair and twisted it into a knot without looking. Even after fifteen years of running the business, she was still excited about what lay ahead, as she stepped into the shower and began her day. She was grateful for how far they'd come. Her love of the business was the driving force in her life. She knew she had single-handedly kept it alive for the past fifteen years, and she had saved and improved the company she had inherited, with love and hard work.

Her family and their business were her life.

Chapter 2

Olivier Bayard sat in his office in Paris on a warm June morning, and looked out the window, feeling like a lucky man. His company's offices took up five floors of a renovated building on the Left Bank, which they owned, and they rented out the rest of the office space to an ad agency and a successful law firm. Olivier owned real estate all over Paris and was a consummate businessman. He owned the largest, most successful handbag company in France, and his bags were sold in department stores all over the world. The company owned factories in France and Italy, where they produced their more expensive bags. At the lower price point, they manufactured part of their line in China, which allowed them to sell at accessible prices, while still maintaining the trendy, fashion-forward look of the better bags. What they made was modern, had a big audience, and sold extremely well.

Olivier had come to the fashion industry in his

youth as an entrepreneur. He had an instinct for business, and had gone to HEC, the Harvard Business School of France. His family had been the discreet owners of a famous haute couture house, and he had understood early on that haute couture was a slowly dying part of fashion, exquisite custom, hand-made clothes at high prices for an ever-shrinking group of wealthy women he firmly believed would disappear in future generations. He had been right. His family had held fast to their beliefs and principles and refused to enter the ready-to-wear market. They thought it vulgar and common, and his family's noble, historical haute couture house had died a quiet death twenty years earlier.

Olivier had wanted to hire young designers and head up a commercial ready-to-wear line for them, to save the business, and his father had refused to "cheapen" their name. So Olivier had used his entrepreneurial skills to start a handbag line of his own. Twenty-five years after he launched the brand, they were the highest selling commercial line of handbags in the world. They were mid-priced, mid-range, trendy, fashionable bags women wore for a season and then replaced with something new.

Long after the family haute couture house of beautiful women's clothing was forgotten, Bayard was a household name. His father hadn't lived long enough to see his son's commercial success, which Olivier often thought was probably just as well. The new offerings four times a year were enticing in colors women couldn't resist and shapes young women felt they *had* to have. Their typical customer was much younger than their haute couture clients had been. With today's rapid transitions in fashion at midrange prices, the bags were almost disposable. Young women weren't looking for bags to keep forever. They wanted the hot new fashion *now*. Olivier had never gotten into the flimsy low-end lines that looked cheap and fell apart in a short time. Bayard bags were durable, but didn't need to be, because the women who bought them moved on with a new season and didn't keep them for long. The bags were all about look, and not the highest quality. They weren't junk, but they had nothing to do with bags like Hermès, or Saverio in Italy. They closely imitated some of their styles from time to time, in fun fabrics or outrageous colors, which gave them a fresh twist, and they flew off the shelves as soon as the stores that sold them put them on display.

In his heart of hearts, Olivier would have loved to own a high-priced brand too, just for the pleasure of it, but the big money was where he had positioned his line. The money was bigger still in the even lower-priced brands, but he had always maintained a certain standard and stuck to it. He wasn't ashamed of the products they sold, but they were a long way from the standards of quality he had grown up with. His dream would have been to establish and own a high-quality brand as well, in addition to his original one. Financially, he couldn't justify owning a brand that would be prestigious but less profitable. So he stuck with the lines he sold so well all over the world. It was business, not love. He was admired in the trade for how smart he was in business, how good his instincts were, and how honest he was.

Olivier had been less judicious in his personal life and had gotten off to a bumpy start. While at university, he had gotten a student at the Sorbonne pregnant. She was beautiful and sexy, and from a different world. Both his parents were well educated. His mother was from a fancy aristocratic family and exquisitely elegant. His father was from a respectable bourgeois family, and had studied to be a doctor, until he gave up his studies and went into his family's haute couture business. They surrounded themselves with intellectuals and dignified people.

Olivier had never dated girls from his own background and preferred girls who were pretty and looser with their favors than the ones he had grown up with. He was briefly infatuated with the girl he'd been dating, but not enough to want to marry her. Her mother worked in a florist shop. Her father was a dispatcher at a trucking company and had been a trucker himself before he injured his shoulder. They were both decent people and Monique was the first person in her family to go to university, determined to better herself. She wanted to be an actress but had been wise enough to go to university first. It ruined everything for both her and Olivier when she got pregnant. Her father had landed a punch squarely on Olivier's jaw, which even he felt he deserved for being careless. They were both eighteen and had been equally cavalier about the risk of pregnancy. Her family was staunchly Catholic, and an abortion was out of the question. She didn't want one anyway. Olivier had done the honorable thing, much to his family's dismay, and married her. Their brief marriage gave them both ample opportunity to discover how little they had in common. She hated being married and being held to Olivier's standards for what he expected in a wife. She cheated on him several times soon after the baby was born. They separated when their son, Maxime, Max, was six months old.

Olivier's parents paid for childcare for their grandson but didn't want him living in their home. Monique's parents grudgingly allowed the child to live with them, with the nanny the Bayards provided. Monique never went back to university, and soon left Paris to pursue her acting career around Europe with stars in her eyes. She got into drugs and died of an overdose when Max was two. He continued living with his maternal grandparents, and Olivier supported him as soon as he had a job and had done so ever since. Olivier saw Max regularly when he was a child, though not as frequently as he would have liked. Eventually he paid for a series of boarding schools for Max, most of which expelled him for cheating and stealing from other students and even teachers. Max was jealous of the other boys, and well aware that his father had money and he had been an early mistake. His maternal grandparents had explained that to him bluntly. He turned his relationship with his father to his advantage and played on his father's guilt, but he had never been a loving, appealing child. He had his mother's worst traits, and as he got older, he always hung out with the bad boys at school. Olivier had done his best to turn him in the right direction with no success. Hoping to guide him, Olivier had given Max a job at twenty-five, working for him.

Now Max was thirty and Olivier was forty-nine. Their relationship had never been easy. Max always felt cheated, and Olivier still felt a responsibility to him, even though his son had not turned out as he hoped. He did his best for him. Max was clever in business, but always looking for a shortcut, a fast deal, an easy way to get what he wanted. Olivier paid him a handsome salary to work in the marketing department of Bayard Bags. Max was abrasive and unappealing, but he was good-looking and used charm and lies to get what he wanted. To him, the end always justified the means. He spent all his money on women and flashy cars, and he loved to gamble. Olivier wasn't proud of him, but took full responsibility for him, and Max made full use of it in any way he could.

Two years after he and Monique had divorced,

when Max was two and a half, Olivier fell madly in love with a young artist. He was twenty-one and Héloïse was two years older. She lived in a garret with no heat and worked as a nude model in her art classes when she needed money. He fell in love with her, and they were inseparable from then on. He was still a student, and much to his family's despair, he married her, and she got pregnant immediately. They had a son named Basile, and he was everything Max never had been, an easy, happy, sunny child who was easy to adore, and they both did. Olivier's younger son was the sweet spot in his life.

His second marriage barely lasted longer than the first. Héloïse ran off with her drawing professor a year after Basile was born and took the infant with her to live in Italy. Olivier traveled frequently to Puglia, the small town where they were living, and did his best to stay present in Basile's life. But eventually, once he started his business, the trips became less frequent, and eventually stopped entirely. As he grew up, Basile became a talented artist himself, and when he was eighteen he returned to Paris to continue his studies at the Beaux-Arts. He was curious about his father and looked him up, and Olivier really got to know him then. And with time and evenings spent together, they became good friends. Basile made it rewarding and enjoyable for Olivier to be a father. Olivier got him a small studio apartment near where he lived, and they saw each other often.

Olivier's two sons were three years apart. Basile had eventually left the Beaux-Arts to become a street artist, starting with graffiti, and now, at twenty-seven, his work had matured and evolved, and he was becoming successful. He had the rare combination of his mother's artistic talent and his father's head for business. Olivier went to his shows whenever he had them and was impressed at how strong and whimsical and appealing Basile's art was. The two half brothers had met several times and didn't like each other, part jealousy and part just too different. Olivier got along brilliantly with Basile, and they never lacked for things to talk about on subjects that fascinated them. They were surprisingly alike and admired each other, whereas Max was jealous of both of them. He had an envious, greedy nature. And even though Olivier and his older son worked together, they still had little in common. Their perception of the world and philosophies of life were total opposites. Max was always on the lookout for situations that would benefit him, no matter how shady they appeared, and Olivier's efforts to lead him to the straight and narrow were fruitless most of the time. In contrast, Basile was full of humor and charm, and had the same generous, honorable, honest, warm heart as his father. Basile was easy to love, and Max an eternal challenge.

Olivier had seen recent photographs of Héloïse, Basile's mother, his great love, and had been shocked to see that she had aged badly, and looked nothing like the beautiful girl he had fallen in love with in his youth. She was still with her former art teacher, who was now in his seventies and looked like an old man, and she was unattractive and looked ten years older than her age at fifty-one. She always told their son that she still had warm memories of Olivier and that he had been a lovely man, but the art instructor she had left him for, and never married but still lived with, was the love of her life. Her union with Olivier had served to produce Basile and nothing more. Basile wasn't resentful of any of them. He had enjoyed a happy childhood in Italy, and loved living in Paris now and seeing his father for dinner at a neighborhood bistro from time to time. Basile wanted nothing from Olivier and was doing well on his own. Olivier marveled at times at how different the two boys were. He got along with Basile and truly enjoyed him, but seeing Max at work every day was never a pleasure. Their relationship had been tense and awkward for all of Max's life.

Max wanted to start his own company but was waiting for his father to pay for it, which Olivier wasn't inclined to do. In his opinion, Max was always looking for an easy ride and wasn't a hard worker. He took too many risks, and his gambling habit worried Olivier. Olivier had no desire to set him up in business and considered him a poor risk. He had terrible judgment. So Max was riding his father's coattails until he got a better deal. He had no desire to do the heavy work himself. Unlike Basile, who worked hard and was starting to sell his street art for high prices, which impressed Olivier. Just talking to him, one could sense that Basile was destined for success.

After Olivier's second unsuccessful marriage, he came to the conclusion that long-term commitment wasn't for him. He was twenty-three when Héloïse ran off with her art professor, and although he'd had relationships later which had lasted for a few years, particularly one that had lasted for seven years with a married woman when he was in his thirties, he had no desire to marry or have more children. He had been single now for more than twenty-five years and was content.

He had an apartment he loved in the 7th Arrondissement, along the quais overlooking the Seine. He went to Italy frequently to visit their factories there, he went to Asia twice a year, and enjoyed a small amount of exotic travel. He did extensive business in the States and had friends there. His life seemed perfectly balanced to him, and he could think of nothing he was lacking, or he would have changed if he had the chance. He still shuddered at the early memories of how unhappy both of his marriages had made him, and with the vantage point of age, he could easily see how he would have been even more miserable if those unions had lasted. Monique had turned out to be a nightmare. Her parents had died, so he didn't have to deal with them, and Héloïse had no family to speak of and Olivier had never met them. She had turned into a blowzy, unattractive housewife who had lost her looks at a young age. She had been a good mother to their son, so he was grateful for that. His own parents had died when he was relatively young, and he was an only child, so he had no family now except his two sons, and as far as he was concerned, they were enough. He saw enough of each of them, so he was satisfied and not hungering for more contact. Basile had never wanted anything from him, he wasn't greedy or grasping, his art sold well, and he was self-supporting. But Max was a frequent headache even now, when they clashed over the business, which happened often. Olivier had long since accepted that he and Max were never going to see life the same way. And neither of his sons seemed to have any inclination to get married. He felt an obligation to give Max a role in his business, but he kept a close eye on him to make sure he didn't do any serious damage.

Max chased anything in a skirt indiscriminately, if she was good-looking. He had a weakness for Russian models. They used him and were even greedier than he was. Basile always seemed to have a girlfriend of the moment, and appeared to be serially monogamous, but the faces changed every few months. At twenty-seven, he was enjoying being young and single and had no urge to settle down.

He said he had no desire to even think about it until he was at least thirty-five, which was eight years away. The timing sounded about right to his father too, much better than fatherhood at nineteen and twenty-two, and responsibilities he couldn't handle at the time. Olivier thought that if he had been smart enough to wait too, and had chosen more carefully, he might have ended up with a partner who would have lasted and not cheated on him almost immediately. They had all been too young for marriage and children. His parents had said it at the time, but he hadn't listened. Monique's father probably would have killed him, or done him some serious bodily harm, if he hadn't married her when she got pregnant, so Olivier had complied, much to his parents' chagrin.

Max appeared to have the same short fuse as his maternal grandfather and wasn't shy about landing a good punch now and then too. Olivier still remembered vividly Monique's father punching him squarely in the face when she told him she was pregnant. Her father had grown up in a rough neighborhood and what he'd learned there had stayed with him for a lifetime. At the time, Olivier had never met anyone like him, or like her. In his more genteel family, punching someone wasn't an option. Monique had hit him a few times too, and he had let her because she was a woman. He was sorry when she died, but he never missed her once they parted, and Max was a great deal like Monique and her family despite the education and advantages Olivier had given him. He had never become a nicer person, or a gentleman. And he was drawn to the lowest element of society among his friends.

Max marched into his father's office late that afternoon, looking as he always did, like he was spoiling for a fight. He was always ready to attack and on the defensive. Olivier was gracious and polite, and seemed relaxed, even when he was stressed. He tried not to let it show. Max waved his emotions like a burning flag.

"Did you see the new fluorescents?" he asked Olivier, sure his father would hate them. They had been his idea.

"I did."

"What did you think?" Max asked, frowning, his body language tense.

"I liked them. Much better than I thought I would. You were right." Max's face broke into an unexpected smile, like sunshine between storm clouds. He had been braced for thunder and lightning, and sometimes enjoyed it. He wasn't afraid of a good fight. "I think they're going to be a huge hit. Particularly in the States, California, Florida, and Texas, where they love bright colors."

"We should have had them made in China," Max said, scowling again. "Why waste money on production?" He had his father's dark hair, and smoldering dark brown eyes to go with it. Olivier's eyes were a warmer brown. Max was taller than his father and powerfully built. He went to a gym often and had broad shoulders. Olivier was tall, strong, and thin, and looked younger than his forty-nine years. They could almost have been brothers, since Olivier was so young when Max was born.

"The fabric would have been as durable in China, but the colors wouldn't have been as vibrant." They'd had the bags made in their factory outside Florence, which was Olivier's decision, to upgrade their look.

"But the profit margin would have been better," Max said.

"We can afford the margin we've got. You can't always sacrifice quality for price, Max."

"If we produced more in China, we could sell to H&M, Zara, Mango, and all the low-end outlets. We'd make millions."

"That's not what we do, or who we are," Olivier reminded him, as he did often. Max wanted to turn Bayard Bags into a high-volume business and give up the price point and standard of quality Olivier had established years before and stuck to.

"We're not Hermès," Max said tartly.

"No." His father smiled at him. "I wish we were."

"This isn't haute couture, Dad. And think of where that went. Down the tubes. If you were still in haute couture, you'd be broke by now." Instead Olivier was a rich man with a booming business, but Max wanted more, no matter what he had to sacrifice to get there, including his reputation and his father's, which meant nothing to him.

Olivier didn't argue the point. It was a conversation they'd had many times before. "What are you doing this weekend?" he asked his son, always trying to bond with him, improve the relationship they had, and find common ground. Max was his son after all, which meant a lot to Olivier. Fatherhood was a commitment he had honored for all of Max's life, and Basile's. Max's sentiments for his father weren't as strong. He worked for him because he paid him well, not because he admired him or even loved him, or liked his job. He didn't. Whatever Olivier had done for him, Max felt was his due. He felt entitled to whatever he had, and not grateful for it, unlike Basile, who was always touched by anything his father did, even the smallest gesture. But Héloïse had been a cut above Monique and had brought Basile up well, and genes played a part in it too. Olivier was a kind, generous man, and Basile resembled him more than Max did.

"Why?" Max answered him about the weekend, as though he was afraid his father wanted something from him, instead of the reverse, which was more usual. There was always something Max wanted from Olivier, money mostly, or any perks he could get.

"I have to go to Florence to see the factory tomorrow. I've got a meeting about next year's spring line." They were already working on it, and were always several seasons ahead, like ready-to-wear. "The Johnsons from Dallas are having a party to celebrate the palazzo they rented and redecorated in Venice. They begged me to come. I'm not dying to, but I think I should." They were Bayard's biggest buyers in the U.S. and bought a huge number of their bags every season. "Do you want to come?" Olivier was always anxious to introduce his son to better people than the sleazy crowd he hung out with and preferred.

"Hell, no," Max said with a grimace. "Sit around with a bunch of deadly old Texans, in some crumbling palazzo half under water, on a foul-smelling canal, no thanks."

"Knowing the Johnsons, and having seen their home in Dallas, and their estates in Lyford Cay and Palm Beach, I don't think a waterlogged palazzo on a foul-smelling canal is a high probability. I think we're talking more like Versailles or a Medici palace, or maybe the Sistine Chapel. She's been working on it for months and this is the unveiling."

"I met them with you before. They bore me to death," Max said, annoyed. "They're tedious and old."

"They bore me too, to be honest. But they're good people and among our best customers. I have to go, and I'll be in Florence anyway. It isn't a big deal to go to Venice after that. It only takes two hours by train. I was thinking of spending the weekend. And I might go to Saverio in Venice, just for the sheer pleasure of it."

"You'd like to buy it, wouldn't you?" Max asked him, although he knew the answer.

"Of course, who wouldn't? But they're as tight as the Dumas family who own Hermès, and the Wertheimers who own Chanel. Some businesses will never be for sale. Saverio is one of them. But I would leap at the chance if it ever came up," Olivier said. "They don't need me. The Saverios own it, and it will always stay that way."

"Do they have kids?" Max asked, not very interested in knowing. It was a dead end.

"I don't think so. It's owned by the third generation. As I recall, the oldest one runs it. They must be fairly young. I don't think any of them are married or have kids."

"Maybe they'll die out," Max said hopefully for his sake.

"Not in my lifetime. I don't know how old they are, but Saverio has been around for years, for over a century, and I've never heard any rumors that they'd sell. I just like going to see the workmanship. I learn something every time. And the original store is in Venice. It's small but beautiful, almost like a church," Olivier said, with a wistful expression.

"There's a good casino in Venice," Max said, more interested in that. "I won't go to the party, but if I meet you in Venice, I can go to the casino while you kiss the Johnsons' asses. You're better at that than I am." It was true, but Olivier wasn't crazy about encouraging his son to gamble in Venice. That hadn't been the point of the invitation. "I'll see what else comes up, and if I have nothing to do, I can meet you there on Friday, and fly back with you on Saturday or Sunday." Olivier nodded and Max left his office a few minutes later. Olivier doubted that Max would join him, and he wasn't sure he wanted him to now. He didn't want to be the one to facilitate his son's gambling. But that, chasing women, and easy money were all Max cared about. Olivier wanted to go, out of respect for one of their biggest customers, and for the beauty of Venice, which he had always loved. A quick visit to Saverio would be a private treat he always enjoyed, just to see what they were doing now, their latest interpretations of their classic designs.

He usually stayed at the Cipriani, across the lagoon, and one had to get there by boat, but this time he was staying at the Gritti Palace, in all its newly renovated fifteenth-century splendor. It was exquisite and had so much history. It would be more convenient to get to the party by gondola instead of speedboat, and more elegant. He was looking forward to it, even if the party would undoubtedly be full of old, wealthy Texans, many of whom were coming for the event, and others who already rented palazzos there. He was sure it would be an all-American crowd, as Max said, but they would be pleasant and charming, and it was a duty he felt obliged to perform for his customers and old friends. Max didn't have either the sense of duty or tradition, or even good manners, that his father had.

Olivier was just leaving his office that night to go home when he got a text from Max. "Okay, I'll come, but not to the party. See you in Venice Friday night." Olivier was surprised, but he had no illusions about it. If it weren't for the casino he liked in Venice, Max wouldn't be bothering to come. Olivier texted back the name of the hotel and left a message for his secretary to get Max a standard room at the Gritti Palace, and not a suite. He was staying in one of the best newly renovated suites himself and could hardly wait. It would be his reward for spending a hot day at the factory in Florence and going to a party which might prove to be dull. But a night at the Gritti and a visit to the original Saverio store would be ample reward.

Chapter 3

As she tried to do every morning, Cosima stopped at the door to Allegra's apartment on the way to her office. Unless she had an early conference call from abroad or a meeting, Cosima had a cup of coffee with her sister on her way to work every day.

Allegra was still in her nightgown, as she usually was at that hour, when she opened the door to Cosima and greeted her with a broad smile. There was a young woman who helped her get ready for work every day, tidied her apartment, and left a meal for her for dinner at night, unless Allegra was going out with friends. The woman didn't arrive until a little later, so the sisters enjoyed their morning visit alone. Allegra had coffee ready for her sister and poured it into a cup as Cosima sat down at the kitchen table. It always touched her how cheerful and upbeat Allegra was. She had been that way since she was a child, even after the accident.

Allegra had scars on her arms and her back from the burns she'd had, but she usually wore long sleeves to cover them, and her lovely face had been untouched. She had the face one saw in Italian Renaissance paintings of cherubs and madonnas. There was a look of peace and joy to her. Allegra always saw the bright side of things, and never complained about her fate, being in a wheelchair since she was fourteen. Fifteen years later, she could hardly remember being any different, although she had walking dreams once in a while, but not very often anymore.

"What are you working on right now?" Cosima asked her. Allegra was always sketching, and had unlimited design ideas, many of which she put away in a folder, knowing that they were too avant-garde for her sister to include them in their line. She was saving them in case she had a chance to use them one day. Her tamer designs, usually based on historic bags they had produced previously, Cosima was delighted to include in what they offered in the store, and she loved that they both worked in the family business.

"I just did a series of six clutch bags for next spring. They're all variations of the same theme, but slightly different from each other. I'd like to do them in pastels, maybe two in alligator, the others in smooth leather." Allegra had an infallible eye for what colors and textures worked with their basic designs. "I left the folder on my desk in the studio,

I can show them to you later," she promised. "What are you up to?"

The two sisters had been very close ever since the accident that killed their parents, kept Allegra in the hospital for months, and ultimately confined her to a wheelchair. She had had therapy at the time but had adapted well since then to her limitations. She had never been angry or bitter and didn't have a depressive nature. Cosima worried much more than she did, about the business, their family, and having enough money. Cosima had all the responsibilities and tried to shield both her brother and sister from them, since she was the oldest.

She would have liked more help and support from Luca, but he offered her none, and added to Cosima's stresses with endless demands of his own, mostly to help him cover his debts.

"Have you heard from Luca this week?" Cosima asked. He was more likely to call his younger sister, who never asked him to be accountable. He viewed their older sister as the police, and strongly resented her questions about his life. He had essentially avoided work for the past fifteen years and hadn't had a job since he dropped out of school at eighteen. He had just turned thirty-three. He wasn't in the least embarrassed by not doing anything productive and had no interest in entering the business. He considered his sisters both slaves to their parents, fifteen years after their deaths. He had no appreciation for how well Cosima ran the business that had met his needs all his life.

"I heard from him last week," Allegra answered her sister's question about Luca, as they finished their morning coffee. It was strong Italian espresso, the way they both liked it. "He said something about going to Venice."

"I'm going on Friday. Maybe I'll run into him. Lucky for him he has time to float around and do whatever he wants while the two of us are working," Cosima said with pursed lips. Allegra nodded, knowing how much their brother upset Cosima at times. He was shameless about how lazy and self-indulgent he was. He was in the newspapers constantly, at some party, ball, or sailing race somewhere in Italy, always with a beautiful woman on his arm. He acted like the heir to a vast fortune, when in fact at times they were pressed for money because Cosima had to put their profits back into the business to help keep it afloat and growing. They had never had a huge fortune, even when their father was alive, although her parents had lived as if they did, and had spent money irresponsibly. Cosima had discovered it later, when putting things to rights had fallen to her so they didn't lose their home and the business. Renting the palazzo had been a wise decision, and gave them some additional income, with the huge rent the Johnsons were willing to pay. "I'm going to the Johnson housewarming party on Friday. Do you want to come?" she offered Allegra, who shook her head, looking pensive.

"I think it would make me sad to see other people living at the palazzo, even if we still own it. And the entrance and main floor are so complicated with all the different levels and my chair." She didn't look sad about it, just matter of fact, which was her nature. And it was true. There were staircases all over the place, to make for dramatic entrances into the reception rooms. Cosima had had ramps built, and chairs that ran up and down the stairs electrically, to give Allegra easy access when they went there, which wasn't often anymore. The sisters were busy in Rome. Their parents had used the palazzo more, to entertain.

Sally Johnson had asked permission to remove the ramps and electric chairs for her long-term rental. Cosima had allowed her to remove some of them but not all, provided she replaced them when they left the palazzo at the end of their lease. Allegra couldn't be there without them, although she much preferred her cozy apartment and studio over the store in Rome. It was easier for her, and she was at home there. Cosima had set up the apartment for her when she was in design school and old enough to live alone. And Cosima was only a floor away if she needed help. Allegra was very independent, and she never called her for assistance. Whatever the problem, she was proud of working it out on her own.

She went out a lot with friends and had a special car Cosima had gotten her with manual controls when she was old enough to drive. Her whole apartment had been installed with everything at her level in the kitchen and bathroom, and she could control curtains, stereo, lights from an iPad. She led a full life and had friends in for dinner frequently. Cosima could hear music coming from her apartment at times and loved knowing that she was having fun. She had too much wine with her friends once in a while, and those were the only occasions Cosima had helped put her to bed, and teased her about it in the morning, and called her a hopeless drunk, which she wasn't. Allegra led a full life for a young woman her age. She'd had a boyfriend once when she drank too much, and Cosima had found them both sound asleep on the couch, tiptoed out of the room, and left them there. At twenty-nine, Allegra admitted that she'd never been deeply in love, but she had dates, and was a beautiful girl. Her disability weeded out the good guys from the bad, and most of the men she knew found her fun and attractive. She just hadn't met the right one yet to spend a lifetime with. Neither had Cosima, who Allegra had long suspected had a "friend," and she could guess who it was. Cosima didn't talk about it, and Allegra didn't ask her. Cosima was so secretive about it that Allegra knew the subject was taboo. Cosima considered herself married to her family and the business, and if she had a romantic secret in her life, Allegra thought she was entitled to it and was happy for her. Allegra hoped her sister would marry one day but had the feeling she wouldn't and didn't want to, for reasons of her own. Allegra respected her sister's secrets. If she had guessed correctly who it was, she knew why they weren't together. Some things were better left alone.

When Cosima got to her office that morning, she had a full day's work ahead of her, with conference calls and design meetings. She met with the designer of their clothes and looked over the cashmeres and fabrics they were going to use in the next season. They only used manufacturers in Italy, and their own workrooms for leather goods. They had discussed adding a few items of jewelry at some point, and Cosima had decided not to. Another possibility was a perfume, but Cosima thought it too risky, and didn't want to lose money on an expensive product that might not do well. She was extremely conservative about the business. Allegra wished she'd take a little more risk at times, but Cosima was slow to move into new areas and was afraid of losing money. She preferred to stay with what they knew worked well for them.

Cosima left the office at eight o'clock that night, she had been invited to a party but decided not to go. It had been a long day and she was tired, and didn't have the energy for a late night, and she was leaving for Venice in the morning. She was taking work with her to do on the train. The trip took just under four hours. She rarely wasted a moment when she could work. She answered her emails the next morning from the train.

She got to Venice after lunch and smiled when she saw the station. Although Cosima had lived in Rome all her life, it was as though her soul and body knew this was home too. She took the boat from the Santa Lucia station to the small hotel where she stayed now, enjoying the familiar sights and sounds of her second home. She had time for a quick visit to the store and toured the workrooms there. After she had seen everyone she wanted to, she looked at the displays of newly finished merchandise. She walked to the Piazza San Marco, sat down at a café, and had a cup of coffee on her own, enjoying the magnificence of St. Mark's Cathedral and the Piazza, just as she did the boats on the Grand Canal when she walked to the Piazzetta San Marco. It was an unbelievably beautiful city, and she loved it. There was a magic and mystery to it that existed nowhere else. Rome had its own special charm, with its history and atmosphere of joyous chaos, but Venice was unique, built on the water, with a Renaissance feeling to it.

She got back to her hotel at six o'clock, in time to return some phone calls from Rome, bathe in the enormous bathtub of her hotel room, and dress for the party. The hotel had arranged for a private boat, and at nine o'clock she was at the Palazzo Saverio and could feel her heart soar as she looked up at it. This was her home, her roots, and her history, and she could imagine her parents waiting for her in the doorway, greeting their guests as they had before the balls and glamorous parties they had given there when she was growing up. She remembered the evenings perfectly, the women in sweeping gowns, her mother in the grandest one of all made for her in Paris, or by couture designers in Rome. Some of the parties had been masked balls, which were even more extraordinary and a favorite in Venice. Cosima had watched the guests from the top of the grand staircase when she was a child. The memory was imprinted forever on her heart. The others had their memories of those nights too. It made Cosima miss her parents acutely, and the loss seem fresh again.

Her breath caught as she walked through the front door and instead of her incredibly elegant parents, she saw Sally Johnson standing there, a very large black taffeta dress covering her sizable figure, with an enormous emerald necklace she had had made by a famous Venetian jeweler, and her tall, portly husband just behind her in white tie and tails. They were way overdressed for the occasion, and the invitation wasn't black or white tie, but they were nice people, honoring the house as well as their guests, and Cosima was touched when she saw them. It brought tears to her eyes as the image of her parents faded and reality struck her.

There was music coming from the distant ball-room and about a hundred people milling around as waiters served caviar and champagne from silver trays, using the Saverio family crystal, silver, and china, which were all part of the rental. The silver trays bore the coat of arms of the Saverios, the same as the signet ring on Cosima's left hand. The house was filled with flowers, and Cosima was star-tled by the new décor, as she descended one of the grand marble staircases to the main living room. The house was built on many levels, which would have made it difficult for Allegra now without most of the ramps.

Cosima glided smoothly down the marble stair-case after greeting Bill and Sally warmly at the door. She was startled by the new decorative addi-tions, which consisted of enormous antique crystal chandeliers hanging from every ceiling, in addition to the original ones, tall antique Venetian lanterns, and oversized reproductions of Venetian grotto fur-niture encrusted with huge pearls and coral. There was a turquoise-encrusted sedan chair at the en-trance to the ballroom, which was even more over-the-top than Cosima had expected, with hanging crystal drops, oversized candelabra, and Fortuny fabrics in gold and coral tones. Some of it was beautiful, but all together it was too much. But the Johnsons were ecstatic, and proud of what they'd done. And their friends were dazzled. Just being in a palazzo impressed them and would have been enough.

There were original antique mirrors propped up along the walls, multiplying the images of the guests, and the dining room table, which seated forty-eight, looked like Alice in Wonderland goes to Venice. There were statues of Roman heads and busts, encrusted with crystal, turquoise, coral, and pearls, all provided and designed by the Dallas decorator. It took a while to take it all in. Cosima circulated in the crowd and recognized a handful of big Saverio customers, who were friends of Sally's, and she made a point of talking to each of them.

Cosima was wearing a one-shouldered column dress in the palest ballerina pink, which molded her perfect figure, and high-heeled silver sandals. Her hair was swept up in a simple impeccably smooth French twist, with small diamonds that had been her mother's in her ears. Her arms were thin and bare, and the only ring she wore was her gold signet ring with the family crest. She looked as elegant as her parents had been, in a more contemporary way. She remembered her mother wearing the same delicate color, which suited her so well with her blond hair, like Cosima's.

After she had circulated for a while, on several levels, she walked out onto the terrace outside the ballroom, admiring the beauty of Venice, and breathing in the cool night air. She stood at the rail of the balcony, her thoughts drifting after the excesses of the décor, which was an assault on the eyes and senses. She didn't notice a man watching her the entire time. Her back was turned, her thoughts were a million miles and twenty years away, to when her parents were still alive, and she was only eighteen. The Johnsons had a Venetian orchestra at the party, and it was easy to pretend for a moment that it was an evening long ago, in a different time.

"It's a beautiful view, isn't it, and a beautiful city," a deep male voice said softly just behind her. She was so exquisite to look at that he couldn't resist talking to her. She could hear that he was French as soon as he spoke, although he had spoken to her in English. She turned toward the voice and smiled mysteriously, slowly pulled back from the revelries of the past. He was tall and handsome with dark hair, wearing a dark blue suit, a meticulous white shirt, and a navy tie she recognized easily as Hermès.

She answered him in French, which she spoke fluently, and for an instant he thought she was French, then heard the faintest accent in otherwise flawless French, and realized she was Italian. He spoke enough Italian to manage at the factory, but he was fluent in French and English, and so was she.

"The house is amazing," he added in French, and she smiled. "I've never seen anything like it,

even in France. It's a bit like Versailles gone mad."
It was a perfect description of it.

"I was born here," she said in a soft voice, addressing him smoothly in French, which was easy for her.

"In Venice?" She nodded.

"In this house." She didn't comment on the décor, which they both knew was excessive, but neither of them wanted to be rude to their hostess. She was so excited about her new Venetian home and décor. "It has belonged to my family for six centuries. I spent time here with my parents for holidays as a child, but we moved to Rome when I was very young." He hadn't paid attention to the name of the palazzo, so he still had no clue as to who she was.

"It must have been a wonderful way to grow up." He smiled at her as they stood in the moonlight with the backdrop of Venice all around them, like a stage set or a movie.

"My parents were very glamorous," she said, smiling. "Life isn't like that anymore, even here in Italy. People live more simply. My parents died fifteen years ago, and even then they were a throwback to another time. They used to give balls and wonderful parties and dances. My mother used to wear the most beautiful gowns she bought in Paris." He was mesmerized by Cosima, and he could visualize the scene she described.

"She might have bought them at my family's

couture house," he said with a shy smile. "Bayard," he volunteered, and Cosima looked startled.

"Yes, of course, she had several of them in her closets. She was still quite young. They died in an accident." She was telling him more than she usually disclosed to a stranger, but there was something so open and gentle about him, and being in her own home made her open up about her history.

"I'm sorry to hear it, about your parents."

"Does the couture house still exist?" She didn't wear clothes like that, so she didn't know if it did or not. He shook his head in answer.

"No, it closed. Haute couture is part of another world. It's history now. What was your mother's name?" he asked, increasingly curious about her.

"Tizianna Saverio." His eyes opened wide when she said it.

"Saverio? The leather goods?" He looked like someone had shot him, and she laughed in answer.

"Yes, and the palazzo." She wondered if he had a wife who bought from them, or if he bought their saddles and hunting clothes. He looked like a gentleman.

"I am your biggest fan. I've been in love with everything you do since I discovered you. I visit your store whenever I'm in Venice or Rome. The workmanship is unique and incredible. Half the reason I came to this party was so I could visit the store tomorrow."

"I was just there today. I try to come to Venice

every week or two to keep an eye on the store. My grandfather Ottavio founded the one here, and my father built the one in Rome. He was Alberto. I have lived in Rome for almost all my life, since my childhood. It's my home. But my roots are here, in Venice."

He looked surprised again then. "You don't sell at Johnson and Dean, do you?" He didn't think so.

"No, we only sell in our own stores, here in Italy. But Sally is one of our best customers, so I wanted to come and see what she did with the décor. She's renting the palazzo from us. She seems to have had quite a lot of fun with it," she said with a shy grin. "I'm not sure what my parents would say, or my grandfather, but I quite like it. It's very lively and cheerful," and very showy, she didn't say, a lot like the Johnsons themselves. It was over-the-top, but they were obviously enjoying the palazzo so much that one couldn't hold the excesses against them.

"I would have loved to see the original," he said, fascinated by her.

"If you come to the store, I can show you some photographs of my parents' masked Venetian balls. They were quite something."

"I've read about them," he said, and then she had a thought.

"Would you like a tour of the original workrooms tomorrow? They have changed very little since my grandfather's day. It's all still entirely artisanal."

"I would love it," he said.

"Eleven o'clock?" she suggested, and he looked enchanted, by her as much as by the invitation.

"That would be perfect. I have been obsessed with your family's work for years. It is legendary."

"We are very bound by tradition," she admitted. "My brother and sister think too much so. I run the business now, and I'm trying to preserve what my father left us, without violating it, but we have to modernize somewhat. It's hard to know how much. It's a delicate balance." He looked interested in what she said and was fascinated by her. He was impressed that she was a Saverio.

"I think you've done it beautifully." He didn't dare tell her that he made handbags too, which were embarrassingly commercial compared to hers and in an entirely different category. She was like Renoir or Degas in his mind, and he compared what he did to cartoons. His bags would be discarded in a year, which contributed to his success. Hers would last for generations.

They continued to chat on the terrace for a while, then went back inside. She shook his hand before she left, and said she'd see him at the store at eleven o'clock the next day. And then she discreetly disappeared and took the boat waiting for her back to the hotel. She glanced at her watch on the way. She was meeting someone in the bar at the hotel at eleven-thirty.

She walked through the lobby and into the bar when she arrived. It was twenty to midnight, but she knew he'd wait. She hadn't seen him in a month. He lived in Rome, but had business in Venice too, and had said he'd be there that night. She saw him immediately when she walked into the bar, her heart pounding as it always did when she saw him. No matter what they had said or agreed to, that never changed. They had promised to stop seeing each other a dozen times or more, but couldn't stick to it, although he was stronger than she was now. He had been determined to end it, although they still loved each other. He stayed seated at a dark corner table when she walked in, and didn't stand as she approached, so as not to attract attention. People knew him in Venice, and all over Italy. He was an important man and had the aura of power about him.

As soon as she sat down, he kissed her, and there was no doubt in either of their minds that he still loved her, and she loved him. She had never loved anyone as she loved him, or known anyone like him. Gian Battista di San Martin had been a close friend of her father's and was his attorney. He had helped her settle her parents' estate and take charge of the business. He had advised and supported her and been there for her in every way after their deaths. She was in love with him long before he admitted it to her. He had waited three years to declare his feelings for her and had begged her forgiveness when he did. She was twenty-six then and he was sixty, now he was seventy-two, and as handsome as ever.

Their affair had been the most passionate either of them had ever known. But it had no future right from the beginning. He was married, although he and his wife had been ill suited from the start and lived separate lives under one roof for their entire marriage. It was a union that had been fashioned by their families when they were young, too young to realize that it was wrong and always would be. His uncle was a cardinal and his family was closely tied to the Vatican. He had a brother who was a bishop. Gian Battista and his wife had no children, but divorce was never going to be possible for them. His wife would never have agreed to it, nor his own family forgiven him the disgrace. Gian Battista had warned Cosima of it right from the first day, and she said she didn't care. Divorce was legal in Italy now, but not for him. A little of him in the shadows was better than none at all. And she knew she had his whole heart. She had the business to run, she had vowed she would never marry once they loved each other. What they had, however limited, was enough for her.

They met in London several times, and in Paris. He met her in Rome discreetly, sometimes with the excuse of seeing her for business. They came to Venice separately, and stayed at the palazzo alone, listening to the sounds of the canal lapping against the outer walls in the winter. And they had met in exotic places for unforgettable romantic vacations. She had never regretted what they did for a minute. And three years earlier, after nine years of their affair, he had stopped everything, and said he wouldn't see her anymore. She was thirty-five and he said he wanted her to find someone her own age, marry, and have children. She even wanted his child out of wedlock, but he wanted a better life than that for her. They had tried not seeing each other at all, but couldn't do it, and for the past three years, their relationship had been chaste. He refused to start up again, he said he was robbing her of her youth and her future and wouldn't do that anymore. So they saw each other rarely now, when they could, and he tried to force her to look to the future, not the past, nor into their hearts.

Cosima had loved Gian Battista for fifteen years. At thirty-eight, she still wanted no one else, but he wouldn't have her, except as a woman he loved from a distance. He said he knew he shouldn't see her at all, but he wasn't brave enough, so they lived with the tiny fleeting moments that were left to them now. Her feelings for him hadn't changed, nor his for her. She could feel it and knew him well. This was all they had left. Stolen moments now and then, which she said were enough. She had stubbornly refused to move on once he changed the ground rules three years before. A stolen, stealthy kiss was all she had now, and it had to suffice. She said it did. No one knew their secret and never had, nor suspected.

They spent two hours together in the bar of her hotel that night, and as always Gian Battista refused to come upstairs with her when she asked him. He left her at the elevator and went out to the boat he had come in alone. He drove the short distance back to his own palazzo, with their secret wrapped around him like a magic cloak which gave him life, and Cosima rode upstairs in the elevator to her room, with an aching heart, which was so familiar to her now.

Chapter 4

Max Bayard arrived at the Gritti Palace half an hour after his father left for the Johnsons' party. Olivier had left Max a note at the front desk, and had paid for his room, adjoining his suite. Max checked in with the small bag he'd brought, and already knew which casino he would go to. He had been there before. It was supposedly one of the oldest casinos in Europe, a seventeenth-century gaming palace, the Ca' Vendramin Calergi, on the Grand Canal, a few minutes' boat ride from the Piazza San Marco. It had all the gambling pursuits he liked, blackjack above all, roulette, Punto Banco, which was the original version of baccarat, and poker. Along with its venerable history, it had been very elegant at one time, but was more informal now. It had changed with the times. It was one of two casinos in Venice, and the one Max preferred. There was another casino closer to the train station, before one reached the canals, but the historical one had brought him luck before.

He ordered a light meal from room service, and at ten o'clock he left for the casino. Things were a little slow that early in the evening, and once he got there, he started with roulette. He usually did well at that. Not tonight. He lost five hundred euros in half an hour, watched a poker game for a while, and moved on to the blackjack tables, which were his drug of choice. He took a seat when a player left at a table that looked like it was running hot. He bought a thousand euros' worth of chips and jumped in. Three hands later, another player left and went to cash in his chips. Max hadn't gotten lucky yet, but he knew he would soon, he could feel it. The new player next to him looked at him with a nod. The dealers seemed to know him. He was Italian, a striking-looking man around Max's age. He asked for five thousand euros' worth of chips, and they let him sign for them. It told Max immediately that he was a known gambler and played for high stakes.

They played consistently until midnight, side by side, and drank while they did. Max drank champagne, and the player next to him drank straight whiskey. Neither of them was drunk, but they had both lost a fair amount of money. Max had lost his thousand euros' worth of chips, and bought two thousand more, and had lost most of them by midnight. The handsome Italian had lost twenty thousand by then and didn't seem to care. Max was surprised that the man hadn't left the table and gone to one that brought him more luck. As though reading his mind, the Italian said to him in English, so the other players wouldn't understand, "My sister pays my gambling debts." He had guessed that Max spoke English. He was cocky and Max was impressed. He usually lied to his father about his debts, but sometimes Olivier found out. Including his initial loss at the roulette table, Max had lost thirty-five hundred that night, which was a lot even for him. And by the time he stood up, the Italian had lost fifty thousand, and looked drunk by then.

"Want to have a drink at the bar?" he asked Max in French when he was leaving. Max took the few chips he had left and followed him to the bar. Luca had realized earlier that Max was French, and Luca spoke fluent French. Max didn't speak much Italian, only French and English.

"You must play here a lot," Max said to him, as they ordered scotch on the rocks, and the Italian grandly paid for them both.

"Luca Saverio," he introduced himself. "I play here once or twice a month. In San Remo too." It was one of four cities in Italy that had legal gambling.

"I play in Paris, and Monte Carlo when I can get there. Max Bayard." The two men shook hands. "What do you do?" Max was curious about him. He had a bold, devil-may-care style about him that

Max admired. He had the feeling that Luca was slightly older than he was, but not by much. In fact, Luca was three years older but didn't look it. Luca was confident, friendly with Max, and arrogant.

"My family is in leather goods," Luca said, and then the name clicked with Max.

"Saverio leathers?"

Luca nodded. "And you?" Luca asked him.

"I work for my father in Paris. My father is crazy about what your family does. He makes handbags too, but nothing as fancy as yours. We have a commercial line that sells pretty well. Bayard." Luca didn't recognize the name because he didn't work in the business, and Bayard wasn't a competitor of Saverio. Only Hermès was, and a few other brands around the world. "His dream would be to buy you out," Max confided, and Luca shook his head. He liked the young Frenchman. He seemed like a cool guy to him, even if a little young.

"My sister will never sell. She kills herself trying to keep our business alive. She loves the business more than anyone, except maybe my younger sister. The older one works hard, though. Do you want to go back to the game, at another table?" he suggested. Max wanted to look like a big shot to him.

"Sure. Why not?" They finished their drinks, stood up and left the bar.

They picked another table, where someone had just made a big win against the house, which Luca said was a good sign. They sat down and Luca played his losses for double or nothing, and within minutes, he owed the house a hundred thousand euros. By two A.M. it was two hundred thousand. Max had lost ten thousand, a month's salary, and they were both drunk.

They left the casino together and Luca laughed and was leaning on Max when he said, "My sister will be so pissed." It didn't seem to worry him at all.

"Will they let you leave without paying up?" Max asked him, impressed. Two hundred thousand was big money.

"They know me well. I'll come back in a few days. They know where to find me."

"Do you live here?" Max asked him, as they walked outside on unsteady legs.

"I live in Rome. I just come here to gamble a few times a month." Luca pulled out his wallet then, took out a card, and handed it to Max. "Call me sometime if you want to come to Rome. I know a lot of hot women. I'll fix you up. If my sister hasn't killed me by then." He laughed when he said it.

"She sounds tough," Max said.

"She is," Luca agreed. Max handed him his card then, and Luca slipped it into his pocket.

"Call if you come to Paris," Max invited him.

"Where are you staying?" Luca asked him.

"At the Gritti Palace, with my dad. He came here for a party. I'm glad I went to the casino and met you tonight."

"Me too. I'll drop you off. I'm staying at a small

hotel with my sister." Luca made a deal with a speedboat driver. "We have a house here, but it's rented to some Americans." It didn't click with Max after all he'd had to drink. He was feeling woozy as they headed to the Gritti Palace, and the driver dropped him off a few minutes later. Luca waved as they sped away. He knew he'd have to face Cosima in the morning, and ask her for big money this time, but he wasn't worried about it. Tomorrow was another day. By the time Luca got to the hotel where Cosima was staying, Max was already sound asleep, fully dressed on the bed in the room next to his father's. He'd have to get an advance on his next month's salary when he got back. He had done it before. He just hoped his father didn't find out, or he'd lecture him again about the evils of gambling. Max hated working for his father, but Olivier paid him well.

Both gamblers were dead to the world.

Olivier hadn't heard from Max yet by the time he left to meet Cosima at the Saverio store off the Piazza San Marco. He took a boat to the square so he wouldn't be late, and he arrived just as she did, on foot. She was smiling and looked beautiful in a pale blue cashmere blazer with jeans and a white shirt. Her blond hair was long down her back, and she was wearing a beautifully made pair of Saverio loafers that looked like a work of art. She looked casual and chic, and carried one of their signature bags. She was still wearing the diamond studs in her ears from the night before. She led Olivier into the store and let him enjoy all the beautiful new merchandise they had on display. Most of it was their classic bags, and the signature bag she was wearing. There were a few styles he hadn't seen before, which she explained were remakes of old designs. She let him examine them closely and she could see the admiration in his eyes, as he murmured and handed them back to her like precious objects, and then she took him to the workrooms upstairs. Several of the craftsmen were hard at work, using all the old precise techniques and old-fashioned tools. The bags they turned out were perfection. Even the insides of the bags were beautiful. Then she led him to her grandfather's personal workshop, which they kept like a museum now. All the tools he had used were there on his workbench. Olivier touched them with awe, and looked at her with amazement.

"I never thought I'd be lucky enough to meet you last night. I had no idea you'd be there." It had been the high point of his trip, and worth coming just for that.

"You seem to know a lot about leather goods, Olivier," she said, curious about him. He had handled each piece with such reverence that she was touched, and he looked like he was about to cry in her grandfather's workroom.

"I've admired everything you do for as long as I can remember. I think it's fate that we met. You inspire me whenever I see something with your name on it."

"It's nice to know that it means so much to some people. I feel that way about our work too. It makes it all worthwhile," all the headaches and worries, and decisions she had to make every day.

"I'm almost ashamed to tell you that I make handbags too. The Johnsons are one of our biggest clients, which is why I was invited last night, and why I went. But I'm not in your category, nowhere near it. We make commercial bags, at a very different price point. They're good for what they are, but not even remotely in your league," Olivier said humbly. "Bayard, you may not even have heard about them."

"I have. I'm not sure I've seen them, though. I don't see other merchandise much. I'm too busy with our own."

"I would have loved to start a firm like yours, something to be proud of, work that will last for generations. What we do is gone in a few months. They vanish in the night."

"There's room for all ranges in the market," she said. He was a nice person and she didn't want to offend him. "Not many people can afford what we do," she said honestly.

"Your bags are what my family's haute couture clothes used to be. But there's so little market for it anymore. They sold the business when it began to fail, and I was hungry for commercial success when I established our company. I wanted to leave a viable company to my sons. But one of them is only interested in low-end mass production in China, and my younger son is an artist and isn't interested in the business at all. So I'm not sure what point there is to it anymore. I've thought about doing a small collection of truly fine bags, but I don't think the stores we deal with would buy them at the prices we'd have to charge. I've discussed it with the Johnsons. They're happy with what we do now, but it's not much of a challenge for me." He hesitated for a moment and then added, "If you ever want an investor or a partner in your business, I'd be first in line." It was a bold statement and she smiled graciously and declined his offer quickly, as he knew she would. He understood that even better now, after seeing the store in Venice, her grandfather's workroom, and the quality of the bags he'd just seen.

"It's a family business, Olivier," she said gently, "I'd sell my soul before I'd give up any part of it or sell a piece of it to someone outside the family. And I'm in the same situation you are. I have a brother who is irresponsible and wants nothing to do with the business, and a sister who is a talented designer and understands our old-fashioned techniques, but she's young and she's dying to make fashionable bags for young people at prices they can afford. She really doesn't want to design for our market. She's frustrated working for me. We all three own the business equally, but I'm the only one who wants to keep it the way it was, with all the old traditions and styles."

"You're doing the right thing. It's working for you," he reminded her. "Just like Hermès. They don't want outsiders in the business either. They'll never sell any part of it, and they don't need to."

"I may need to one day," she said with a sigh, "but I won't sell it if I can do anything humanly possible to avoid it." He believed her, and he understood it better now. She looked passionate and intense whenever she spoke of the business.

They sat at a café for a cup of coffee after he had seen the workrooms and the store.

"Now I'll understand your work even better when I see it." She was so fluent in French that they opted for his language and not hers. He spoke some Italian, he'd had to learn from talking to the workers in his factories, but it wasn't as good as Cosima's flawless French.

"Do you come to Rome?" she asked him.

"Occasionally. We have factories near Florence. I visit them fairly frequently."

"I'll have to watch for your bags now," she said kindly, but she was interested in his work too. He was clearly very knowledgeable about their business, at any level, whether his or hers. "Let me know if you come to Rome," she said. It had been fun meeting him. She was glad she'd gone to the Johnsons' party and so was he.

"When are you going back to Rome?" he asked her. He and Max were flying back to Paris that night.

"Sometime this evening. I have to catch up with my brother. He was supposed to arrive last night but he wouldn't come to the party. He said he was going to the casino. Unfortunately, he likes to gamble."

"So does my son," Olivier said, obviously unhappy about it. "And fast cars and racy women."

"They must be twins," Cosima said with a rueful smile, thinking about Luca. "At least your son has a job, working for you. My brother doesn't. And at thirty-three, he's getting to be too old to play around all the time and be so irresponsible."

"It sounds like you've got a lot on your shoulders," Olivier said sympathetically. And he only knew the half of it. She hadn't told him about Allegra, since they had just met the night before. "If I can ever do anything to help, let me know. I'd be honored," he said sincerely, and she was touched.

They finished their coffee and he walked her back to her hotel, and said he'd find his way back to the Gritti Palace. He had a map of Venice in his pocket. He hugged her before he left, and she wondered if she'd see him again. She liked him, he seemed like a decent man. She was thinking about Gian Battista as she went to her room. She wanted to call him before she left Venice. She had just gotten to her room when Luca knocked on the door. He looked seriously hungover when she opened it and took a look at him.

"You look like you had a rough night," she said. "I hope you didn't lose a lot of money." He didn't answer her at first, and sat down heavily in a chair while she closed her suitcase with the pink dress in it. His silence seemed ominous and she turned around to gaze at him again.

"I need some money," he said without preamble. In the cold light of day, almost sober, it was harder to say the words than he'd anticipated.

"How much money?" Her heart beat faster as she waited for the answer.

"You can take it out of my share of the profits," he told her. He hadn't brushed his hair or shaved, and she noticed the dark circles under his eyes.

"You already spent your profits for this year." He lived on an allowance but was always borrowing money from her.

He said something she didn't hear, and she stared at him. "What did you just say?"

"Two hundred thousand." Her eyes flew open wide, and she sat down with terror etched on her face.

"Please tell me that's a joke and you're not serious."

"I am serious, and I need it in a few days, or they'll send their goons after me." She was surprised they'd let him leave at all without paying.

"Are you insane? Where do you expect me to get that kind of money? I can't just pull that out of thin air."

"Take it out of the business."

"I can't do that. Sell your cars." He had a Ferrari and a Lamborghini.

"I won't get the money fast enough," he said, looking worried. "Sell the palazzo to the Americans. We don't use it anymore anyway."

"I'm not selling our family home to pay your gambling debts." She was angry and disgusted, but she knew that if she didn't pay, they might kill him. She had his life in her hands, and he had her by the throat. She couldn't put the business at risk by taking that kind of money out of it. It was out of the question. And the only thing she had to sell was the palazzo. She was furious with him. "Get your bag, we're leaving."

"I haven't eaten yet," he complained.

"I don't care. We're going back to Rome."

"Don't you have to go to the store or something?"

"I already did. If you're coming with me, I'm leaving in five minutes." He slammed the door on his way out, and she called Gian Battista on her cellphone. He answered as soon as he saw her number. "I'm leaving, I just called to say goodbye." He knew her well and could tell that she was upset.

"Did something happen?"

"Luca lost two hundred thousand at the casino last night. He's out of control."

"Oh God. One of these days you should let him deal with his own debts. It would teach him a lesson."

"He says they'll kill him if he doesn't pay soon."

"They might," Gian Battista admitted. "He can't keep doing this to you, though. It's not fair." He sounded as unhappy as she was.

"I don't think fair is the issue. He's going to ruin us one of these days. I can't afford it."

"What are you going to do?" He couldn't free up that kind of money without explaining it, but she wasn't asking him to, she was just sharing her miseries with him, as she always did.

"I'll have to think of something. He told me to sell the palazzo."

"He'll just blow that money too. He knows you'll bail him out. You ought to let him solve his own problems for a change. You can't mother him forever. You've been cleaning up his messes for fifteen years. I can lend you a small amount, but not that kind of money," he said.

"I know you can't, and I wouldn't let you. I just wanted to tell you that it was so nice to see you last night," she said. He had been missing her all day too.

"One of these days, you should count this against his shares of the business, so you get something in exchange."

"He always says it's a loan and he'll pay me back one day. I think he believes it but I know he never will."

Gian Battista agreed. "I'll see you in Rome soon," but she knew he wouldn't. He'd been trying to stay away in recent years, to encourage her to lead her life without him. It was hard for both of them.

"Take care of yourself," she said sadly. Seeing him was always like having a taste of a drug again. She was still addicted to him, and now she had to solve her brother's problem. Gian Battista told her he loved her and they hung up. Luca was waiting for her in the lobby, and she said not a word to him as they got into a boat to take them to where they could find a taxi for the airport. They were flying home.

All the way back, she thought about where to find two hundred thousand euros. There were only two possibilities. Take it out of the business or sell the palazzo. Luca was right, and she was furious with him. She left in a separate cab from the airport in Rome, telling him to get home on his own. She had told him on the flight that if this was another "loan," he should sell his fancy cars and pay her back eventually. She was sick and tired of paying his gambling debts. He didn't answer. He was never accountable and didn't want to pay her back.

When she got back to her apartment, she called Sally Johnson to thank her for the fabulous party. And then she hesitated for a moment, and leapt in.

"You know, you've done such a fabulous job with the place, you've brought it back to life. We're not ready to do it, but I was thinking last night. If we ever decide to sell the palazzo, would you and Bill be interested in buying it?"

Sally let out a scream before she answered. "Oh my God, yes. We'd love it. And there's so much more I could do if it were ours." It broke Cosima's heart to think about it, after all that she'd seen the night before. How many more pearls and crystals, coral branches and turquoise beads and Roman statues could they add to what their decorator had already done? Cosima shuddered at the thought. But her brother's life was at stake through his own stupidity, and if she didn't save him, it could be truly disastrous this time, for that amount of money. She felt responsible for him, as though he were a child, and she, his mother. "Bill will be thrilled to hear it," Sally went on, breathless with excitement.

"We haven't decided," Cosima said quickly, "but my brother and I were talking about it today, and he thinks we should. I'll give it some more thought and call you," she promised.

She had a splitting headache after that but went to check on Allegra anyway. Allegra said she'd had a busy weekend and had gone out to dinner with friends both nights. She knew all the young designers in Rome and hung out with them regularly. One of them wanted her to design bags for them, but she knew Cosima wouldn't like it so she had refused.

After Cosima listened to what Allegra had done all weekend, she told her about Luca's disastrous loss in Venice.

"What are you going to do?" Allegra looked panicked. "He's right, they probably will kill him if he doesn't pay up."

"It's so wrong to sell the palazzo to cover his gambling debts. And he'll do it again, you know it," Cosima said angrily. Allegra didn't disagree, but he was her brother and she loved him, no matter how derelict and irresponsible he was.

"You can't take it out of the business, just borrow it, and pay it back later?" Allegra asked her.

"I can't run a business that way." Cosima was frustrated.

"Then I suppose you have to sell the palazzo." Allegra had tears in her eyes as she said it, and so did Cosima. They both knew that Luca expected Cosima to come through for him. She always had before, but not for an amount like this.

Cosima went back to her apartment and tossed and turned all night. She barely slept, and sat on the terrace looking at the city before the sun came up. She knew she really had no choice, but she would warn Luca that this was the last time she would bail him out. She knew her father would have expected her to help him. Luca wasn't the head of the family now, she was, and had been since their parents had died. The idea of Luca as the head of the family was a bad joke.

It was all she could think about on Sunday, and she waited until nine o'clock Monday morning, called Sally Johnson from her office, and gave her the good news. For the Johnsons, not for the Saverios.

"We've decided to sell the palazzo if you and Bill are really interested. I spoke to my brother and sister, and we all agree." She didn't tell her why they were willing to sell it, or what a lowlife her brother was. She would never forgive him for this. "If Bill is agreeable, I'd like to have two hundred thousand fairly quickly, as a nonrefundable deposit and gesture of good faith. We can work out the final price later, after we get a proper estimate of what the palazzo is worth," which they both knew would be a great deal more than the deposit she had asked for.

"Of course," Sally said without hesitating. She didn't want Cosima to change her mind. She knew how much she and her family loved their palazzo. She considered it a great stroke of luck that they were willing to sell it. She thought the new décor might have convinced Cosima that they were worthy owners and would do an even more spectacular job once they owned it. "I'll have Bill write you a check today and put it in the mail. Is that fast enough?" Sally wondered for an instant if the Saverios had money troubles. She thought it unlikely. Their family business was such a successful and expensive brand.

"It's fine," Cosima said in a dead voice. She texted Luca as soon as she hung up. "You'll have your money in the next two days. You don't deserve it. I'm not giving you another penny after this. We're losing our family home because of you. You're a disgrace to our name and to yourself. I hope you learn your lesson this time. Don't ever ask me for money again. And you'll have your third of the money from the sale. I'll take the two hundred thousand out of your share, and you'd better not blow the rest at the blackjack table."

She had a heavy heart all day, just thinking about it. Luca hadn't answered her text. He'd had an idea and had dug in his pocket for Max's card. He found it in the pocket of the jacket he'd worn at the casino. He called Max as soon as he found it.

"How did your sister react when you told her what you lost at the casino?" Max asked, curious, still impressed that he could cover such a loss, and that the casino gave him credit. But he imagined that the owners of Saverio were rolling in money, so he wasn't entirely surprised.

"The usual. She had a fit, and read me the riot act, but she's going to cover it. I had an idea, though. I'd like to come to Paris to discuss it with you," Luca said in a silky tone that intrigued Max. He liked Luca. They'd had a good time together, despite their losses. And apparently Luca's weren't a big deal to him. Max had borrowed against his salary as soon as he got back to Paris, so he'd have money to live on for the next month. He had lost every penny he had in his bank account, and he didn't want his father to know. Olivier would have been furious with him.

"Sure. That would be fun," Max said with a grin. "I can take you to the casino at Enghien, but it's not Venice or Monte Carlo. It's pretty boring. And there's a small club on the Champs-Élysées."

"Sign me up," Luca said enthusiastically.

"When do you want to come?" Max asked him.

"How about this weekend? I have to take care of business here first," and pay his debt as soon as the Johnsons paid the deposit.

"You can stay at my apartment if you want," Max offered.

"Sounds perfect," Luca said. He had a brilliant plan and couldn't wait to tell Max. If it worked, he would even be able to give Cosima back the money and she wouldn't have to sell the palazzo. He didn't see why it wouldn't work. In his mind he was doing her a favor in the long run. He didn't want to tell Max on the phone what his plan was. He was waiting to tell him in person. As soon as he hung up, Luca knew he had the answer to their money problems. He was sure that it was providence that he and Max Bayard had met.

Chapter 5

Cosima deposited the Johnsons' check into Luca's account as soon as it arrived. They had sent it immediately, and Cosima felt sick when she saw it. It was the first step toward the saddest thing she'd ever done since burying her parents. But she had no other choice, with her brother's life on the line. It broke her heart to sell the palazzo, but she had no other way to cover his debt quickly. They had no spare money in the business. Everything they made they poured back into it, except what they needed to live on. She calculated it very tightly. They needed all the money they had to pay for the high-quality materials, operating costs, publicity, advertising, payroll, their expenses in both locations. The profits from the business supported Cosima, Allegra, and their brother. He was the greatest money drain of all. And the rest they put back into the business. She couldn't understand how he could gamble for such a large amount, knowing full well he didn't have the money to pay for it if he lost. He always thought he would win, but more often he lost, not knowing when to get out of the game, and not setting any limits for himself. He had no income other than his allowance since he didn't work. He was shameless about relying on his sister to cover his gambling debts. This time he had gone too far. The fallout from his recklessness was just too great, and the stress for her. Cosima swore she'd never pay another debt for him again, and meant it.

Luca flew to Paris on Friday night, and arrived in Paris at nine P.M. He went straight to Max's apartment in the 7th. His father had bought the apartment for him when he was twenty-five. It only had one bedroom, but there was a pullout couch he had invited Luca to sleep on.

They went out for a late dinner at a neighborhood bistro and shared a bottle of wine. Then Max took Luca to the gambling club he'd mentioned on the Champs-Élysées. They only stayed for an hour, since luck wasn't with them that night, and Max couldn't afford another heavy loss. Nor could Luca, but his slate was clean now, since Cosima had given him the money from the Johnsons' deposit to pay his debt, and he had taken care of it before he left Rome and made the deposit at his bank.

They were back at Max's apartment at one A.M. He poured them both a drink, although they'd been drinking steadily all evening, and they were both feeling jovial and in good spirits. After their night at the casino in Venice, they felt like they were old friends.

"So what's your brilliant idea?" Max asked, slurring his words a little, but his head felt clear, or he thought so at least. Luca took a long sip of the brandy Max had poured him and smiled.

"It's incredibly simple. I thought of it when my sister had a fit about covering my debt. She says she'll have to sell the palazzo. She won't even have to do that if we do this right. You said your father would do anything to buy into our business." Luca looked serious when he said it.

"And you said your sister would die first." Max remembered it distinctly.

"That's true. Except she doesn't own the business. We all do. We each own one-third of the business. I found an old copy of my father's will in my desk, and I read it the other day. There is nothing in it that says I can't sell my shares to whomever I want. I could sell them to you if I want." His eyes gleamed and he sounded victorious as he said it.

"I don't have the money," Max was quick to tell him.

"No, but your father does. I could sell him my third of the business, and he'd be a partner with my sisters. And there's nothing Cosima can do to stop it." Max grinned as he heard it. He liked the idea of being a hero in his father's eyes when he offered him the opportunity to make his dreams come true and own a major share in Saverio. It would be like owning a share in Hermès, an opportunity which was never offered to outsiders.

"Wow, my father would go nuts and leap at the chance. He'd pay you damn near anything for it. You don't need your sisters' permission?" Max was surprised at that, with a family as protective of their ownership as they were, and as closed about it.

"Nothing in the will says so. It says I can sell my shares to one or both of my sisters if I want to. But it doesn't say a word forbidding me to sell to someone else, and I don't have to give my sisters right of first refusal. There is no reference at all to selling my shares outside the family. I can sell to anyone I want."

"What will your sister say? I don't think she'll be too happy about it."

"She'll be happy to have a lot of fresh money to help pay operating costs. She's always crying poor about the business and whining about how expensive everything is. She'd be happy not to have to sell the palazzo, and she can give back the deposit that just paid my bill at the casino. It solves all the problems. She'll thank me for it one day." They finished their brandies toasting Luca's brilliant idea, and Max couldn't wait to tell his father. He was sure Olivier would want to buy in immediately, and Luca was always hungry for money. He wouldn't have to ask Cosima for a dime for a long time if Max's father paid him a handsome sum for his share of the business, and Max said his father was rolling in money. Their business was very profitable, probably much more so than Saverio. They'd have to have Saverio appraised to establish the market value of Luca's shares, but that didn't seem like a big deal to either of them.

Max and Luca fell asleep on the couch with another brandy, and woke up hungover the next morning, still excited by Luca's brilliant idea. They both agreed that Max's father would be over the moon at the prospect of becoming a part owner of Saverio, and Luca was thrilled at the prospect of an influx of money. He was tired of being broke and at Cosima's mercy for extra money. And at thirty-three, he didn't want to live on an allowance. He wanted to live like a rich man, just as he felt he deserved.

They went to the casino at Enghien that night, after nursing their hangovers all day. Luca won two thousand euros, and Max lost a small amount again. He was being very cautious. They went home early, and Luca flew back to Rome on Sunday morning.

Max was going to announce the good news to his father on Monday morning and could hardly wait. He was well aware that his father disapproved of many of his activities, and this was going to buy him Olivier's approval and gratitude forever.

Olivier had just sat down at his desk, when Max walked into his office with a broad grin on Monday morning.

"You look like you've had a good weekend," Olivier said to him. "Not gambling again, I hope."

"Of course not," Max said primly. "I have some very good news for you." Olivier looked at him, wary of what might come next. Their view of what constituted good news was rarely the same. "What would you say if I told you that I could present you with a one-third ownership in Saverio?"

"I'd say you've been drinking heavily at breakfast. I met Cosima Saverio last weekend in Venice. She runs it and is one of the principals. She is never going to sell. I have no doubt of that now. The family is deeply attached to the business. Who have you been talking to?" Someone was obviously leading Max astray, possibly for an up-front commission. Olivier wondered who it was.

"I met someone very interesting last weekend in Venice too, while you were at that party. He can make your dream happen."

"I strongly doubt that. He doesn't know what he's talking about." Olivier was definite about it, and Max was annoyed by how skeptical he was. He wasn't the least bit enthused and dismissed the possibility out of hand as pure nonsense.

"He's one of the owners, Dad," Max insisted. "He owns a third of the business, and he'd be willing to sell you his shares."

"That's not possible. What about his sisters? They'd never give their consent, at least not the sister that I met with, and she runs it."

"He doesn't need their consent. According to their father's will, they can sell to whomever they want. And he wants to sell to you." Olivier stared at him as though he didn't understand.

"Why does he want to sell to me, an outsider? According to his sister, that's not how the family operates."

"I guess he wants the money. He probably won't want to sell cheaply. But he flew here from Rome to offer it to me. I had told him that you're in love with their business. He researched it after I left and offered to sell his shares to you. It's an incredible opportunity that might never come again."

"Does his sister know? Cosima, the one who runs the business."

"No one knows right now, except you and me," Max said proudly, waiting to see the look of victory, elation, gratitude, and pride on his father's face. It didn't happen. Olivier frowned, looking gravely concerned.

"I would like to see documents showing me that he has the right to sell. I seriously question it, and he's walking himself, and me potentially, into a massive lawsuit. That's the last thing I want, or hostile partners. I told Cosima Saverio myself that I would love to invest in their business, and she brushed me off immediately. There's something very smoky going on here. What kind of guy is he? You met him at the casino?"

"He's a great guy and the head of the family. He can do whatever he wants."

"But he hasn't told his sisters. It sounds like desperation or an act of war to me. How much did he lose at the casino?"

"Not that much," Max lied to him, as he did about his own gambling debts. "He's a smart guy, and he wants to make a deal with you. What should I tell him?" Max was getting nervous. His father hadn't reacted as he had expected him to, which surprised him. He'd been sure Olivier would leap at the deal and thank Max profusely for making it happen. Instead, he looked like there was a bad smell of something rotten in the room.

"Tell him I'll think about it," Olivier said noncommittally, and looked busy at his desk. "Thank you for making me aware of it. Tell him I'll be in touch very soon," was all Olivier would say to him, and he waited for Max to leave. After he did, Olivier closed the door to his office, took out his wallet with Cosima's card in it, and dialed the number in Rome. He called her cellphone, not wanting to alert anyone in her office to the nature of his call, and she sounded surprised when she answered. She had just left a meeting and was on her way back to her office. She was going to let it go to voicemail until she saw who it was.

"Cosima? Olivier Bayard."

"Hello, how nice to hear from you." She was surprised.

He got straight to the point. "I'd like to have a private conversation with you." She was back in her office by then and sat down at her desk.

"On what subject?" She was curious, although she thought she could guess. He wanted to dazzle her with an offer to invest in her business. She needed the money, but she wanted no outside investors, and what they would want from her in exchange.

"It's a private matter, and I'd rather discuss it with you in person. I can fly in to see you for a few hours if you tell me when you're free. I don't want to discuss it on the phone." She could tell that he wanted to convince her about something and thought he could do so more effectively in person.

"I don't want to waste your time, Olivier. I meant what I said last weekend. I won't sell participation in the business to anyone outside the family."

"I understood that," he said, "but I've become aware of some facts I think you ought to know about." His call was sounding more mysterious by the minute, and it was clear he wouldn't discuss it on the phone. "Would you be free anytime tomorrow?"

She glanced at her calendar before she answered. "I can cancel my appointments in the afternoon," she said hesitantly.

"I'll do the same. I'll let you know when I'll be arriving, and I'll try not to take up too much of your time," he said politely. What he had heard from Max he wanted to tell her face-to-face, and offer his help to deal with her brother, who was clearly a loose cannon. If Luca was offering Olivier his shares, he could offer them to anyone else, and sell them to the highest bidder. For the safety of her business, Olivier wanted to warn her. Her brother, who was offering Max the deal, sounded like a scoundrel, and Olivier was sure it wouldn't be good news to her. "See you tomorrow then," he said. His gentle, friendly, warm tone when they'd met had disappeared and he was all business. She couldn't imagine why he was coming to see her, except to try to pressure her to let him invest in her business. Before he hung up, he said something that frightened her. "Don't tell anyone I'm coming until you hear what I have to say and decide how you want to proceed." His mission remained a mystery to her, and it was a long twenty-four hours waiting to see him. She couldn't guess what it was about, but she followed his request and didn't tell anyone she was meeting with him. She canceled her afternoon meetings for the following day, claiming a schedule conflict, and Olivier did the same. He had his secretary book him on an early flight to Rome and sent Cosima a text with what time he'd be at her office. He told his secretary not to tell a living soul that he was leaving town for the day. She was to tell people that he was at their factory outside Paris, resolving problems with the union.

He arrived at Fiumicino Airport at twelve-thirty the next day, and was at her office an hour later, right on time.

Cosima had skipped lunch and was waiting for him when her secretary ushered him in, and stood up to greet him with a warm smile. He looked serious and businesslike. He was carrying a briefcase with papers he had to read on the plane. He was thinking of going up to Florence the next day to visit one of their factories there, as long as he had come this far and was in Italy.

"You're very kind to come and see me," Cosima said politely. "I have to admit, it's a mystery to me. Would you like coffee, by the way? Or something to eat?"

"I'm fine," he said, relaxing a little as she led him to a couch and comfortable chairs in her office, where she held informal meetings. They both sat down, and Olivier took a deep breath. He hated telling her what he felt he had to, out of fairness to her.

"As I mentioned to you on Saturday, I have a somewhat badly behaved son," he began, "or let's say he has some bad habits. He likes to gamble. He was in Venice with me when I came for the Johnsons' party, and I believe he met your brother, by pure chance, at one of the casinos in Venice the night of the party."

"I'm sorry about your son," she said kindly, and then frowned. "My brother has the same bad habit, to a rather extreme degree. He's in disgrace with me at the moment. He lost a great deal of money that night, which he expected me to cover, since I often do. This time the amount was exorbitant, and I had to pay his debt to protect his life."

"I'm sorry to hear that too," Olivier sympathized. "I think the two of them hit it off. Your brother came to Paris to visit my son a few days ago and made him a proposition, which was actually meant for me. I learned of it yesterday, and wanted to make you aware of it immediately, face-to-face, because I suspect you're unaware of it, and it could put you and your business in serious jeopardy. Your brother offered—via my son, I never met him—he offered to sell me his share of your business, a third, I believe." His words hit Cosima like a bomb as she stared at him in disbelief.

"What? But that's not possible. He has said nothing to me, and he would require my permission and my sister's to sell his shares to anyone outside the family."

"He claims that's not true, and that he can sell his share of the business to anyone he wants, without your or your sister's consent. He seems very definite about it, or he may be lying to my son."

"Then he's lying. I'm sure there's a clause in my father's will that he can't sell his shares to anyone outside the family, although I haven't read the will recently." She looked devastated and as though she were about to cry, just at the thought that Luca would try to sell his shares to strangers. It was the ultimate betrayal in her eyes.

"I assumed as much, which is why I wanted to speak to you, and I didn't want to give you news like this on the phone."

"That's very kind of you," she said, still looking shocked and dazed. "I'll check, but I'm sure he's wrong and he needs our consent."

"If he doesn't, what worried me is that he could sell them to anyone disreputable, and just to the highest bidder, if he needs money. Gambling is a very dangerous thing. I had an uncle who was a gambler. He ruined his family and left them destitute."

"My brother is irresponsible in every possible way," she said with a sigh. "Thank you, Olivier, for telling me. What do you suggest I do?" She felt at a loss just thinking about it, and she knew Olivier was an honest man, since he had come to warn her, and hadn't seized the opportunity. "What did you tell him?"

"I told my son to tell him I would think about it. I didn't want him running off to sell to someone else, so I didn't close the door on the deal. I wanted to speak to you first, and I said I wanted to see documentary proof that he doesn't need the other heirs' consent, i.e., you. I think the first thing you need to do is check the will carefully and see if he's right and telling the truth. And then you need to confront him, and maybe make some kind of deal with him preventing him from selling to an outsider in future, but that might cost you, if he's greedy. Can you buy him out?" He felt sorry for her. She looked devastated.

"I can't afford to," she said honestly. "Everything is tied up in the business. Our operating costs are enormous. I suppose I'll have to buy him out at some point, but I can't do it yet and I can't believe he doesn't need our consent. I have to make sure my sister doesn't sign anything she shouldn't. She's young, and she loves him. He can be very convincing, particularly if he tells her his life is at risk in some way. She's an artist, not a businesswoman, she has a kind heart, and she's naïve. I'm at my wits' end with him, especially after his recent disaster. He owed two hundred thousand euros to the casino. I agreed to sell the palazzo to the Johnsons. I had no other way to cover his debt." She looked sad as she said it, and he felt terrible for her. He understood now what the palazzo and the business meant to her. They were her heritage, and she had dedicated her life and soul to preserving them for future generations that didn't even exist yet.

"Well, take a good look at the will, and call your lawyer."

"I'm actually a lawyer, or almost. One semester short of being one. I went to law school, but I didn't finish. My parents died and I came into the business. I never thought I would do that."

As they were talking, there was a knock on the door, and a beautiful young girl in a wheelchair rolled in. She was wearing a red sweater and jeans, and had long dark hair cascading past her shoulders and a beautiful face. She looked vaguely like Cosima, with a wide friendly smile and big blue eyes. She looked startled as soon as she saw Olivier and Cosima deep in conversation on the couch, and she thought her sister looked upset.

"Oh, I'm so sorry. Your secretary is out, I didn't know you were in a meeting." She started to roll her chair away and Cosima smiled and indicated for her to stay.

She turned to Olivier. "This is my sister, Allegra. She works with me, she's a designer."

"All I do is dust off our classic models and modernize the hardware a little," Allegra said modestly, but it was in great part true. She leaned over to shake Olivier's hand, and Cosima explained that he owned Bayard Bags. Allegra knew instantly what they were and her face lit up.

"They're fantastic! I buy a new one every season. I get them sent from the Bon Marché in Paris, and Harrods in London. They're my favorite bags, other than ours, of course," she said with a glance at her sister. "Are we going to do some kind of collaboration?" she asked hopefully, and Olivier laughed.

"Not if your sister has anything to say about it. I'm just an admirer of everything you do. But I'm glad you like our bags. I'll send you some of our new ones, for the fall line." She was exactly their market, young, chic working women, millennials who wanted fashion that changed frequently but not at insane prices. They didn't want bags that would last a lifetime, although that was Olivier's preference, and why he loved Saverio and Hermès. Allegra left them a few minutes later, and Olivier looked at Cosima. "She's a lovely girl and incredibly beautiful."

"She's fantastic, and a brilliant designer. She's wasted here, but I love having her in the business." She could see the question in Olivier's eyes that he was too polite to ask, what had happened to her to put her in a wheelchair. She was so vital and enthusiastic that she didn't look as though she belonged there. "She was in the boating accident with my parents and another family. Six people died. She was the only one who survived, with third-degree burns and a severed spinal cord. She's amazing, and incredibly brave. She was fourteen when it happened. She leads a full, busy life, but the damage isn't reparable. She never complains about it, and never has. She's twenty-nine now. I always feel guilty not giving her a free hand with her designs, but that's just not what we do. She's wasting her talent here, but it's a family business."

"Are you going to tell her what your brother is up to?" he asked, curious, impressed by both women.

"I will warn her not to sign anything. She still has some illusions about our brother. I don't. I know who he is, especially now, after what you told me." It was a shocking, dishonorable thing for Luca to do, and probably dishonest too.

"You have a lot on your shoulders. I'm sorry if I added to it, but I thought you should know as soon as possible. You have to stop him from selling to anyone who'll pay. I can string him along for a while if you want me to, so he doesn't go out shopping for other buyers. My son told him I would do anything to participate in your brand, so he thought I was a sure thing. I can keep it that way for a while. And I want you to know that under no circumstances will I buy his shares from him. I respect what you've done, and your philosophy, and I won't do anything to violate that." He stood up as he said it, and she stood too. He was an honorable man. He had just demonstrated that to her, and she trusted him.

"Thank you, Olivier." He had proven that he was a friend and an ally. "I'm going to get the will out and read it carefully and call my father's lawyer. There has to be a way to stop my brother. We'll find it." He hoped she was right, because if not, an out-sider could cheapen, commercialize, and destroy her business and the legend she had protected so carefully for fifteen years. He thought of something then.

"As long as I'm here, I'm going to go to Florence tomorrow to see our factories. We've had some production problems. Would you like to have dinner tonight if you're free?" He didn't want to be intrusive, but every time he saw her, he wanted to know more about her. She gave up no personal information, only about the business and the family. She was very discreet. She hesitated for an instant and then nodded. He had done her a huge favor and she felt as though she owed him a debt, or at least dinner.

"Why don't you come for a drink before dinner? Allegra and I live above the store, in our own apartments. I have a rather nice view from mine," she said shyly. "We grew up in this building, in the apartment I live in now. My brother has a house on the Appian Way, but Allegra and I stayed here."

"I'd love to see it," he said, fascinated by their history. The sisters were steeped in the traditions of past generations and yet were strong, modern women with minds of their own. He was intrigued that Cosima had studied law, and that her sister was a talented designer. It was a shame that their brother wasn't as decent as they were. Luca seemed to have taken a wrong turn somewhere along the way. Olivier worried about Max doing something like that, out of greed or weakness, by following someone else's lead or poor advice. Neither of them seemed to have a strong sense of morality, and it was odd that they had found each other at the casino, two spoiled young men with families that indulged them and their weaknesses. Max's mother had been cut from the same cloth, but apparently not Cosima's parents.

They agreed that Olivier would come for a drink at seven-thirty, and she explained to him how to access her apartment via the private elevator, from a side door with a code, and up a short circular stairway at the top. It sounded very romantic to him, although Cosima wasn't seductive. She didn't flirt with him. She was straightforward and friendly, but businesslike. It made him wonder if there was a man in her life. She didn't send out vibes that said she was available. He wondered if she was married to the business, or if there was someone or something else. Everything about her intrigued him. She was so attractive but seemed just out of reach. He was looking forward to spending the evening with her. He was staying at the Hassler, in walking distance from the store.

They shook hands when he left, and she went straight to the safe in her office, dug through some papers in a folder, and pulled out her father's will.

She sat down at her desk and read it carefully. Her stomach was in a knot as she did. Luca was right. There was absolutely nothing in the will that would forbid him from selling his shares to whomever he wanted, any stranger, at fair market value.

She couldn't understand why there was no protection in the will, and had never noticed that before. She picked up her phone as soon as she had read it carefully, twice. She called Gian Battista, who had been her father's attorney. He would know why the will was written that way, and how to stop Luca. Gian Battista always knew the answer to everything. When he saw that Cosima was calling, he answered on the first ring.

Chapter 6

Cosima told Gian Battista what Luca had tried to do, and that Olivier Bayard had come to warn her.

"He sounds like a decent human being," the lawyer said quietly. "He could have just bought Luca's shares."

"Could he? Is that right? Why in God's name didn't Papa write some language in to prevent that? How is it possible that Luca can sell to any stranger who comes along?"

"Because your father was an honorable man, and he assumed his son was too. We talked about that language in the will, and I wanted him to add a clause just as you said, and he told me it was completely unnecessary and even insulting, that no one in the family would ever sell their share of the business to an outsider. He wouldn't let me write it. I was afraid of just such a scenario as this one day. If one of you went bad, or got involved with a bad spouse or partner, you could be influenced to sell your part to a stranger. And now that's exactly what Luca wants to do." He didn't sound happy to be right.

"How do I stop him?" Gian Battista always had all the answers for her, to protect the family, but he didn't this time. Their father had left them wide open to exactly what Luca was trying to do with the Bayards. Fortunately, Olivier was an honest man and wouldn't do it. He had too much respect for Cosima, and the house, to buy into the business deceitfully or exploit the sisters as a result of their brother's greed.

"You can't stop him," Gian Battista said bluntly. "Unless he makes an agreement with you now not to sell, except to you and Allegra, or with your written consent." He thought of something then. "You pay him an allowance, don't you? Do you still?" Gian Battista had disapproved of the allowance ever since Luca turned twenty-one. He thought Luca should have a job, in the family business or elsewhere, but not collect an allowance to do nothing except spend money and get into trouble.

"I do," Cosima confirmed.

"That's not in the will. It's at your discretion." Gian Battista knew their father's will by heart and had written it at Alberto's request just as he wanted it. "Tell him there will not be another penny until he signs an agreement that he cannot sell his shares to anyone outside the immediate family, you and

Allegra in other words, without your written consent. That will tie his hands very effectively. He may not want to sign it, but he doesn't want to go to work either. In my opinion, he'll sign."

"Will you draw it up? I want to confront him soon, before he looks for other buyers if the Bayards take too long to respond or turn him down. He may have other debts I don't know about, and has no way to repay them, since I told him I won't cover his debts again." Luca would have no big influx of money now until the sale of the palazzo closed.

"I'll write something today," Gian Battista promised. She noticed that he sounded tired. "I'm sorry you have to go through this. There was always a bad element somewhere in Luca. I could smell it even when he was a boy. Your father didn't want to believe it, but it was there. He used to cheat other children in school, and steal money from the servants. They were always petty crimes that took advantage of someone weaker than him. You're not weaker than he is by any means, but your father left you and Allegra exposed by that flaw in his will. We'll try to correct it now."

Cosima hoped that Luca would sign the agreement. She was still worried about it when Olivier arrived at seven-thirty for a drink. He followed her directions and came past Allegra's door and up the narrow stairway to Cosima's penthouse apartment with the terrace. The view was spectacular, and the gilded domes of Rome's myriad churches shimmered in the setting sun.

"Oh my God, this is fabulous." He stood admiring the view as she offered him champagne, and they sipped it together.

"I love watching the sun come up here every morning. I used to give big parties on this terrace when I was younger. Now I enjoy it by myself. It's so peaceful, and so joyous. Rome is so alive at any hour." She loved the vibrancy of it. Venice was mysterious, and Rome happily chaotic.

"Rome is a beautiful city. I love the atmosphere. There's just enough mischief and magic to be fun. Paris is more serious," Olivier commented, "and not as exciting."

"But also very beautiful. It's my favorite city, after Rome."

"I love Venice too," he added, "and Florence. I'm always happy to have an excuse to go there for work."

"I've agreed to sell the palazzo to the Johnsons, as I told you earlier," she reminded him. "We haven't signed the papers yet, but it was the only way I could pay off my brother's casino debt."

"You can't do that," he said sternly, sad for her. "You have to cancel the sale."

"I have no choice. And the Johnsons love the palazzo."

"It's your history."

"It's more important to protect the business. We

live from that, and we don't use the palazzo now, which is why I rented it to them. Times change," she said philosophically, as they sat down on chairs on her terrace and looked at the view together. It felt peaceful being with him, and safe. He had protected her from her own brother with what he told her. He had come to Rome to help her defend herself and their business, and she was grateful to him. There was no doubt in her mind that he was a friend, and he had strong protective instincts. Gian Battista was like that too. They were both good men. "I spoke to our attorney today. He wrote my father's will. My father thought it unimaginable that any family member would sell to an outsider. I will have to make a deal with my brother to prevent him from selling his shares in the business. I may need the money from the sale of the palazzo now to pay him." It was a devastating situation for her.

They left as the evening grew darker, and he took her to Pierluigi on Piazza de Ricci, a chic trattoria that was one of the most fashionable restaurants in Rome. He talked to her about Basile, his younger son, over dinner, and it was obvious how proud Olivier was of him. He was everything that his older half brother wasn't, hardworking, warm, affectionate, honest. Basile wasn't jealous or greedy. He led the life of an artist in a small, simple apartment and created his street art almost every night. It was starting to sell at high prices. He had had a show a few months before, and every piece sold, Olivier told her.

"It's amazing how different the two boys are," he commented to Cosima. "Their mothers were too. I was married to each of them for a very short time. Youthful mistakes that cured me from ever wanting to marry again. I don't think marriage is my strong suit," he admitted. "But I'm lucky to have two sons out of it. I worry about Max, though. I think he could easily be led in the wrong direction, mostly for money. He always hung out with bad boys when he was young too."

"It's interesting that he and my brother found each other. Luca was always that way too. My parents made excuses for him, which were more acceptable when he was younger. He got worse after they died. I guess I wasn't tough enough with him either."

"I never had those problems with Basile. He was always a good boy. He's a good man now and has so much talent. Max is always looking for the shortcuts to big money. I suppose that's why he gambles."

"He and Luca have a lot in common," she said unhappily.

"Your sister has the same kind of open joie de vivre my son Basile does. Maybe it's because they're artistic and have talent. They're not chasing after money. Basile is shocked by what his paintings sell for now. It's street art and I think he'd do it for free.

He did actually for several years before he started selling his work."

"It's so complicated being a parent," Cosima commented.

"Especially at nineteen." Olivier smiled at her. "And I was no better at it at twenty-two when Basile was born. I was ridiculously young when I had both of them, and even more inept as a husband, although the two women I married weren't ready to settle down either. I shouldn't have married them. They both left me. We were children playing at marriage. I was always sorry that I didn't do it right, with the right woman at a more reasonable age. But by the time I was old enough to be a decent husband and have kids, I felt so burned by my earlier experiences that I never wanted to be married again. I'm not sure if I missed out or not. My relationships have been pretty sensible and sane ever since. None of them were destined to last, but they went on long enough and we always managed to end things cleanly on good terms. And now I'm happy as I am." He looked content as he said it and seemed to have few regrets except about his early marriages, and he was a loving father to both his sons, but he wasn't blind to Max's flaws.

"Me too," Cosima said, about being happy as things were. "The business keeps me busy and fulfilled. I took on the role of mother with Allegra when she was fourteen. Luca was eighteen, which was harder. I feel as though I've done all that. I wouldn't want to do it again." Although she would have for Gian Battista, but only for him. And he wouldn't. So children were no longer an option for her, nor was marriage. She wasn't seeking either one.

"You're still young enough to marry and have children of your own," Olivier said. It was what Gian Battista had said to her when he ended their affair three years before. But she wanted neither marriage nor children, except with him. She had known a great love in her life from twenty-six to thirty-five, and she still loved him. Gian Battista had filled her heart in ways that she didn't think any other man could. He had freed her so she could marry and have children, and she didn't want to. Just seeing him now and then was enough. She wasn't expecting more from him or out of life. Olivier had the feeling that there was a part of her that she didn't reveal to anyone. Cosima was a woman with a secret of some kind, and he didn't pry. She said she was happy as she was, and he believed her. But there was something sad in her eyes.

"I'm not sure I could ever have swayed Luca from the bad path he was on, even at eighteen. There was something deeply wrong in him, even as a boy," she said pensively.

"I feel the same way about Max," Olivier said seriously.

They spent a lovely evening together and found that they had many interests in common. He was hoping to see her again, even as a friend, if she would allow it, and he had proven himself worthy, warning her about Luca.

They strolled through the streets of Rome after dinner in the warm night air, and she told him about the agreement that Gian Battista was going to draw up for her, to have Luca sign. Olivier was relieved that she was going to deal with it before Luca ruined things completely by selling his shares to a stranger.

"I'll be coming back to Florence in a few weeks," he told her when they reached her private door on the street. "I'd love to see you again, if you have time." She was a busy woman with a big job, a demanding life, and heavy responsibilities, but there was something so feminine and appealing about her. She was a gentle person, and he had enjoyed the evening with her.

"I'd be happy to see you. I owe you a huge debt for telling me what Luca is up to. And thank you for not buying his shares."

"I couldn't do that to you," he said with a warm smile, and then he surprised her, and bent to kiss her gently on the mouth. She stunned herself by responding to him and kissing him back. She hadn't kissed any man except Gian Battista in twelve years, but it seemed entirely natural with Olivier. She wasn't sure if she should be angry at herself or not. It had taken three years after Gian Battista left their relationship to be open to another man, and she didn't even know if she was open to Olivier. But he had taken the first step. She looked up at him and smiled.

"Thank you for a lovely evening." She pressed the code panel and opened the door. "Goodnight, Olivier," she said softly, and then she was gone, back to her own life, and he walked to the Hassler nearby.

As she walked up the stairs to her apartment, she wasn't sure if she was glad he had kissed her. But it was the first time her heart didn't ache for Gian Battista, so maybe that wasn't a bad thing after all.

Gian Battista had the agreement for Luca to sign the next day, and he brought it to Cosima's office himself. He seemed tired and she thought he didn't look well. He said he'd had the flu recently, and she was happy to see him.

The agreement for her brother to sign was straightforward and simple, and made things clear. It closed the gap their father had left. Other than his sisters, Luca couldn't sell his share of the business to anyone, without their written consent. And she would give him no money or financial support unless he signed the protective agreement. She hoped it would be enough to convince him. Cosima and Gian Battista talked about Luca for a few minutes, but she didn't say anything more about Olivier.

She felt mildly guilty about kissing him when she saw Gian Battista, and he kissed her before he left her office. But his lips on hers seemed more nostalgic than passionate suddenly. She wondered if kissing Olivier had been a mistake and had changed things between her and Gian Battista.

After he left her office, she sent Luca a text, and asked him to call her. He didn't call until late that night, when she was in bed but still awake, reading some reports from her office.

"What's up?" He sounded like he was at a party and said he had just seen her text. She could hear noise and music and laughter in the background.

"I need you to sign some papers at the office," she said casually, not wanting to alert him that she knew what he'd been up to.

"Can you send them to me?"

"No. They need to be witnessed," which wasn't true. "Can you come by tomorrow?" She didn't want to let another day go by, waiting for him to sign the agreement. He had to sign three copies.

"Okay, fine. I'll come by sometime in the afternoon," as though she had nothing else to do but wait for him.

She thanked him and hung up. She could hear a woman laughing next to him.

He showed up at five in the afternoon the next day and looked like he had just climbed out of bed.

"So what am I supposed to sign?" he asked as he sprawled on her office couch. He looked handsome and disheveled and as though he'd had a lot to drink the night before.

"I got a call from a French lawyer," she said coolly, lying to him to protect Olivier, "wanting to confirm that you didn't need my permission or Allegra's to sell your share of the business. He represents the Bayards. I checked Papa's will, and apparently that's true. But I'm not going to work as hard as I do and have you sell out to a total stranger who could destroy our business. I spoke to Gian Battista, and he said that it never occurred to Papa that you might do such a thing. It's very simple, I'm stopping your allowance and all support until you sign an agreement that you need our consent in writing to sell to anyone other than Allegra or me."

"That's ridiculous. I can sell to anyone I want to," he said, laughing at her. "And Olivier Bayard has a ton of money and is crazy about what we do. He'd be a perfect business partner for you."

"I don't want a business partner, and you know it. And this business is what Allegra and I do, not what you do," she said coldly. "You don't have to sign, but there will be no more funds to you, no allowance, and I'm not paying any of your bills or debts until you sign. It's up to you." She saw fury in his eyes then as he looked at her. She had him cornered. He couldn't live without the allowance she gave him and had since he turned eighteen. He spent every penny of it every month. And if he signed the papers, he couldn't sell his shares to whomever he wanted for a lot of money, and the sale of the palazzo would not close for several months. He would have no money until then. None, without his allowance.

"Oh, for God's sake. I was trying to do you a favor, selling to Bayard," he said grandly.

"Behind my back, without our consent? That doesn't sound like a favor to me."

"If you let me sell to him, you can give the Texans back their deposit and don't have to sell the palazzo. I thought that would be more important to you."

"Keeping the business healthy and growing and in the family is more important," she said quietly. He stood up and grabbed a pen from her desk, thinking of the allowance he'd lose if he didn't. He had no choice. He needed the allowance to live as he chose. He signed all three copies, threw them at her, and stormed out of her office, slamming the door. She sat with the agreements in her hand for a long time, hating what he had become, but relieved that he had signed. He led a worthless life, content to be supported and do nothing and play all the time, gambling and chasing women, and buying expensive cars. It made her both angry and sad thinking about what a wasted life he led. Her parents would have been so disappointed in him. But at least their business was safe, now that he had signed. Olivier had warned her of impending danger and protected her from her own flesh and blood.

She sent Olivier a text in Paris saying that Luca had signed, and the same one to Gian Battista. She had two protectors now. One from the past, and one in the present. Gian Battista had shielded her when she was very young, after her parents died and for many years after. And now Olivier had appeared and protected her from Luca's malevolent intentions and shady deals and warned her. They were good men, and she was grateful to have them in her life. She wondered if it would be possible to love them both.

Olivier answered her an hour later, telling her how relieved he was. He told her to call on him if there was anything he could do to help her. But he had already helped her enormously.

She heard from Gian Battista late that night. All he said in his text was "Happy to hear it. Sleep tight." The ache she felt hearing from him was gentler now. But it was hard not to remember the passion they had shared for nine years.

Luca was at a party that night, with the usual flock of women around him. He offered to take one of them to Venice with him the next day. He had a hunger to go to the casino to play. He'd be more careful this time, so he didn't owe his bitch of a sister money again. She was hell on wheels to deal with. But at least he hadn't lost his allowance. And when she sold the palazzo, he'd have his share of that money too. He had another idea he wanted to share with Max Bayard. They were kindred spirits, and Luca had a plan. All he wanted was money now, big money, and as much as he could get. As far as he was concerned, he deserved it. He would have the money from the sale of the palazzo, and possibly even more than that to top it off. He smiled thinking about it. The good times were coming. And to hell with his sister. He had no feelings for her or anyone else, only himself.

Chapter 7

Cosima waited until the following week to meet with Sally and Bill Johnson. She'd had time to speak to Allegra in the meantime about selling the palazzo. It had been the only way she could cover Luca's outrageous gambling debt fast enough to save him. She couldn't pull two hundred thousand euros out of the business with no justification for it, and she was meticulous with their books and their money, and ran the company honestly and responsibly. The palazzo was an enormous asset, which brought them rental income now. But there was more to be gained by selling, no matter how painful for them. They all remembered the time they had spent there with their parents, the elegant parties they gave and the magnificent balls. They had been dazzling hosts, surrounded by glamorous people, royals and socialites and movie stars. It was a forgotten era now. A time of dazzling social life in Rome. And the upkeep of the palazzo was enormous, in a city with difficult weather conditions and the sea and the canals eroding the historic buildings.

Selling the palazzo had been the only solution Cosima could think of to solve Luca's pressing need, and possibly save his life, and selling would bring them each a sizable amount of money, even if it pained her and Allegra to sell.

Luca's most recent escapade had made her realize that at some point it would be wise for her and her sister to buy him out of the business. He would be happy with the money, and they'd be better off without his ability to interfere.

Allegra didn't disagree with her, but she was sad to lose the palazzo that had been in their family for centuries. She was more romantic and sentimental than Cosima, who saw the practical side of things as well. Allegra always trusted her sister's decisions, but she was sad about this one. Selling the Palazzo Saverio seemed like an enormous piece of their history to give up, but out of respect for her sister she didn't oppose the sale, although she was unhappy about it.

"If we don't sell it, I'll owe them the two hundred thousand euros they gave me, which I had to give Luca," Cosima said with a sigh. "We have no other way to cover it. I can't take it out of the business," and they both knew they didn't have that kind of money lying around. Their father had always impressed upon Cosima never to borrow money. But he couldn't have imagined that they'd have to sell the palazzo, and all because of their brother's folly and vices. He had demonstrated that he would do anything for money.

"Luca will be happy with the money when we sell it," Allegra said wistfully.

"He never cares where the money comes from, as long as I pay his debts," Cosima said angrily. Countless times she had had to cut back severely on something for herself or Allegra, to cover him, and he barely thanked her. He expected to be taken care of and didn't even pretend to have an interest in the business that supported them all.

The meeting with the Johnsons went smoothly. Cosima had had time to consult several realtors and had an idea now of what the palazzo was worth in the current market. It needed repairs and modernizing. There was maintenance they had deferred because the careful work it required, given the palazzo's age, was expensive, and they couldn't afford to keep it in pristine condition. But with its history, and how beautiful it was, and its size, it was worth a great deal of money. Cosima wanted to put some of the money into the business, but the sale would give each of them more than they had in the bank now, and a cushion for the future. Before they'd rented it to the Johnsons, it had been a constant drain on them with repairs they couldn't avoid, and

Cosima had been responsible about keeping it in the best condition they could afford, with the help of their two old caretakers. The repairs they had done served them well in the negotiations with the Johnsons, and they settled on a price which seemed fair to all of them. They were going to have reports done on the health of the structure and the stone, but there were few surprises. Cosima and the Johnsons were well aware of the palazzo's weaknesses and its strengths.

The Johnsons wanted a ninety-day closing on the sale, which would take them into September, and at the end of September they were going to bring their architect and their decorator back to outline their plans for remodeling and renovation, and all the modern touches and elements they wanted to add once it was theirs. The timing sounded right to Cosima. Until then, the Johnsons were going to sign a "promise of purchase," establishing the price and their intention to buy the palazzo in three months. No further money would change hands until then, since the Johnsons had already given her the two hundred thousand as a deposit. They intended to pay the balance in full at the end of the ninety days. Until then, the Palazzo Saverio would belong to the three Saverios, and after that it would change hands. The two hundred thousand euros already paid was a nonrefundable deposit if they changed their minds or defaulted on the sale, and the deposit was to be returned in full by the Saverios if they decided not to sell. But both sides had ninety days to change their minds. The Johnsons were worried that the Saverios would back out before the end of the waiting period, but Cosima assured them that she couldn't imagine a circumstance that would induce them to keep the palazzo. It was a practical although painful decision for them. The Johnsons had unlimited funds to spend to bring it back into pristine condition, the Saverios didn't, and the family hadn't lived in Venice for thirty years. However much the family regretted it, and however attached they were to the palazzo, it seemed like a wise decision to sell.

Allegra was satisfied with the conditions Cosima had agreed to, and when she informed Luca, as usual he complained.

"Why didn't you get a bigger deposit? They can afford it, and why not shorten the waiting period?"

"We don't need to," Cosima said simply. "Ninety days will pass quickly enough," and they all needed time to adjust to the idea of the loss. They didn't need the palazzo, but they loved it.

"It would have been nice to have the money sooner," Luca said. They didn't need it any sooner, and Cosima was sure that Luca would spend his share in a matter of months, knowing how irresponsible he was with money. She hoped he wouldn't gamble it away, but she had long since learned, and again recently, that she couldn't protect him from himself.

It was painful to listen to the Johnsons' plans and their elation at the prospect of owning the palazzo. But at least they loved it, and she knew that the palazzo would be in good hands. There were no future generations of Saverios to pass it on to. Realistically, it didn't seem likely that any of them would have children, or perhaps even marry. Allegra had a wide circle of friends, but no serious suitors. Her circumstances were complicated since the accident. Men still found her beautiful, but a wife with a serious spinal cord injury was a major undertaking, and she'd never come close to marriage with any of the men she knew, or even had a long-term relationship. She was capable of having children, but it didn't seem likely. And Cosima had given up the idea of marriage once she'd fallen in love with Gian Battista and knew he'd never divorce. No man had come close to meaning as much to her, and she still couldn't imagine it. Marriage was the farthest thing from Luca's mind in his self-indulgent, hedonistic life. So there were no Saverio heirs to be considered, present or future, and no spouses on the horizon either.

The Johnsons were planning to go back to Dallas for July, and then to a home they had in Aspen for August, to avoid the crowds of tourist season during the summer in Venice. They'd be back in September in time to close the sale.

"I could have chartered a yacht this summer if

they closed sooner," Luca said to Cosima, which irritated her again.

"You're ridiculous. You can charter one next
summer, if you have any money left. When are you
going to grow up?"

"Hopefully never. You don't make it look like
much fun," he said, bitter about the agreement
she'd made him sign to protect the business and
prevent him from selling without her and Allegra's
permission.

"We're getting a good price for the palazzo. And
none of this would have happened if you hadn't been
an idiot at the casino with Olivier Bayard's son."

"You should have let me sell my share of the
business to him. You could have paid the Johnsons
back their deposit and kept the palazzo you and Allegra love so much." He had no sentiment, only an
unquenchable thirst for money he could squander.
How he got it didn't matter to him. "I might still
charter a boat in September, to celebrate." He had a
vast entourage of hangers-on to draw from whenever he had some money. "Don't you ever want to
have fun, Cosima? You can't be dutiful all the time."
But she was, in part thanks to him.

"I love the business. That's fun for me."

"You should have a good time for a change. Allegra has a better time, and she's stuck in a wheelchair. She goes out more than you do."

"She's younger and she doesn't run the business,"
Cosima responded. "Thank you for your advice," she

added coldly. She was utterly fed up and disgusted by him.

It was easy to have fun and be young and carefree when someone else was paying the bills, which was the role she'd been assigned when their parents died. He had never stepped into their father's shoes. He had left that to her. And their father hadn't been so wise with money either. They lived well beyond their means, and the scope of the business at the time. It was Cosima who had put the family business firmly on its feet. Luca always said she lived like a nun. She and Gian Battista had kept their affair a secret, and as far as Luca knew, there had never been a man in her life. Luca had always thought her strange.

Allegra had suspected that there was someone, had guessed that he was married, and possibly who it was, but Cosima had never told her the truth. She kept her secrets to herself. Luca just thought his older sister was dull. Allegra had always sensed that there was a mysterious side of Cosima she never shared, and didn't question her about it. Just as Cosima never asked Allegra how far things went with the men she saw her with. They respected each other's privacy. Everyone in Rome knew what Luca was up to, and who he was with. He hung out with the worst elements in Rome.

Luca went to Paris again once Cosima had made the deal with the Johnsons and set the price for the palazzo. Luca knew just how much he was going to get out of the sale. It was a very sizable amount, and he was looking forward to it. But he wanted more. He knew how fast money could evaporate, and how quickly it was spent. He saw an opportunity around every corner.

He stayed with Max Bayard again while he was in Paris. They went to the casino in Enghien together and had a few minor wins, nothing to get excited about. Max had been cautious since their night of mad excess at the casino in Venice. Paris was lively and entertaining, and Luca liked French women. They were dazzled by his looks and fell prey to his charms. He spoke French fluently, which made it easy. Word of his reputation hadn't traveled as far as Paris, and Max didn't mention to his father that he had seen Luca again. They made plans to meet again in Venice in July. Luca had a friend who was away for the summer and had loaned him an apartment. They were planning to go to Saint-Tropez afterwards. Max had a friend they could stay with there. There would be plenty to do. They were similar in their pursuits and an unholy pair.

Luca was tempted to ask the Johnsons if he could stay at the palazzo, since they'd be back in the States for the summer and the place would be empty. But he knew that Cosima would be furious if he did, and he wanted to stay away from her for the moment, so he settled for the friend's apartment in Venice on one of the smaller canals. Max was going to stay with him there. Max had five weeks' vacation by law in France, and Luca had no obligations. He usually floated around Europe in the summer, staying with friends, pursuing easy women, and gambling when he could.

As they did every summer, Cosima rented a house in Sardinia for two weeks and took Allegra with her. It was lively and fun, and they had friends there, many of whom had boats and invited them to spend the day on them. The time away from Rome did them both good.

They'd been there for a week when the store manager in Venice called Cosima at midnight, sounding panicked.

"I'm sorry to wake you," he apologized.

"You didn't. We just got home from dinner." They had dined late on a friend's boat in Porto Cervo and had had a good evening.

"I just got a call from the fire chief. There's a fire."

"At the store?" She was instantly alert as she listened intently.

"At the palazzo. He thought you should know."

"Oh my God, there's no one there. The Johnsons are in Aspen. How bad is it?"

"It sounds serious. It's not contained yet. I'm going there now, but I wanted to call you first."

"Let me know as soon as you get there." The palazzo wasn't far from the store, and Cosima sat for the next hour with the phone in her hand, waiting for news. She told Allegra as soon as she ended the call, and they sat together, waiting, until the store manager called them back.

"The fire is almost contained now. The palazzo isn't destroyed, but there's considerable damage, and probably a lot of water damage. They wanted to put the fire out as quickly as they could. One of the firefighters told me that most of the contents of the first floor are damaged, the furniture and the art. They won't let anyone in for several hours until they're sure it's safe and the fire is out. I can't really talk to them yet. I'll call you back in the morning when I know more." Cosima looked shocked when she hung up and reported to Allegra, who was distraught. As they talked, Cosima changed from the Pucci silk pajamas she'd been wearing into jeans and a T-shirt, a safari jacket, and sneakers.

"Where are you going?" Allegra asked her.

"To the airport. I want to be there when it opens. I'll catch the first flight out to Venice. I want to see the damage myself. We still own the house, and I don't know what the Johnsons will want to do if the house is badly damaged. They may back out of the sale. Can you manage without me for a few hours?" Cosima asked her, but she knew she could, and the housekeeper who came with the house would be there in the morning to make breakfast and clean the house and help Allegra if she needed it.

"Do you want me to come with you?" Allegra offered.

"No, stay here. I'll call you when I get there. And I'll try to come back quickly, depending on how bad it is." It was at times like this that Cosima was sorry she didn't have a man in her life, to lend a hand and be there with her. Gian Battista had always been such a strong support for her before, and still was to some extent. But it was late and she didn't want to wake him. He was at his family's home in Tuscany for the summer, and there was nothing he could do from there. Like everything else, she had to deal with the fire on her own.

She left in a cab to the airport in Olbia twenty minutes later, waited until the airport opened, and was able to catch a flight to Rome at six-thirty, and from there caught a flight to Venice. She couldn't even get a cup of coffee while she waited in Olbia, and had dozed in a chair for five hours before her first flight. Both flights were on time and she landed at the airport in Venice at ten A.M. and took a cab to where she could catch a speedboat into the city. She was already tired when she got there, and tears stung her eyes when the Palazzo Saverio came into view.

Many of the windows were broken. Some of them had been made of antique handblown glass. There were black streaks on the façade where the flames had been. Firefighters were still coming in and out of the house, and there were piles of debris in the garden, made up of priceless antiques and the Johnsons' new decor. There were people on the street staring at the activity, and one of the fireboats was still in the canal in front of the palazzo. The smell of smoke was acrid and heavy in the air. Cosima got out of the boat and ran up the dock to the house. Two firefighters stopped her, and she explained that she owned the palazzo. They stood aside then and let her peek inside. Much of Sally Johnson's recent decorating had been destroyed, and the antique furniture was either burned or soaked. The wood paneling in the main living room had badly burned, and Cosima felt sick as she saw it. The damage looked devastating, although it might not be as bad as it looked at first, but the house had been heavily affected by the fire and the powerful water hoses used to put it out.

"You can't go inside yet," one of the firefighters told her. There were still firefighters everywhere checking for pockets of fire and embers that could burst into flame again. Cosima looked through all the windows that remained. Some rooms were better than others, and the ballroom appeared to be untouched. The fire hadn't reached it yet. Some of the Johnsons' decorative statues had melted, and others had exploded in the heat of the fire.

The palazzo had been saved, and the roof was intact, but it would take a lot of work to restore it to the condition it had been in. Cosima had no idea what would happen to the sale now, and how the

Johnsons would react. It had become a much bigger project than even they had been planning to undertake. If they didn't repair the damage, Cosima would have to. It was a daunting prospect, as she sat down on a garden chair in the midst of the debris in the garden. She called Allegra at noon, after she'd seen as much as she could. The caretakers had been away for the weekend.

"It's a mess," Cosima said, trying not to cry. She didn't want to scare her sister, and knew she had to be strong.

"Is the house burned to the ground?" Allegra asked, panicked. She'd been up for hours, waiting for news from her sister.

"Several of the rooms are badly burned, especially the ones with wood paneling. There's water damage everywhere. The tapestries, curtains, and antique chairs are ruined, one of the big chandeliers fell, and a lot of the windows are broken. It's going to cost a fortune to repair it, and take a long time. I don't know what condition the upper floors are in, but the fire got to the second floor before they put it out. It may not be as bad as it looks right now, but it's pretty awful," Cosima said. "It's not safe to go in until tomorrow, so I'll stay here tonight. And I want to get some kind of cleanup started before I come back."

"Do you want me to fly in?" Allegra offered.

"No, I want you to stay in Sardinia." It would be too hard for Allegra to try to deal with it from her wheelchair. "I'll get Tomaso and Guillermo to help once we can go in. They'll be back tonight." They were the caretakers they'd had for years, and they were devoted to the family. "I'll call you tomorrow once I've been inside and seen how the rest of the house looks. The first floor looks pretty bad. They're investigating what started the fire, whether it was electrical or something else." Some of the wiring was very old, and none of it was recent. That was part of the work that the Johnsons were planning to do, replacing a lot of the wiring to make it safer.

"I'm so sorry, Cosima. Let me know if you change your mind and want me to come and help," Allegra said.

"Just stay at the house in Porto Cervo. We have it for another week." Cosima didn't bother to call Luca because there was nothing he could do either, and he probably wouldn't offer to help. She didn't even know where he was, on his summer rounds to visit friends. He was never a help in a crisis and wouldn't be now.

Cosima had a long talk with the head of the fire brigade after she hung up. They were checking the house for signs of arson, which Cosima considered unlikely. She explained that the house was unoc-cupied for the summer. She was sure the wiring was the culprit and felt guilty that she hadn't dealt with it before, but it was so expensive to replace and everything in the palazzo still worked, even if it was antiquated.

She hung around the scene of the fire all day, and finally at six o'clock they were sure it was safe and let her go in. They assigned a firefighter to go with her, so she wouldn't get hurt. There was broken glass everywhere. She went from room to room carefully. The top two floors were unaffected, except for smoke damage, and the smell was awful. The bottom two floors had sustained the greatest damage. It took her an hour to check the house from top to bottom, and she took many photographs with her cellphone to show Allegra and their insurers in Rome. It was going to be a costly venture repairing it. The brigade chief was on the scene and spoke to her when she emerged.

"We have our answer," he said with a stern expression. "We found oil-soaked rags in three of the rooms. It was arson." He looked grim.

"That's impossible. Who would do that? Vandals? Do you think they broke into the house?"

"Arson happens for a lot of reasons," he said. The police were on the scene then too, and the brigade chief informed them that it was arson. A more extensive search would be made once the embers were colder, but they no longer had any doubt. Someone had set the fire on purpose, out of pure malice or for other reasons. Usually for insurance money. Cosima was shocked. The fire brigade took the rags as evidence and commented that whoever set the fire hadn't tried to remove them once the fire had caught. They said it must have gotten hot very quickly, and the flames had caught on the antique draperies and upholstery. The police marked it as a crime scene, and they wouldn't let Cosima go back in.

She eventually went to the small hotel near the house where she often stayed, checked in, called Allegra again, and reported to her that the fire had been set intentionally.

"What a horrible thing to do," Allegra said in a choked voice. Cosima sounded numb. She had barely slept the night before, except in an airport chair, and had been on her feet at the scene all day. And she was in shock over the cause of the fire. The police and fire brigade were sure it wasn't an accident and had opened a full-on investigation.

Cosima had just hung up with Allegra when Olivier Bayard called her. He sounded cheerful and in a good mood.

"I'm coming to Rome tomorrow. I have meetings in Florence the day after, even though the factory is closed. Would you like to have dinner tomorrow night? I'm sorry it's such short notice."

"I can't. I'm in Venice," she said, exhausted. "There was a fire at the palazzo last night. Allegra and I were in Sardinia. I've been here all day. It's a disaster." She hadn't seen him since he'd left Rome a month before. He said he'd been swamped in Paris with a huge workload. He had texted her a couple of times just to say hello.

"I'm so sorry. How did that happen?" he asked her. "Careless? A lit cigarette? Electrical?"

She hesitated, but she didn't want to lie to him.

"They think it was arson. They found evidence. I can't understand why anyone would do that."

"People do it to commit insurance fraud sometimes. Are the police being helpful?"

"More or less. They've been busy, and the arson issue makes it a much bigger deal. I hope they don't think I set the fire."

"Of course not. They must know who you are. I take it you still own the house and it hasn't changed hands." He knew she was selling it, but not if the sale was final yet.

"I still own the house," she said, feeling like a zombie. It was all catching up with her and she felt like she might faint. She hadn't eaten all day either, and no one had thought to bring her something. The store manager had come and gone. And Tomaso and Guillermo, the guardians, had been busy as soon as they arrived.

Listening to her, Olivier made a decision. "I don't need to be in Rome, and I can put off my meetings in Florence for a day or two. I was coming to Rome to see you. I'll come to Venice tomorrow in case you need a hand. This sounds complicated, if it's arson. You shouldn't be there alone. Is your sister with you?"

"She's at a house we rented in Sardinia. She wanted to come, but it's too difficult with her chair.

There's debris all over the place on the ground outside the house." The caretakers were going through it for anything valuable.

"Where are you staying?" She gave him the name of the hotel. "I'll be there tomorrow morning. I'll find you."

"You really don't need to do that. I'm fine here on my own," she said bravely, but he could hear how upset she was.

"I'm sure you are, but I'd feel better seeing you." He was matter-of-fact about it, and she didn't argue with him, and was grateful. She took a long shower when she hung up, to get the smell of smoke off her and out of her hair. No amount of soap and shampoo did it. She bought a sandwich at a nearby trattoria, ate it quickly, and went back to the hotel and to bed. As she lay there, she felt guilty for letting Olivier Bayard come the next day, but relieved too. She could manage on her own, and five minutes later, still in her clothes, she was sound asleep.

Chapter 8

Cosima was back at the palazzo at eight o'clock the next morning. There was a police officer outside the house to prevent looting. She told him who she was, and went in. She had been pawing through debris with heavy gardening gloves for two hours when she heard someone call her name from the floor below. She had started at the top where there was the least damage and was working her way down, when she saw Olivier come up the stairs. He looked tall and solid and sympathetic when she saw him, and he gave her a hug and held her for a minute, and then looked her over. Her sneakers were wet and she was filthy, and had smudges of ash on her face.

"I'm sorry I let you come," she apologized. "This is an awful project. I don't even know where to start. It's a disaster downstairs on the first floor. The fire didn't get up here."

They walked down the stairs together, and he

looked around as they got to the more affected areas. "Once you sift through it for anything you want to save, you need one of those companies that come in and clear it all out for you," he said practically. It was much too big a job for her, the two old caretakers, or anyone but professionals. But he was glad he had come to lend her support. She looked as overwhelmed as she felt.

"I left a message for our insurance company yesterday. I think they arrange things like that." But it was the weekend and the office was closed. There was only voicemail. It was Sunday when Olivier arrived.

He went through some of the debris with her and had been working for two hours when one of the police officers came into the house and told her that the detective in charge of the case would like to meet with her at the police station after lunch. He looked ominous as he said it, and she whispered to Olivier after the officer left them and went back to his post outside.

"What do you suppose that's about?"

"Standard procedure. They want information from you, or anything you might know about a potential arsonist."

"He didn't look friendly."

"He's a police officer, he's not supposed to be," Olivier said calmly. "Have you told your brother about the fire? He might have some ideas. I hope he's not in debt again."

"Me too. And I haven't called him. He's never any help when something bad happens. He figures it's not his problem and disappears. I don't even know where he is right now. He's been floating around visiting friends. He does that every summer. He could be anywhere, France, Greece, Turkey, Italy. He usually goes to the best places." Olivier didn't comment but he thought less and less of her brother the more he heard about him, from her and his own son Max, who said he liked Luca. From all he had heard of him so far, Olivier didn't. He seemed to leave his sisters high and dry at every opportunity. Olivier was very glad he had flown in from Paris. If nothing else, Cosima needed a friend with her.

He convinced Cosima to stop working for long enough to go to the trattoria with him for a quick lunch, and then he went to the police station with her. They made her wait for half an hour, and then eventually called her in to the chief detective's office. They were polite but not pleasant, and Olivier was surprised by how little compassion they showed her. Her home had been badly damaged, and Olivier could guess that she was in shock, and the discovery that it was arson was traumatic, although she was calm and polite when addressing the police. They asked for their full names, Olivier's as well, and to see their identification. They made note of it and asked her if she was the sole owner of the house. She said she wasn't. She owned it with her brother and sister. She said the house was currently rented to Americans, and they were away, back in the States for the summer, and they had taken their employees with them. The chief detective then asked the whereabouts of her brother and sister.

"My sister is in Sardinia, at a house we rented for two weeks, and I have no idea where my brother is. He travels in the summer." The officers wrote down that information too, along with Allegra's and Luca's names and cellphone numbers so the police could reach them if necessary.

"Were you aware that the house was unoccupied and the renters were away?"

"Yes, of course. I'm in regular contact with them."

"Why were you in Venice if you rented a house in Sardinia?"

"I came when the manager of my store here called me on Friday night to tell me about the fire. I flew in yesterday morning."

"What flight did you come in on?" the detective asked her, and she told him and glanced at Olivier. The questions seemed odd to her, and he didn't comment. "Is the house insured? And the contents?"

"Yes." She gave the police the name of her insurance company.

"For what amount are the house and contents insured?"

"Five million for the contents, and ten for the

house itself." The detective nodded and wrote it down, and then asked Olivier why he was there. Olivier said that he was a friend and had come to help her.

"From Paris?"

"Yes, I have business in Florence next week. I have factories there." He gave the detective his business card then, which showed that he was the CEO of the company. Cosima didn't have her business cards with her.

"And you own a store here?" the detective asked Cosima. Her name had apparently not rung any bells for him.

"Yes. And one in Rome." He nodded and made a note.

"Can you think of any reason why someone would have wanted to set fire to your palazzo?"

"None at all. It must be the work of vandals, who just wanted to damage my property," she said quietly.

The chief detective went on questioning her for an hour, and then informed her that she had to stay in Venice while the police continued their investigation. He asked if there had been any similar incidents at her store, and she said there hadn't been. Two hours later, she and Olivier were free to leave the police station, but not the city, in her case. Olivier appeared to be of no interest to the police. They went to a café after that for a cup of coffee.

"Why do you think they asked all those questions? Do you think they suspect me of starting the fire?" The idea was insane, but people committed insurance fraud all the time for the money.

"They probably want to rule out insurance fraud, which won't be an issue in your case. He obviously isn't a customer at Saverio, but when they check it out, they'll know you're respectable." She nodded. It made sense, although it wasn't flattering to be treated as a potential criminal.

"I should probably call Luca and tell him what's happening and find out where he is. He might even be in Venice, for all I know. Hopefully not at the casino. He doesn't usually like being here in summer. It's too crowded with all the tourists." She took out her cellphone and called him and was surprised when he answered. He usually let it go to voicemail when she called him, unless he wanted money from her.

"Why are you calling me?" he said bluntly.

"Because I wanted to know where you are. There was a fire at the palazzo on Friday night. It's badly damaged, the police have said it was arson, and they want to talk to all three of us. Where are you?"

"In Saint-Tropez. I just got here. I'm staying with friends," he said casually, as though a fire in the palazzo wasn't his problem. "Can't you handle it?"

"They want to talk to you too."

"Why would I know anything about it?"

"I don't know. They asked a lot of questions

about our insurance, and how much coverage we have on the house."

"How much do we have?" Luca assumed Cosima insured the palazzo for a great deal of money, but he didn't know the exact amount. Cosima was careful about those things. Their stores were insured for a fortune.

"Ten on the house, and five million on the contents."

"Fifteen million?" He sounded pleased. "Good for you. So we'll get fifteen million?"

"Not unless we lost everything, which we haven't, thank God. The insurance people will send out appraisers to assess the damage. I'd say it will cost one or two million to repair the damage and replace what we lost."

"That's not a lot, but it's better than nothing," he said, which irritated her. He didn't sound upset about the fire at all. "With the sale, you can collect the insurance, and let the buyers do their own repairs, and we can keep the insurance money." He had it all figured out. He had an angle for every situation, for personal profit.

"If the Johnsons do the repairs, they'll deduct it from the purchase price," she informed him sensibly.

"They're rich. They can afford the repairs," he said smugly. She felt sick listening to him. His greed knew no limits.

"You may have to come back here if they want to

interview you too. They told me I can't leave Venice until they're through."

"Tell them I'm busy," he said lazily. "I'm not coming back for that. They can talk to you."

"Thanks a lot."

"What do you want me to do? Shovel out the burnt furniture? You can hire people to do that."

Cosima hung up a minute later. As usual, Luca was no help. She called the Johnsons that afternoon too, and they were shocked. They immediately confirmed that they still wanted to buy the palazzo, no matter how damaged it was. They loved it, and they said the décor had only been temporary while they rented it. They had much more elaborate plans for after they bought it. And they were going to redo the wiring, the floors, and the moldings anyway. Cosima didn't mention it, but she was sure they would want a reduction of what they were going to pay now that the house was damaged. And they were willing to undertake the repairs, which would save her the trouble and the expense. They said they wanted their workmen to do it, and their architect to oversee it.

Olivier and Cosima had done all they could, for now anyway, until the insurance appraisers came to see it for themselves. And Cosima and Olivier had taken a lot of pictures with their phones. They went back to her hotel, and Olivier took her to Harry's Bar for dinner that night, which was one of her favorite restaurants in Venice. He was staying at the same hotel she was, so he could be near her, and he told her he had canceled his meetings in Florence the next day. He was a steady, solid, reliable person, not showy or exciting, but someone she could count on. She liked how calm and reassuring he was.

They went for a walk after dinner, and she never got lost in the maze of little narrow streets, it was her second home and all of it familiar to her. Then they went back to the hotel and went to their rooms. She was up early again the next day, and the police called her and asked her to come in again that morning. When she told Olivier, he offered to accompany her again.

The detective in charge was even less pleasant than he had been the day before, and after another hour of questioning, he informed her that she was under investigation for insurance fraud, and the possibility that she had hired someone to set the fire so she could collect the insurance. What the detective said sounded just like the scheme Luca had described to her, for the insurance money. She was shocked when he told her, and Olivier saw her go pale. He tried to reason with the detective and explained that she owned two of the most important stores in Italy, and was an honest, respectable citizen. The detective wasn't impressed. And she told him that the house was currently about to be sold.

"Insurance fraud is a very profitable business. People make millions at it if they can pull it off. And there's no question that the fire was due to arson.

We have the evidence," the chief of police told her. Cosima didn't say anything, but she called Gian Battista as soon as she left the police station, and she told him what was happening. Olivier was with her when she called, but he could only hear her half of the conversation. He understood enough Italian to get the gist.

"I'll make some calls," Gian Battista said immediately. "I know two very strong judges in Venice, and the police chief. I hate to ask, but where is your brother?"

"In Saint-Tropez, with friends."

"You don't suppose he had anything to do with it, do you?" She thought about it for a minute and shook her head.

"No, I don't. He's not that crazy. And why would he?"

"Money, of course, this kind of thing is right up his alley. I hesitate to say it, but I wouldn't put it past him."

"Gian Battista, that's a major crime. He's a jerk, but he wouldn't do that. He could go to prison for it. He's not a fool."

"Let's hope not. But let's see if I can get you off the hook at least." Gian Battista sounded concerned for her.

Allegra had decided to go home to Rome by then. It was no fun being in Sardinia without her sister, and it didn't look like Cosima would be coming back anytime soon. Allegra called Cosima and said she wanted to relinquish their rental and go back to Rome that afternoon.

"I'm sorry I'm stuck here," Cosima apologized to her, but by late that afternoon, the police called Cosima and told her she was free to leave. Gian Battista had worked some magic, and they said they would contact her in Rome if they needed to. They said nothing else. The investigation into the arson had only just begun, and the insurers were doing their own, independent of the police.

"What's happening?" Max asked Luca in a whisper after he hung up from talking to his sister. They were in Saint-Tropez together, staying with Max's friends. Max had been with him since Venice.

"Nothing. They figured out that it's arson, and they're investigating my sister for insurance fraud. That's pretty funny. It'll do her good to be on the hot seat for a change," Luca said harshly. He wasn't concerned.

The police weren't naïve, and they sent detectives out to various quarters of Venice, to see what they heard about Luca Saverio. They checked the casinos, and discovered that Luca was well known at the Ca' Vendramin Calergi and had been there on Friday night. The casino management said he was a high-stakes gambler, and he had been there with a friend. They vaguely remembered that his friend was French, but not much more about him.

It wasn't a long jump from that to Luca's chronic gambling debts and his two-hundred-thousand-euro loss two months before, and the police rapidly put together a portrait of a rich boy who was frequently in financial trouble, although he didn't have a criminal record. But he had a dicey reputation as a bad guy, and a heavy drinker and gambler.

The police went back to the house to investigate further, and found cigarette butts in the rubble, and a silver flask near where the oil-soaked rags had been found, with Luca's initials clearly engraved. LAS, Luca Alberto Saverio. It was incriminating evidence. They called the police in Saint-Tropez and had them pick Luca up for questioning. The Venetian police checked the flask for fingerprints. There were two sets, and they made due note of both and emailed them to the police in Saint-Tropez. Cosima had been fingerprinted too.

Cosima called Gian Battista again after they told her she could go home to Rome. She thanked him and asked him what he thought was happening. He had been making calls to officials he knew to find out.

"They're trying to build a case for insurance fraud. I just hope your brother had no part in this. If he did, and they prosecute him, he'll go to prison. The insurance companies don't take this lightly, and neither do the police."

"Have I been cleared now?" she asked, worried.

"No, you're still implicated, but they don't think you're the prime suspect, and they don't have enough evidence against you to win a case. Luca may be what they're looking for. I just don't want it to be you, and have you become his victim."

"I don't see how this could happen. And why me?"

"Because you're related to someone who is capable of it, even if you're not, and you could have planned it with him. I hope he has a rock-solid alibi for that night. He was at a casino earlier in the evening, with a friend, before the fire." The police chief had shared the information with Gian Battista confidentially, and none of it sounded good.

Luca made light of the police questioning him in Saint-Tropez. He acted as though he thought it was amusing, but the police were less than amused. Luca was haughty, cocky, and rude to them. They asked him who he had been at the casino with earlier on Friday evening, and he said he couldn't remember. They asked him about the silver flask, and he said it had been stolen out of his pocket at the casino that night. They hadn't gotten the fingerprints yet, and they hadn't fingerprinted Luca at the station, since he hadn't been accused of a crime so far. They let him go after questioning him for an hour.

Luca went out to dinner that night with the group of people he was staying with. They went to the Gorilla Bar in the port for drinks first, and visited friends on various yachts. They knew most of the people there. It was a rich man's playground, and Max Bayard looked uncomfortable all evening. They eventually went to Club 55 at Pampelonne Beach for dinner, and dancing afterwards at Les Caves du Roy, and got back to the house at four A.M. One of them had bought cocaine at the nightclub, so they all shared it and finally went to bed at seven.

Luca was sound asleep at nine when two detectives showed up. His host, Max's friend, went to wake him. Luca staggered out of his bedroom, still drunk from the night before. They had come to fingerprint him and had permission from a judge to fingerprint everyone in the house, to see if they got a match for both sets of prints on the flask found at the scene. Max looked panicked when one of the other guests came to wake him.

"Is it a raid, because of the cocaine?"

"No, some dumb thing about a fire in Venice," the housemate told him. "They've got an order to fingerprint all of us. They're talking to Luca now." Max nodded and was speechless with fear. The whole thing had been Luca's idea. Since he was part owner of the palazzo, he said he would collect a third of the insurance money and he had promised to give Max part of his share. It would give both of them easy free money they could spend on whatever they wanted. Luca was convincing, and Max had agreed. Luca said they'd never get caught. And since the palazzo was being sold, they could keep the insurance money and the new owners could do the repairs. Luca had called it "gravy" with the sale, a bonus. But setting the fires was more complicated than Max had expected, although they had gotten into the house easily with Luca's key, and there was no alarm, just as he had said. They had to leave the burning oil-soaked rags, but they'd gotten away with no problem. Max had burned his arm when they set the fires. He put on a long-sleeved shirt before he joined the others to be fin-gerprinted. They all looked rough after the drugs and alcohol the night before. They were a sorry-looking group the next morning, but none of them looked like criminals. Just a sleazy bunch who had partied hard all night, which wasn't unusual in Saint-Tropez.

The usual wild bunch of badly behaved rich boys gave the local police a headache all summer, but rarely with serious offenses, mostly with drugs and drunk driving, the occasional stolen vehicle, or women claiming they had been drugged, date-raped, or coerced into having sex with them, which the police were taking more seriously now. Or one of the hookers they brought with them shoplifted a bathing suit from a store, which the men paid for to avoid prosecution. The arson case in Venice was the most serious one they'd had in months.

The two detectives took the prints and left, and everyone went back to bed for the rest of the day to sleep off the revels of the night before and start again that night.

Olivier insisted on flying back to Rome with Cosima, although she said it wasn't necessary, but he could see that she was shaken by the events of the weekend. They arrived in Rome that evening. Allegra wasn't home yet when he accompanied Cosima back to her apartment. He'd called the Hassler to reserve a room and postponed his meetings in Florence for another day.

"You didn't need to come with me," Cosima said, embarrassed, and he opened a bottle of wine for them, to settle their nerves. He knew she was going to have her hands full with the insurance company, the police, and the future owners of the palazzo, and getting the house as cleaned up as possible before they returned.

"I know you can do it all on your own," he said. She was a proud woman. "But a little help never hurts." He smiled at her. "Your attorney did a good job, convincing them to let you go home." He could tell from her tone when she spoke to him that she knew the lawyer well.

"He's always been there for me. He and my father were close friends. He handled everything for us when they died. He's been like a father to me." For the flash of a moment, Olivier wondered if he was something more to her as well. Olivier had seen her whole face soften when she spoke to him on the phone, and she sounded very familiar, even intimate, to Olivier. He wondered if there was more to it, but didn't know her well enough to ask, and didn't want to be presumptuous or intrusive. "He's very well connected with local government here in Rome, and some very high-up politicians. His family is powerful in the Vatican, and he knows important people in Venice too."

"He sounds like a good man to have in your corner," or your bed, he wondered, and felt guilty for what he was thinking. He had no idea why he thought it. It was pure instinct, but he had an odd feeling about her lawyer. She looked pensive as she sipped her wine. She was worried about her brother, and the fact that she was under investigation about the insurance. Nothing like it had ever happened to her.

"My brother has always been a problem and hard to manage, but he's not a criminal. I don't think Luca would even be capable of what they suspect us of."

"I hope not," Olivier said sincerely, not quite as convinced as she was of her brother's innocence. Trying to sell his shares in the family business behind his sisters' backs was certainly dishonorable, though not criminal. "Do you have anything to eat here, or do you want to go out?" he asked her. She wasn't hungry, but he thought she should eat something. She looked worn out by what she'd been through for the past few days.

"It will be a terrible scandal in the press if they press charges," she said softly, her mind fixated on the arson fire at the palazzo. She couldn't stop thinking about it, and how ravaged the palazzo looked now.

"Hopefully, it will never come to that. They're obliged to investigate something like this thoroughly. But if Luca's innocent they'll look for other explanations for the fire." Olivier had no doubts about Cosima's involvement. She seemed like the most honest woman he'd ever met, and his admiration for her had grown even in the past few days with her in Venice, seeing how graciously she handled the police suspicions and the firefighters checking through the debris. She was a decent person in a bad situation, and he was glad to be with her, and to get to know her better. In a crisis, he got to know her faster than he would have otherwise. He liked everything he discovered about her, even the things she didn't tell him. He still had the impression that she was a woman with secrets, but not criminal ones.

He finally convinced her to go to a trattoria he knew in Trastevere, the more bohemian section of Rome, like the area around Saint-Germain-des-Prés in Paris, where young people went for a simple meal. It was easy to get lost in the crowd there and go unnoticed.

Olivier talked about his travels and his factories to distract her during dinner, and asked Cosima questions about her grandfather. She was an endless source of information about the social history of Rome and Venice, and had grown up surrounded by it, until her parents' deaths. After that, she was too busy with the business to have any social life at all. Olivier had done the same with his own business, always chasing success, and had sacrificed other things for it. He thought it was worth it, although at times he questioned that now. Approaching fifty, what mattered to him had subtly changed. At thirty-eight, she was too young to have experienced that yet, and was still set on her path at full speed, protecting her business and trying to make it grow within the parameters her grandfather had established.

"I'm the first woman in my family who ever worked," she shared with him over dinner of pasta alla primavera, while he ate spaghetti vongole, his favorite, with clams. "I'm not sure my father would approve," she said shyly, "and I know my grandfather would be appalled. But someone had to do it, and Luca wasn't capable of it, and never wanted to be in the business. He even said it as a boy. My father thought he could change his mind, but I don't think he ever could have. Luca has wanted to be a playboy all his life," and he had achieved it. It didn't enhance Olivier's impression of him.

"My son Max is always looking for the short-cuts, the fast track to success and get-rich-quick schemes too. There are no shortcuts. Hard work is what pays off in the end." Olivier and Cosima had both learned that lesson and accepted the personal sacrifices they'd had to make. He was sorry to see her hit a bump now and have to deal with arson at the palazzo and the investigation, which put the spotlight on her. She didn't deserve it, and it was a headache she didn't need. He hoped the police would move on quickly, find the real culprit, and leave her alone. After all she'd been through and was carrying, a business, a sister with a disability, and a spoiled profligate brother, she had enough on her plate without this. His own life seemed easy by comparison.

Cosima looked exhausted by the time she got home, and she could see the lights on in Allegra's windows. She knew the police wanted to interro-gate her too, but assumed they would drop their suspicions of Allegra quickly when they saw that she was in a wheelchair. She was unlikely to have set the palazzo on fire, and too naïve and innocent to plan it. Cosima and Luca were their main sus-pects for now.

"I guess I'll go to Florence tomorrow," he said hesitantly. He hated to leave her. "But I can be back in a few hours if you need me. Don't hesitate to call if something comes up," he said, and meant it.

"I think the investigation will take some time. Gian Battista doesn't seem to think they're going to come to any rapid conclusions, and I told the police everything I know." Olivier had that same odd feeling when she said her lawyer's name again. There was an unspoken intimacy about the way she said it, almost as if they were married. He told himself he was probably wrong. He had gathered that her lawyer was the same age as her father, which put a thirty-year gap between them, or more. It made his suspicions seem less likely.

Olivier took her upstairs and left her at her apartment. She was going to check on her sister and make sure she had gotten home safely. She said that Allegra didn't mind traveling alone, but it always worried Cosima, who mothered her probably more than she should, she admitted. She had said that Allegra hated to be fussed over, and liked fending for herself, and did it well. "I'm too much of a mother hen," Cosima said, smiling at Olivier. "It's a good thing I never had children. I would have driven them crazy."

"I do the same with my boys. Basile, my youngest, thinks it's funny and indulges me. Max hates it and thinks I'm trying to control him when I give him fatherly advice. As a result, he's always secretive about his life. Basile is an open book. He's just a big friendly guy. He wears his heart on his sleeve and says whatever he thinks or feels. He's uncomplicated to deal with. I enjoy that a lot."

"I hope I meet him sometime," she said politely. There was so much about Olivier that she liked, especially his solidity and stability, and his kindness to her. He wasn't glamorous, pretentious, or overly sophisticated. He was real, which she liked better. He came from a normal background, not an illustrious one like hers, and he tried to be a good father to his sons, even though both their births had been unwelcome accidents, and the marriages that spawned them hadn't been successes. Like Cosima, he was a responsible person, and had made the best of difficult circumstances, and didn't try to blame anyone else for it, even his ex-wives.

"I hope you meet him too," Olivier said about his son. "You'll have to come to his next art show. Let me know what's going on," he said to her and hugged her, enjoying the feel of her in his arms for a minute. He hadn't pressed her or tried to take advantage of the situation to make romantic advances, but he was powerfully attracted to her, and kissed her in his arms before he left. "Take care of yourself," he said softly, and she nodded.

"You too," she said with a wistful look in her eyes. She didn't want it to be that way, but they both had the feeling that there was a third person in the room with them, standing between them. Cosima knew it was Gian Battista, even with their chaste relationship now. Olivier wasn't as sure, but he had begun to suspect who it was, and wondered if that would change. She appeared to be alone, but he didn't know how true that was. He could almost feel Gian Battista looking over his shoulder like a ghost when he kissed her.

Chapter 9

Luca was thinking about leaving Saint-Tropez in the next day or two, but the pleasures he encountered there were too appealing. Drugs were plentiful, nights were long and highly entertaining, the women were beautiful, easily seduced, and practically naked all day long on the beach. He was in no rush to leave, although the police visit to the house where he was staying had been unpleasant.

The police returned the next day. His fingerprints were a match with those on the flask found in the palazzo.

"What does that prove?" he said boldly to the detective, seeming fearless and innocent. "I told you the flask was stolen out of my pocket at the casino that night. Maybe the person who took it was the arsonist, or sold it on the street. Carrying a flask doesn't make me an arsonist." Or maybe just a drunk. The evidence was damning, but not conclusive. Max's fingerprints were on the flask too, and

Luca now "remembered" that they had been at the casino together early that night, and shared sips from the flask. Previously, he had forgotten, or said he did.

"Shit," Max said to him before they left Saint-Tropez, "they're getting close." He didn't like it and was panicked.

"They don't know squat, and what I told them is true. If someone stole my flask, it could have been the arsonist. There's no proof that it was us. There are no surveillance cameras in the house, or even an alarm." They had never bothered to put one in. Installing a proper one was too expensive, so they'd never done it, or even smoke alarms. The wiring at the palazzo had been poor for years, with constant short circuits and blown fuses. All of which was why Luca had suggested they set fire to the palazzo for the insurance money he'd get.

So far, the police had no conclusive evidence, just their own suspicions. The police in Saint-Tropez had gone to see Luca twice to humor their counterparts in Venice but weren't really interested. They had enough other things to do. Luca was exactly the kind of guy they hated dealing with. He was arrogant, supercilious, rude, and treated them like dirt under his feet. They would have liked to arrest him just to teach him a lesson, but there wasn't enough hard evidence for an arrest yet. And they weren't sure there ever would be. He was clever, and had explanations for everything, some of which held up.

Later in the week, a number of the group at the house in Saint-Tropez left for Greece on a friend's yacht. Max had to get back to Paris to work, and Luca headed for the Italian Riviera to meet up with other friends. Cosima was back at work in Rome. She hadn't heard from the police in several days, and the insurance adjusters were doing their appraisal of the damage. Olivier had called her several times and was back in Paris. There was a terrible heat wave there and he wished he were on a beach somewhere. He had no plans to go back to Rome for the time being.

He was working late in his office one night when Max walked in. He had just come back from Saint-Tropez the day before and had a good tan. Luca and Max had slept late every day, but they had made it to the beach in the late afternoon.

Max and Olivier both had their jackets off and their sleeves rolled up in the heat. Olivier smiled when he saw him. Max handed his father a stack of marketing reports he'd been reviewing all day. He was bored to tears and missed Saint-Tropez.

"How was Saint-Tropez?" Olivier asked him, and Max smiled in answer.

"A lot of fun . . . and hot girls," he said, and Olivier laughed. Max was good-looking and young. At his age, Olivier already had two sons and had been divorced twice. Max's life was very different, and he had a devoted father who spoiled him. Max had no responsibilities whatsoever, except his job, and his dreams of get-rich-quick schemes so he wouldn't have to work forever, like Olivier, or as hard as he had until now. Max wanted no part of that.

As Max handed him the reports, a long red, raw patch on his right arm caught Olivier's eye. It looked ugly, blistered, and infected. "Wow, what happened?"

"Nothing. Some dumb girl in a nightclub bent over a candle and set her hair on fire. I helped put it out and got burned while I did."

"That looks nasty." Olivier was concerned. "Did you see a doctor?"

"No, it's getting better. I'm fine. Our sales went up seventeen percent this month. The fluorescent bags are a huge hit. We have more reorders than we can fill," Max said to distract him, and Olivier was pleased, but he was still worried about the arm when Max left his office. As soon as he did, Olivier had a sick feeling in the pit of his stomach. Luca and the palazzo came to mind, and he just hoped that the story about the girl in the nightclub was true. He suddenly had the feeling that Max was lying to him, but there was no way to find out.

Olivier called Cosima that night and asked if she had seen her brother. She hadn't, and he hadn't called her. She said it was hot in Rome too, but her offices were air-conditioned, and he said his weren't. The high temperatures were unusual in Paris. He liked hearing her voice, and she said she had no news from the insurance company or the police about the arson investigation.

"If they had any new evidence, you'd have heard from them," Olivier reassured her.

"Maybe they'll never have proof," she said, wondering when she'd see him again. She was surprised that she missed him. But his factories in Italy were closed for the rest of August, so he had no reason to come to Italy at the moment.

She hadn't known him for long, but a lot had happened in a short time, and she found that she had grown attached to him and liked knowing that he was somewhere not too far away, and that she could reach out to him if she wanted to. She wasn't ready to get too deeply involved with him, and didn't know if she ever would be, but there was something special about him that was important to her now. He had filled some of the empty space that Gian Battista had left when he moved slowly away from her to set her free. Olivier was filling the void, but she wasn't ready to let go of Gian Battista yet and didn't want to. Olivier could sense it too and had never questioned her about it. She was like a graceful bird poised for flight and he knew that if he moved too quickly he would lose her completely, which was the last thing he wanted. She was like a wave on the sand he could never quite capture. There was a mysterious, elusive quality to her, which was part of her charm.

Cosima had always reminded Gian Battista of

her mother. Alberto had been much more earth-bound and exuberant. Tizianna had been ethereal, like an angel with her blond beauty. Cosima was so much like her in so many ways.

For both Cosima and Gian Battista, their relationship even in its diminished state was a way of keeping her parents alive. Gian Battista was aware of it. Cosima wasn't. Her love for him was simple and pure and direct and strong, for all that he was. He was nothing like her father. He was a fascinating older man who had mesmerized her for as long as she'd known him. There had never been anyone to compare to him. Olivier was nothing like him, but now she was attached to him too. It was confusing. She was careful not to move forward with Olivier into something she knew she wasn't ready for. Olivier didn't press her. He didn't want to frighten her away.

Luca did some serious playing and partying on the Italian Riviera while he was there. He spent time at the casino in San Remo. He drank more than usual, and was cocky about what he and Max had pulled off in Venice and gotten away with, even though the police had found his flask. They didn't believe his story but couldn't prove otherwise, or hadn't so far. The chief detective in Venice had a theory that all things revealed themselves eventually. For the time being, Cosima remained their prime suspect, but everything about Luca felt wrong to the chief detective, who was like a jackal silently waiting for his prey, ready to strike.

Eventually Luca ran out of places to stay, and friends to stay with. He headed back to Rome and stopped in Venice, and could never resist a visit to his favorite casino. He ran into friends there, drank too much, gambled heavily, had a lucky win that night, and bought drinks for everyone. In a nearly incoherent state, he bragged about what he had done and gotten away with, and said that when the insurance paid up, he stood to make at least half a million euros for his share of the insurance money, in addition to three million for his part of the house sale. He was going to be a rich man now. He was staggering when he left, and slept at the hotel near the one where Cosima stayed.

One of the dealers at the casino had never liked Luca, who had accused him of cheating several times and had almost cost him his job. With a guarantee of secrecy, he reported what Luca had said to the police. The police found Luca at his hotel the next morning, put him in handcuffs, arrested him, and took him to the police station, pending a hearing with the chief prosecutor and a judge. He put up a fight when they arrested him, but two burly carabinieri removed him from the hotel and drove him away, as the owners and guests whispered.

The chief detective was waiting for him at the station, with the statement signed by the blackjack dealer. Luca was stunned. They advised him to call an attorney. He called Gian Battista from jail and was hysterical. Gian Battista wasn't happy to hear from him. Luca insisted that he was innocent and knew nothing of the dealer's sworn statement repeating what Luca had said himself, bragging of setting fire to the palazzo for the insurance money.

Luca claimed to Gian Battista that it was all a trumped-up case against him because of the flask. He denied the charges and demanded that Gian Battista get him out of jail immediately.

"I'll look into it," Gian Battista said in a dry tone. Luca's fall had been a long time coming and didn't surprise him. He knew that if he was found guilty, Luca would go to prison, no matter how illustrious his family was, and Gian Battista personally felt he belonged there.

The attorney called Luca back two hours later, having spoken to the chief detective and the chief of police, his friend. There was no doubt in anyone's mind that Luca was guilty, and they believed they could prove it. They had told him about the sworn statement from the dealer at the casino. It was all hearsay, but it had the ring of truth. Gian Battista told Luca about the statement without giving up the man's name.

"I was drunk," Luca shrieked into the phone.

"I'm sure you were, but you gave them all the information they needed to convict you, and you bragged about the insurance money."

"I need you to come here and get me out," Luca said, sounding desperate.

"I can't. I'll get a good man I know in Venice to be your lawyer. I don't do criminal law. I'd be doing you a disservice if I took the case." He would have done it in an instant for Cosima if she needed him, but not her brother. Gian Battista had a powerful dislike for everything Luca represented, and thought he belonged exactly where he was. He called the lawyer, who took the case as a favor to Gian Battista. Then Gian Battista had the thankless task of calling Cosima and telling her where Luca was and what had happened. She was silent for a moment afterwards, digesting what he had said.

"Do you think the lawyer can get him off?" she asked him.

"I honestly don't know. I doubt it. The evidence is strong against him. He wasn't smart enough to pull it off and not get caught, and if he could have let you take the blame, he would have. That's who he is." She sighed as she listened.

"I know. I don't know if I love him or hate him. Maybe both. I've been responsible for him for fifteen years, but he has never turned into a decent human being, or the man he should have been."

"And he never will," Gian Battista said with certainty, and no pity for Luca. "I don't think you can stop what's coming. He'll probably make some kind of deal with them to get off or reduce his sentence if he's found guilty. Be careful, Cosima. He'll sacrifice you in an instant, or anyone in his path. Keep your distance. You're not responsible for him anymore, and he never lived up to your faith in him, or your parents'. He has to live with that now." She knew he was right, but she felt bad for her brother. She told Allegra what had happened, and Allegra was realistic about it. She saw him more clearly now than her older sister and understood how worthless he was. She had lost all her illusions about him. He had tried to burn down their home and implicated them all. They could all have ended up in jail for arson and fraud, and still might.

Cosima didn't rush to Venice to see Luca, or try to rescue him, and he didn't call her. He knew she couldn't help him, so she was of no use to him.

She called Olivier in Paris that night and told him that Luca was in jail.

"I'm sorry for you," he said sincerely, "but I think he deserves it. Do you think he'll get out of it?"

"No, I don't," she said. She didn't disagree with him. They all felt the same way about Luca. He had committed a crime and had to pay for it now. She thought even her father would have believed that. She just hoped he would learn a lesson and clean up his life when he got out.

Gian Battista informed Cosima when Luca was formally charged with arson and intent to commit insurance fraud. Any concerns about her were dropped, and the entire guilt rested on her brother, where it belonged. Gian Battista said that Luca was trying to make a deal to lighten his sentence if he was found guilty, or even to get them to drop the charges. She couldn't imagine what kind of deal he could make. Luca was trading on his name and his family, which was getting him nowhere, and two days later, Olivier called her, and sounded near tears.

"Max was arrested this morning, at the request of the Italian police. Apparently, Luca told them that Max helped him plan it and set fire to the palazzo with him, hence the flask with both their prints on it at the scene. They were going to share Luca's portion of the insurance money when he got it. Max is being charged with the same crimes as Luca, to a slightly lesser degree because they believe he was an accessory, but not the one who planned it. Luca had already bragged at the casino that he was the mastermind behind it. They could serve as much as ten years in prison," Olivier said, sounding devastated. She felt terrible for him, and guilty that her brother had caused it. But in some ways Luca and Max were equally to blame, looking for fast money, no matter what they had to do to get it.

"They won't serve that in Italy," Cosima reassured him. "People rarely go to prison in Italy. No one was injured, no one died. They didn't get the money. What they did is awful, but at most they'll serve five years or even two." She thought it was disgusting too that her brother had sold out his

friend to save his own skin. That wasn't lost on
Olivier either. Luca was rotten through and through.

"There's a hearing in two weeks. I'm going to be
there. I assume you will too," she said hesitantly.

"Yes, of course," Olivier said. "Let's go together.
Max is on his way to Venice right now. I have to find
him a lawyer in Venice, maybe your friend could
help me."

"Of course. I'll ask him."

"I never thought a child of mine would go to
prison."

"We never thought that either. It would have
killed my parents, but he's been out of control for
years. I wasn't strong enough to rein him in. I wasn't
old enough at the beginning."

"I don't think that's it. I think there is something
broken and deeply twisted way deep down in people like Luca and Max. Max's mother was like that
too, and came to no good. She got into drugs right
after he was born."

"I don't know where it comes from on our side.
Some rotten nobleman in the fifteenth century
maybe. But I think you're right. Luca is broken. He
always has been. I tried to fix him, and I couldn't."

"You can't. It's up to each of them, and they don't
want to be fixed. I'm not looking forward to the
hearing."

"How was Max when he left?"

"Shocked. He didn't say a word." His coconspirator had betrayed him, which shocked all of them too. Luca had no loyalties or decency at all.

"I'm so sorry," she said to Olivier.

"So am I. But at least I have an excuse to see you," he said grimly, with a wintry smile. "I'm glad we'll be there together."

"What's the hearing for?"

"I'm not sure if it's to register their plea, or if they'll be sentenced then if they plead guilty. It won't be good, whatever it is, for either of them."

"Maybe they'll go easier on Max," she said, trying to give him hope, but both situations were fairly disastrous. Neither Olivier nor Cosima had much hope for either one.

Olivier told her he would come to Rome the day before the hearing, and they could fly to Venice together, or take the train. At least they would have each other.

Two days before the hearing, Cosima got bad news from the insurance company, which didn't surprise her.

They told her that since her brother and an accessory were charged with the arson in the palazzo, whether they pled guilty or were convicted the insurance company would not pay for the damage. The family would have to pay for all repairs themselves. It seemed only fair, but it was a terrible blow. They would either have to pay for the repairs or adjust the price accordingly for the Johnsons and sell them the palazzo at a greatly reduced price. It was not good news to Cosima, who decided to tell Sally Johnson after the hearing. She could only deal with so much at one time. The hearing was weighing heavily on her mind.

The day before the hearing, before Olivier arrived, Allegra said something to Cosima about the hearing, which surprised her.

"You're planning to come?" Cosima didn't think she would. Allegra had said nothing about it until then.

"Of course. He's my brother too, but I'm not going for him. I'm going for you."

"Can you do that? With the chair and all . . ." Allegra laughed when she said it.

"Obviously. I'm in a wheelchair, not on life support. I'm coming with you."

The same thing had happened to Olivier, he explained to Cosima later. The day before he was to leave, Basile had announced that he was going to Venice with his father. He had even bought a suit for the occasion and cut his hair. He didn't want to embarrass his father in court. One bad son was enough.

Cosima had had a call from Luca's attorney that morning. Max had given the prosecutor a statement, blaming Luca for everything. Max had sold him out to save his own skin, just as Luca had done to him, which had gotten Max arrested. There was nothing honorable about either of them, not even honor among thieves. They had agreed to lighten the charges against Max in exchange for his statement, and Luca was now likely to face a heavier sentence. The next day, Luca's lawyer said that Luca was considering pleading guilty. He had finally accepted that he couldn't win.

Olivier and Basile came directly to Cosima's apartment when they arrived. They had a light lunch in Allegra's kitchen. They were flying to Venice later that afternoon, staying at a hotel together, and Olivier had suggested they have dinner at Harry's Bar that night to cheer them up and calm their nerves. Cosima and Allegra wanted to visit Luca, but he had refused to see them. He was furious with Max, and hated his sisters too. He told his lawyer they had thrown him to the wolves and abandoned him.

"Your sister Cosima is paying my fees," his attorney informed him.

"She can afford to." Luca had expected her to lie for him and she wouldn't. He tarred Allegra with the same brush as her older sister. Max was too ashamed to see his father and half brother and had refused too. The two men weren't being sentenced to death, "only" to prison. They could see their families after the sentencing if they wanted to.

When Olivier and Basile arrived in Rome, Olivier put his arms around Cosima and kissed her. He looked happy to see her, and he introduced Basile to both sisters. Basile was tall and handsome and athletic-looking, and his eyes lit up when he saw Allegra. He told his father that he had never met a more beautiful woman. They talked nonstop through lunch, as Cosima and Olivier smiled at each other and could hardly follow the rapid-fire conversation about music, art, social media, films they had seen, places they had been, where they'd gone to school, the meaning of art. It was like watching a forest fire begin.

They chatted all the way to the airport, where Basile offered his help to get Allegra into her chair, but she refused. She preferred to manage on her own, which he understood immediately, and he didn't offer again.

Allegra and Basile sat next to each other on the plane, and Cosima and Olivier sat across the aisle from them. Olivier whispered to Cosima halfway through the flight.

"Whoa . . . those two are like a tornado together. They haven't stopped talking and laughing since we got to Rome."

Cosima nodded with a smile. "Allegra is usually pretty lively, but she's lit up like a Christmas tree with him."

"Long may it last," Olivier said in a whisper, and Cosima smiled. Men were often impressed by Allegra, but it rarely went further than that. Her disability scared them. But Basile seemed undaunted by it. He saw who Allegra was, regardless of the chair.

When they got to the hotel, Allegra offered to show Basile around Venice, and she let him push her chair while she gave him directions. He nearly ran her into a statue once while they were talking, and she teased him about it.

"You're a terrible driver, but you know a lot about Renaissance art."

"I majored in art history. They didn't teach street art then," he said proudly.

"Do they now?"

"I teach a class at the Beaux-Arts," he said, grinning, and she was impressed. He was two years younger than she was. She was twenty-nine and he was twenty-seven, which didn't matter at all.

Allegra and Basile were back at the hotel in time for dinner, and they all left for Harry's Bar, as Olivier had promised. For Olivier and Cosima, being with Basile and Allegra made it feel like a happy trip and not a sad one. They were going to watch their brothers get sent to prison. It wasn't a joyful occasion, but Allegra and Basile were such upbeat, ebullient young people that they lifted everyone's mood by just being around them.

By the end of dinner, Basile had invited Allegra to come to Paris sometime, to watch him work in the street. He worked in a studio too, when he worked on canvas, he explained, but he still liked doing street work also. She thought it would be exciting to see him do it.

"I'm so glad they both came," Cosima said in a soft voice to Olivier at the end of the meal. "It's fun just being with them."

"She's an amazing woman," Olivier said with admiration for both sisters, for different reasons.

"She does more than most people who have full use of their legs," Cosima commented. "She puts me to shame."

"Basile is full of life too. He always cheers me up when I'm down. We're going to need them tomorrow. I'm not looking forward to watching Max get dragged off to prison, however much he deserves it."

"I think Luca lured him into it, by offering to share the insurance money with him."

"You can't lure an honest man," Olivier said, and she knew it was true. She had spoken to Gian Battista the day before, who had also heard that Luca was considering pleading guilty, in exchange for less prison time, if the prosecutor would agree. Gian Battista had wished her luck but didn't offer to come to court with her. She said that she and Allegra were going with Max's family, and he was relieved. She had promised to call him afterwards and tell him how it went.

They went to their own rooms when they got back to the hotel. Cosima was sharing a room with Allegra, mostly for the moral support, not because

Allegra needed her help. She managed fine on her own, which Basile had noticed all day and commented on to his father.

"It's as if being in a wheelchair doesn't slow her down at all. She acts like it's just normal and she makes it seem that way. What does she do in the family business?"

"Cosima says she's a talented designer, she designs handbags."

"You should hire her," Basile said enthusiastically.

"Her sister would kill me." Olivier laughed. It had occurred to him too.

They all went to bed early, met in the lobby in the morning for croissants and coffee, and were on their way to the courthouse half an hour later. The hearing was at the Ordinary Court of Venice on Santa Croce at the end of the Grand Canal, near the train station. Both lawyers were waiting for them, and Luca's took both of his sisters aside.

"He's going to plead guilty," he explained to them. "The prosecutor made a deal with him." Cosima knew it meant he would have a criminal record forever, but he also would if he pleaded not guilty and they convicted him. A deal had been his best chance for a slightly shorter sentence. And Max had already made his deal when he made the statement accusing Luca of his crimes. The hearing that morning was more of a formality than a surprise, but it was daunting anyway, as the four of them filed into the courtroom with the two lawyers. The two defendants were brought in a few minutes later, in handcuffs, but wearing suits and ties. Max looked imploringly at his father, as though begging him to rescue him, which brought tears to Olivier's eyes, and Basile gently patted his father's shoulder to give him strength. Luca walked in with averted eyes and went right past his sisters without even glancing at them, defiant and hostile to the end, as though it was all their fault and not his own. He took responsibility for nothing and never had.

The judge dealt with Max's case first. For accessory to arson, and intent to be an accessory to insurance fraud, he was given a year's jail sentence, followed by a year's probation. Cosima could feel the tension go out of Olivier's body. At least they knew now what he was facing, a year in prison, and not five or ten. Olivier thought Max could do that without having it ruin his life. It was a powerful and much-needed lesson about the kind of people he consorted with, and the influences in his life.

The judge turned to Luca then and read off the charges, as Luca listened stone-faced. He knew what was coming, and he was very lucky. Gian Battista had intervened as much as possible on his behalf, reminding the court of the honor of his family, and their position in the history of the city for centuries. He wasn't sure it would help, but he had tried. Cosima and Allegra held hands tightly as they waited to hear Luca's sentence, and the judge was kind to him. He got a year for the arson, since he was destroying his own home and not someone else's, because the sale hadn't gone through yet. And a year for the insurance fraud he was intending to commit but had received no money for yet. Two years in prison, and a criminal record forever. Even Cosima thought it was better than he deserved. Olivier, standing next to her, squeezed her hand, and she held tightly to his, with Allegra on her other side. Tears of relief ran down her cheeks. She had been afraid he would get ten years, not two.

Luca never turned to look at them and made no sign as he was led out of the courtroom to begin his prison sentence. Both he and Max had been sentenced to the Due Palazzi prison in Padua, about forty minutes from Venice. As she watched him go, Cosima wondered if she would ever see him again. She felt as though her brother had just died.

Max was crying when they took him away, and Olivier nodded, praying that this would be the last harsh lesson he'd have to learn.

The two families left the courtroom in silence, each of them digesting what they'd seen and what it meant to them. Max and Basile had never been close. Max had always been jealous of Basile but they shared the same father and had the same blood, which counted for something.

They were still standing on the courtroom steps when Cosima's cellphone rang. She didn't look to see who was calling her, and just answered it, in case it was Luca wanting to say goodbye. It seemed so odd to see him leave without even acknowledging them. But it wasn't Luca, it was Sally Johnson, in Aspen, and she was sobbing. Cosima couldn't understand her at first, she was crying so hard. She could only decipher a few sentences between the sobs.

"We were having dinner last night, and Bill looked at me and just rolled out of his chair . . . he was unconscious . . . I thought it was the altitude . . . the paramedics came right away and tried to revive him and couldn't . . . he's dead . . . oh my God . . . Cosima, he died, right there in front of me. . . ." Bill Johnson was dead.

By the end of the brief conversation, Cosima had understood that Sally just couldn't buy the house . . . it would break her heart to be there without Bill. She was so sorry, but she was canceling the sale. Cosima told her she understood completely. What she knew fully by the time she hung up was that her brother had done major damage to the house by setting fire to it, and the insurance company wasn't going to pay them a penny, because her brother had committed arson and was going to prison for it. Cosima couldn't afford to pay for the repairs. The Johnsons weren't going to buy the house, and she now owned a ruined palazzo, with no way to repair it or sell it. She felt like someone had dropped a building on her head.

"That didn't sound good," Olivier said gently, as she ended the call.

"It isn't," she confirmed, and they walked silently to where the boats were to go back to the hotel. She felt dazed. Her brother was on his way to prison, and her life was falling apart at a rapid rate.

Chapter 10

Cosima had big decisions to make after Bill Johnson died and Sally told her she couldn't imagine redoing the palazzo without him, and backed out of the sale. Cosima didn't blame her for it, but it left her in a complete quandary as to what to do.

Without insurance money, which was no longer available to them, she couldn't do any of the repairs for the fire and water damage. And without the Johnsons purchasing the house at the price they'd agreed on, she had no spare money either. Sally had wanted to undertake the repairs anyway, for a lowered purchase price for the palazzo. Now none of that was possible, and no one would buy it in the condition it was currently in, except at a fire sale price. Cosima didn't want to sell it for a ridiculous bargain price. But a new owner would have to handle the repairs, and Cosima couldn't imagine anyone doing so. It would have to be boarded up now, left in its current state of damage and disrepair, and taken off the market. It seemed tragic, and a waste of a once-spectacular palazzo and historic home. But she had no other choice. The idea of selling the palazzo would have to be shelved until she had the money to repair it, and she couldn't see when that might happen, or if she might sell it at a very low price. She always put any profits they had back in the business. At least she wouldn't have to support Luca's extravagant lifestyle now. That was the only blessing, among a series of hard blows and losses.

She had called Gian Battista after Luca's and Max's sentencing to report to him, and he thought the judge and the prosecutor had been very fair. Olivier and Cosima agreed, but Luca didn't. He had sent Gian Battista a scathing letter, accusing the lawyer of betraying him. He had threatened Max's life for selling him out to the prosecutor for a lesser sentence, and he inflicted the harshest cut of all on his sisters, which he knew would wound Cosima to the core. Total silence. He was still trying to wound people even once he was in prison. He hadn't grown up yet and become a responsible adult, willing to be accountable for his own mistakes.

Cosima could remember people telling her over the years that they had an unredeemable rotten brother, and it had seemed so odd to her that they should give up on a member of their own family. Now, with Luca, she understood it. Some people just refused to ever take responsibility for anything they did and expected the entire world to forgive them. It broke her heart to see what Luca had become, and to know he was in prison. She felt as though she had failed him because she hadn't helped him become a better person.

She wrote him a loving, compassionate letter, full of apologies and regrets, that he never answered. She eventually learned to live with it and moved on. She couldn't carry his weight forever, nor the burden of his mistakes and the blame. It took courage to give up on him. She was sad about it, but she had a life to lead, even without him. It had never been her style to give up on anyone, but she knew she had to this time. Allegra took it less personally, and had never been as close to him, or felt responsible for him. Their relationships with their brother were entirely different.

Olivier had promised Max he would visit him once a month. Basile had no desire to see him. Basile and Allegra had similar attitudes about their derelict brothers. They wrote them off and felt free to go on with their own lives and didn't feel sorry for them. Cosima didn't plan to visit Luca either, unless he contacted her and something changed radically. Gian Battista was relieved to hear that she wasn't trying to hang on to him or save him. She had finally given up on her brother.

Cosima called Sally Johnson a few weeks after Bill's funeral, to see if she had changed her mind about

the palazzo and wanted to go forward with the sale
after all, after the initial shock. She didn't. She was
totally devastated by Bill's sudden death. He wasn't
young, but he wasn't very old either, and they had
been very close for all forty-seven years of their
marriage. The idea of continuing their life in Venice
without him was unimaginable. So the sale of the
palazzo to Sally was a dead issue. Cosima knew she
couldn't put it on the market in the condition it was
in after the fire. She had promised to send Sally
what was left of their belongings that had been
damaged. She wanted to go through the house and
see what was worth saving and send it to Sally by
container. It was a sad end to the Johnsons' happy
years in Venice.

Cosima spent a weekend in Venice in September,
identifying their belongings and putting together
what was salvageable, intact, or worthwhile, or
might have sentimental value. It wasn't a large pile,
except for some wardrobe boxes of clothes that had
been upstairs and weren't touched by the fire or the
water. It was a pathetically small pile of boxes and
crates, and Cosima used the opportunity to assess
what to do with her own things.

Once she had packed up what belonged to the
Johnsons, there was little worth saving. The furniture in the bedrooms was of little value, and
reeked of smoke, so she marked it with red tags, to
be thrown away. All of the fabrics in the upper
rooms, used as servants' rooms and guestrooms,

smelled of smoke. The fire had gotten to the main bedroom floor and many things were burned and had to go too. Curtains had fed the flames and were gone, carpets were badly damaged, upholstered furniture had been soaked through and ruined. At the end of her weekend of sorting, there was very little furniture worth storing or reupholstering, and another group of antiques that were water- or fire-damaged but could be restored. The family had sold most of the art a long time before, and most of what was on the walls belonged to the Johnsons. There were beautiful original crystal sconces and light fixtures which were still intact, and Cosima left them in place. Some of the china and crystal had shattered from the heat, but most of it was still good, and she marked it to pack up and store. The family silver was tarnished but undamaged, and there was a lot of it, with the family crest on it. And the miraculous survivor of the fire was the ballroom in the far wing of the house, which was spared almost intact, with only a faint hint of smoke.

Cosima marked everything, and showed it to the two elderly guardians, Tomaso and Guillermo, and asked them to ship the items to Sally Johnson or put them in storage, and throw away what was too damaged. She sent an email asking for instructions.

Cosima planned to leave the house empty rather than filled with damaged items. On closer inspection, there was a fair amount in the end to send to storage for future use or repair. All the floors had buckled from the heat and water and would have to be redone. The burnt moldings would need to be restored. The walls were still drying out from the water a month later and might take a year. But once they got out all the ruined furniture and items for storage, it would be easier to see the work the house needed to restore it to its former beauty.

When she studied the palazzo closely, Cosima was surprised that there was a lot less restoration to do than she had feared. She was sorry now that Sally Johnson didn't want to do it, and that she didn't have the money to do it herself, and there was no insurance money forthcoming, thanks to Luca. A new owner could do it if they wanted to, but it was a big project, and would be expensive and time-consuming.

She worked alone for three days, sorting everything and throwing things away. She had a few boxes of mementos and old photographs she found in an upstairs closet, some old family albums, and several beautiful old Vuitton trunks in the attic, containing her mother's old gowns, some costumes for their masked balls, and her mother's and grandmother's wedding gowns, which were all unaffected by the fire. She was sending it all to storage. She only threw away what was irreparably damaged and couldn't be restored. The china, crystal, and silver could still be used one day if she or Allegra had a formal home. Luca was no longer a consideration.

She'd had the structure checked by an engineer right after the fire, and had some vital areas rewired so they had some light in the house. Surprisingly, the ceilings were all sound, despite the water, and she had all the broken windows replaced that had been blown out by the fire. Just doing that much had been expensive, but it had to be done to protect the house for the winter. She had thrown out all the old kitchenware and faded linens before the Johnsons rented the palazzo, so everything was clean and fresh for them. A lot of the Johnsons' new décor had melted in the heat of the fire and had to be thrown away. Sally was going to be shocked by how little was left. It made Cosima think of the housewarming party after they redecorated, where she had met Olivier, the same night that Max and Luca had met at the casino. It had all started then, only three months before. It felt like a lifetime.

She knew that Olivier was visiting Max the same weekend she was working at the palazzo. He came to see her on Sunday afternoon and was amazed by how much she'd done herself, with the caretakers' help.

He had found her up in the attic looking at her mother's gowns. Even the trunks they were in, which had been her grandmother's, looked like works of art and were worth a fortune. Every room had an echo now, as the two men carried things out and she emptied each room and threw things away.

"It looks better than I thought it would," Olivier said when he found her. She had done an immense amount of work. She was filthy, covered in soot and ash and dirt. She had cut her fingers repeatedly on small shards of broken glass. He hugged her when he saw her, and she was happy to see him.

"How's Max?" she asked him.

"Not bad. He could be worse. It reminds me of when I visited him at camp, which he hated. He says the food is terrible, but he likes his cellmate. He's a Russian forger. Max may pick up some bad skills there." More than a month of his sentence had already gone by. Olivier had brought him cigarettes, magazines, and chocolate. He had his computer, and a job in the kitchen. It made Cosima wonder how Luca was doing. She didn't ask if Max had seen him. The two men hated each other now and blamed each other for their misfortunes. She wondered what Luca would do when he got out, if prison would change him, or make him worse, and turn him into a dangerous criminal. Two years was a long time. And Luca was already far down a bad path, probably irretrievably. She had no hope for him now.

"Can I drag you away for dinner?" Olivier asked her.

"You'll have to turn the hose on me. I'm filthy."

Her clothes and hair smelled like smoke, and she was covered in dust and ash.

"We can tell them you were cleaning house all day and you're a thorough cleaner. The place does look surprisingly good. Are you really going to take it off the market?"

"I don't see who would buy it like this," she said, carefully folding her mother's gowns back into the trunk, and putting a tag on it to send to storage.

"It's not easy to find a historic palazzo in Venice," he said. "Someone might want a project. And only two of the floors were really affected. The ballroom is perfect."

"We won't get a decent price for it like this, and I can't afford to do the restoration now. Maybe later." He nodded, it was a difficult situation, and heartbreaking for her, especially since her brother had done it.

"Your sister is coming to Paris next week, by the way, to visit Basile. They're going to do street art together. He's going to teach her how." It was the second time in a month Allegra had visited Basile, and Cosima smiled.

"They're cute together."

"I had the feeling they'd like each other when I met her. They have the same vibe, full of life, they're like rays of sunshine together."

Cosima nodded. "And I look like a garbage can." She laughed at herself as she headed downstairs with him to the main hall. She came down the grand staircase remembering how her mother had looked doing that at their balls.

"You're just a little dusty," Olivier teased her. He couldn't believe how much she'd done. She was a powerhouse, and so was Allegra. They were strong, determined women, with courage. "Can I get you out of here?"

"I'm done. The rest has to be thrown out, sent to storage, or shipped to Sally in Dallas." She'd spent a productive three days, which didn't surprise him.

She washed up as best she could at the garden faucet. The water was turned off in the house, as was the gas. They went to the closest trattoria and had a simple dinner, which tasted delicious. She'd been living on apples, salami, and bread crusts all weekend.

They went to the airport together after dinner. He took the last flight to Florence, and she took the last one to Rome.

"When am I going to see you again?" he asked her before he left.

"I'm going to Milan next week for Fashion Week. We're doing a pop-up store on the Via Montenapoleone. Allegra is in charge of it. I'm sending her to Paris Fashion Week too."

"Aren't you coming?"

"I might. I have a lot of work to do in Rome, and Allegra seems to be very eager to get to Paris these days." She smiled at him, and he hugged her.

"And I'm eager to see you." He was flying back from Florence to Paris. He had meetings in Paris that week too. "Will you try to come to Fashion Week in Paris?" he asked her.

"I don't want Allegra to feel like I'm checking on her."

"We can leave them alone. I'll try to come to Rome for a night in a couple of weeks." They'd both been busy since the summer, but she was always on his mind. In some ways, she was always so warm and welcoming, and at other times, he could feel her holding back, and she still hadn't explained it. There didn't seem to be an active man in her life, but there was something stopping her, and he knew it. He didn't know if it was Gian Battista or an old ghost, and he was afraid to ask her.

Allegra had stars in her eyes when she came back from Paris the following weekend. It was obvious she was in love with Basile.

"How was it?" Cosima asked her when she stopped in for coffee with her on Monday morning. Allegra had returned late the night before.

"He's incredible," she said dreamily, "and he's such a good artist. He really has talent."

"So do you," Cosima reminded her.

"I'm a designer, he's an artist. There's a difference."

"Talent is talent, it just gets expressed differently by different people."

"What about you and his father? I thought that

was going to turn into a big deal at first, but I have the feeling you put the brakes on. You always do. He's such a good guy, and he's crazy about you. Basile said so too. Why do you stop? What are you afraid of?" Allegra worried about her sister.

"Everything. Men, people, making a mistake, getting hurt. And I have you and the business. I'm busy."

"Don't be too busy to have a life. Why don't we go to Paris to see him sometime?"

"That's what Olivier said. Maybe I will one of these days. He said he'd come to dinner here in a few weeks. I saw him in Venice last weekend for a quick dinner after I cleared the house."

"You need more than that," Allegra said. She loved her big sister and wanted her to be happy, the way she was with Basile. They felt made for each other.

Cosima thought about what she'd said when she got to her office, and then the calls started, and emails and meetings, and conference calls, everything that gobbled up her day.

She got a call from her realtor at noon.

"I cleared the house last weekend," Cosima reported to her. "All the debris is gone, all the burned curtains and broken things. The guardians cleaned it thoroughly last week. They said it looks pretty good. I'm going to board it up now, and get ready for winter, and we can talk about it again in the spring. It needs work, and I just can't do it right now."

"Let's talk about it now. I've got someone who wants to see it," Francesca Viti said with determination.

"You shouldn't show it the way it looks now, before it's restored. I won't get a decent price," Cosima insisted.

"I'm not so sure. I have a new client, from Qatar. He's got a French lawyer looking for him. He seems to be rolling in money, and his lawyer says he doesn't care if the place needs work. He only wants a historic palazzo, whatever the condition. Supposedly he's got great taste, and a decorator and an architect, and would be willing to do the restoration. Should I show it to him?"

"He'll be sadly disappointed. The walls are burned, the floors buckled, there's water damage, one of the big chandeliers exploded and fell. I cleaned it up, but it needs a lot more than that, and I don't want to lose a fortune by showing it in this condition."

"How much do you want for it now?"

"The same amount the Johnsons were willing to pay me before the fire. It's the right price, but not with a lot of work to do."

"Why don't I tell them and see what the lawyer says? If he still wants to see it, I'll show it to him. It can't hurt. I've got two other palazzos to show him, but yours is older, bigger, and prettier, and the guy is apparently a Renaissance buff."

"Okay, but he'll be disappointed when he sees

it." It needed so much work and that would be expensive. And she still wanted a decent price. She would have to do some of the work herself to show it.

"I'll let you know." Francesca hung up, and Cosima rushed off to a meeting before lunch. She saw Allegra in the hall on the way to the design studio and waved. Cosima didn't have time for lunch and stayed until eight o'clock on conference calls. They were launching a new publicity campaign, and Cosima wanted to get it just right. She got home at nine, exhausted, and she had brought work home. She wondered when Allegra thought she'd actually have time for a romance, with Olivier or anyone else. There was no room in her life for a man. There had been when she was younger, with Gian Battista, but after him, she had filled all the gaps so she didn't miss him so acutely. She had been miserable for a long time without him, and at least she could still see him from time to time, for a drink, or lunch, or a kiss that reminded her of what she was missing and no longer had. Gian Battista was adamant about not starting things up again once they broke up. And she'd never fully gotten over him. They both knew it. Olivier was the only man who had appealed to her ever since, and she was afraid to leap in and get hurt, or hurt him. She always thought that if she stayed alone for long enough, Gian Battista might come back, but he never had.

For three long years, even though she knew he still loved her too.

Cosima had a busy week while they got ready for Fashion Week in Milan. She was completely immersed in her work, and forgot all else. A week later, the realtor called her back, right before she left for Milan. Cosima had forgotten all about her and the Qatari with the French lawyer who wanted to see the palazzo. Cosima was sure he wouldn't be interested at a decent price, or at all.

"You were wrong," Francesca Viti said for openers. She had a deep, raspy, sexy voice that always made Cosima smile. She was so Italian. "The Qatari doesn't care about the burnt walls. The lawyer sent him a million photos, I was with him when he took them, and his client is in love with your palazzo. He wants it, at your asking price, all cash, thirty-day closing, as is, damage and all. And you're right by the way. The floors are a mess. I tripped three times on the speed bumps in the dining room." She laughed her deep throaty laugh. "So, what do you think?"

"I think he's crazy," Cosima said, considering it. She had made her peace with the idea of keeping the palazzo now, even in its current state, ever since Bill Johnson died and Sally backed out of the deal. The palazzo was in no condition to show or to sell. And she didn't have the money to restore it. She was prepared to let it sit for years if she had to. The whole idea of selling it had come up when she had to raise money quickly to pay Luca's gambling debt, and selling the palazzo was the only way she could do it, and then she was on the hook to the Johnsons since they had paid her a deposit she couldn't afford to refund. But she had no pressing financial need now, and the two hundred thousand the Johnsons had given her had cleared Luca's debt. Sally had canceled the sale when Bill died, so Cosima didn't have to refund the money to her. She could just keep the palazzo now and decide what she wanted to do about it some other time. She didn't know if she was ready to leap in and give it up with a thirty-day closing, although the price he was willing to pay was a fair one, and more than fair given the fact that two of the floors were badly burned and there was serious repair work to do. "He doesn't mind all the work there is to be done?" Cosima said hesitantly.

"Apparently not. His lawyer said he's not going to rush into it. He wants to buy it so he doesn't lose the opportunity, and take his time doing the work when he's in Europe. He has an apartment in Paris, and another in London and a house in Switzerland. He liked one of the other palazzos, but not as much as yours. The lawyer said he's crazy about it. I didn't talk to him myself. A lot of them do business that way, through lawyers and corporations. I don't even know the man's name. And he's going to pay all cash by bank transfer through his lawyer's trust account. We do that all the time. So?" She had a big commission resting on it, so she was eager to know. But Cosima didn't want to be rushed.

"Let me think about it. I want to talk to my sister. I didn't tell her about him because I figured he wouldn't want it." They needed Luca to agree too, but she could do that through his lawyer, and it would put a sizable amount of money in an account for him to have when he came out in two years, several million euros, and she was sure he would be very pleased with the money. Money was all he cared about.

Cosima told Allegra about it that night before she went out to dinner with friends, and told her the pertinent details. Price, timing, all cash, as is, with a thirty-day closing.

"Wow," Allegra said, "it sounds amazing, if he doesn't care about the fire damage and is willing to pay what the Johnsons were going to pay before the fire. It needed some remodeling then too. Should we do it?"

"I don't know," Cosima said. "I was getting to like the idea of keeping it, even though it needs work and it's a mess right now. And I don't know when we'd have the money to restore it. Not anytime soon. But there's no rush to do it."

"Can we afford to keep it?"

"No more or less than we could before. It takes

money to maintain it. We can't use it now, but I'm sad to let it go." Allegra was less attached to the palazzo than she was and had fewer memories there since she was nine years younger, but she loved it too. She loved the family history it represented for centuries. For Allegra, it was woven into her feelings for her parents and memories of her happy childhood there.

"Maybe we should let go of the past and forge ahead. I thought that's what we decided before, and then Luca screwed everything up and set fire to it. We probably won't get another buyer who doesn't care about the damage," Allegra said sensibly.

"True. Why don't we both sleep on it and see what we think," Cosima suggested.

"I vote to sell it," Allegra suddenly announced. "It would be nice to have the money, as a cushion." It was a lot of money, even divided by three. "Do you think Luca would object and try to block it?"

"Hell, no. He'd love to have the money." Cosima was sure of that.

"Yeah, me too," Allegra admitted shyly. She'd never had a large amount of her own and lived on the salary Cosima paid her for the small amount of work she did. Her apartment was free. And she shared in the profits every year but Cosima always put them back in the business for improvements and operating costs. "I vote yes," Allegra said softly.

"So, it's up to you." They didn't use majority rule, they all had to agree unanimously.

The thought of it haunted Cosima all night. She wanted to call Gian Battista and ask his advice, but that seemed childish, and he had already told her to sell when the Johnsons wanted to buy it. He thought the palazzo was a money pit, and he wasn't wrong, especially now. She thought of asking Olivier too, but she felt stupid not making the decision on her own. She wondered if Allegra was right, and they needed to move ahead into the future and stop clinging to the past.

She tossed and turned all night, tortured by the decision, and woke up early the next morning. She watched the sun come up as she loved to do, squeezed her eyes shut for a few seconds, and picked up her phone and sent Francesca Viti a text.

"It's a go. Sell it. I have to get my brother's permission, but that won't be a problem." She sent his lawyer an email, explaining the terms, and she said she needed Luca's consent to make it legal, soon, if possible.

She had Luca's approval by noon, and she felt as though she had taken a leap out of an airplane and was waiting for her parachute to open and praying it would. She hoped she wouldn't regret selling. She was more attached to the palazzo than either of her siblings was, but it was time. She needed to move something in her life and maybe this was it. Francesca sent her all the papers to sign that afternoon, and Cosima had never made an easier deal. By six o'clock that night, they were selling their family's palazzo to the Qatari they had never even met, and Cosima was surprised that she was excited about it and hadn't even shed a tear. Maybe it was the right thing to do after all.

Chapter 11

Cosima went to Paris with Allegra for Paris Fashion Week, and had a great time going to a few fashion shows. She had dinner twice with Olivier. Milan had gone well too, but she had work to do there. In Paris, she was purely a spectator, and she went to Olivier's office and was impressed by the size of his operation and how elegant his showroom was. It was where they met with buyers and took wholesale orders. His handbags were surprisingly good-looking for the price.

She hardly saw Allegra while they were there. She was with Basile all the time, and stayed at his apartment. Cosima didn't comment on it. At twenty-nine, Allegra was old enough to do what she wanted, and Basile was wonderful to her. Cosima knew she was in good hands.

Cosima told Olivier about selling the palazzo to the Qatari, and that she and Allegra were going to Venice the following weekend to see it for a last

time. She had already moved their remaining belongings into storage, and she just wanted to see it
once more and kiss it goodbye.

"Are you sorry you sold it?" he asked her, over
dinner at Le Voltaire, a chic bistro on the Left Bank
she had always liked. He was a regular there.

"No. It's crazy but I'm excited. Allegra's right. We
need to move ahead and stop hanging on to the
past. And it will be nice to have the money." The
deal was closing in the next week. "It would have
taken years to be able to pay for the restoration."

"Do you have any special purpose in mind for
the money?" he asked her, and she hesitated.

"I'm not sure. I've been wondering if I should
use it to buy Luca out of the business, or keep it and
invest it, or just pour my share back into the business. We can always use the money. I think Allegra
wants to hang on to her share."

"Maybe you should do something special with it
and spoil yourself," he suggested. She couldn't even
imagine what. She had no special needs or desires.

The four of them had dinner together on their
last night in Paris, and Olivier was pleased. Fashion
Week had been a big success for his business and
orders had been rolling in from their usual customers and new ones. He had been wanting to ask Cosima a question all week and hadn't had the
courage. As exclusive as she was with her bags, he
couldn't imagine her agreeing, but he was dying to
ask. He finally screwed up his courage over dessert,

while Basile and Allegra were teasing each other and laughing. They played children's card games every night and screamed with laughter, and Allegra said that Basile cheated constantly, which he hotly denied. They were like two happy children with each other, and best friends. Cosima envied that. It seemed so innocent and uncomplicated.

Over coffee, Olivier finally took the leap.

"Cosima, would you ever consider a one-time collaboration, or more than once if it works, where you'd consult with me on some of our higher-priced styles and give them an extra chic twist? We'd price them at our high end, and make them very exclusive. I want to develop a luxury line," contrary to what Max had always suggested, to go cheap and low-end and mass-produce in China. Olivier wanted to go in the opposite direction. Before she could answer, Allegra leapt into the conversation.

"Can I do it?" she asked. "Cosima never lets me add anything to our classics. I have to keep them very pure. I have a lot of sketches that might work for you."

Cosima smiled. "Maybe that's your answer. And Allegra is right. I'm married to our signature styles, and I'm very resistant to changing them. Allegra is brimming with new ideas, and she knows our style."

"Could we call it a Saverio-Bayard collaboration then, maybe with just six styles, two or three of them in exotic skins, ultrachic for our more sophisticated customers and better stores?" It was a more commercial direction than Cosima usually liked to go in, but she also knew it could be a big money-maker and broaden their client base, and bring attention to their bags in other countries. She knew her grandfather would have hated it, but she liked the idea, and Allegra looked like she was going to jump out of her chair, she was so excited.

"I can start working on them tomorrow," Allegra said. "And I have a file full of designs."

"I have to approve them if our name is on them," Cosima reminded them both. "Nothing too trendy or crazy."

"The whole point is that I want to bring our bags closer to your look, not bring yours closer to ours," Olivier explained.

"I have another idea too," Allegra leapt in again. She was brimming with ideas now and Basile looked at her proudly. He loved how creative she was. "When I get the money from the palazzo, I want to do a line of really out-there, wild, terrific, superchic younger bags in great fabrics and materials, crazy colors, all the things Cosima won't let me do for the house. I want to bring them in at accessible price points, not look cheap, but not be out-of-sight expensive like ours. I want to call the line Allegra, and bring them to Fashion Week next time, and set up my own pop-up store, and see how they sell."

"Are you quitting?" Cosima looked panicked.

"No, I want to do it as a sideline. But I don't know where to have them made."

"I'll tell you what," Olivier entered the conversation again. "I'll do six prototypes for Cosima at our factory, so you can check out our quality and production and workmanship, and I'll do ten or twelve of your own designs for Allegra, and we can introduce both lines, our collaboration and the Allegras, at Fall/Winter Fashion Week here in March. It'll take us that long to get it right." Cosima liked the idea, and Allegra was over the moon at the idea of a pop-up store with her own exclusive designs, with no one holding her back, so she could do whatever she wanted. She had never been able to do that before.

The four of them ordered champagne and toasted each other and their two new projects. Cosima knew that collaborations were one of the more successful new marketing tools, and Allegra couldn't wait to introduce her own designs. Olivier was thrilled with both projects, and was eager to get started on them. Cosima was guardedly excited, as she was about all things that involved the family name, but she liked the idea too, and it was a good experiment to see how their designs would translate to a broader, more commercial market.

"I think we're on to some very exciting new concepts here," Olivier said. "I like our plan."

Basile and Allegra left the restaurant a little while later, still talking about it. She kept turning around to talk to Basile and almost turned her chair over as he reached out and grabbed it. "You're drunk, you're going to get a DUI," he warned her, and pushed her chair the rest of the way home, as she told him all about the bags she was going to design for the new line. It was the most exciting thing that had ever happened in her job, and she'd been saving folders of her designs for years.

"I can't believe that your dad got Cosima to agree to all that. She must be drunk too." But Cosima looked more than drunk. She looked in love with Olivier. Allegra was happy to see it. She was tired of seeing her sister working too hard and always alone. She deserved to be happy too.

Cosima called Gian Battista when she got back to Rome after Fashion Week. The sale of the palazzo was closing in a few days, and she wanted to see how he was. He always sounded tired lately and a little down, and she was worried about him.

"Allegra and I are going to Venice this weekend to kiss the palazzo goodbye. Do you want to come?" He had had so many happy times there, even before she was born. He and her father had been boyhood friends. They had grown up in Venice together.

"I don't need to see it again," he said quietly. "And I don't want to see it now, damaged and injured, thanks to Luca, with all the beautiful furniture gone. That's how I remember it, in all its glory.

I have my memories. That's enough. I'll see you for lunch when you're back," he said, and she suggested the following Monday. She thought he sounded nostalgic, and a little bit morose, which was unlike him. He was a serious person, but not usually so down. But she was looking forward to lunch with him. Any excuse was good to see him. She still missed him so much.

She and Allegra spent a warm, loving weekend in Venice, going to some of their favorite places. They sat in the Piazza San Marco and ate gelato, as they did as young girls, and drank wine, and walked for miles, with Cosima gently pushing Allegra, always ending up in the same place, as one did easily in Venice, but it was hard to really get lost if you knew the city well, which they did.

And on Sunday afternoon, they went to the palazzo, let themselves in, and went quietly from room to room on the main floor to say goodbye, and then Cosima went upstairs alone. She was crying when she came down the grand staircase for the last time, and they hugged each other at the bottom of the stairs and held each other tight. Cosima hoped she had done the right thing and hadn't made a mistake selling it, but practically, it made sense. And they could do other things with the money. The final payment was due in their accounts that week. Cosima closed her eyes tightly for a minute, picturing her parents on that same staircase, and then they went out the front door and locked it behind them. One of Francesca Viti's assistants was waiting to collect the keys from them. Both caretakers had already left, both had retired, Tomaso to Sicily and Guillermo to his hometown, Maratea, a small beach town south of Naples. He had waited all his life to go back. The new owner had hired someone new, and younger, who was starting in a week, to manage the property and the restoration.

"Congratulations," the young assistant said as she put the keys in her purse. "Francesca says you got lucky with the French guy who bought it, he paid the full asking, all cash, even with the fire and water damage."

"He's not French, he's Qatari," Cosima corrected her. "If he were French, he'd have beaten us down on the price," she said wryly, trying not to cry over the emotional moment of leaving the palazzo for the last time. They might never see it from the inside again and probably wouldn't.

"No, he's French," the girl insisted. She was young, talked too much, and was new in Francesca's office, and didn't know what she was talking about.

"His lawyer is French," Cosima said. "The buyer is from Qatar."

"Oh. I guess I got that wrong." The assistant shrugged with a grin. "I thought he was the buyer."

"No, just the front man."

"Why did he need a front man? Is he a drug dealer or something?"

"Some people just like that, if they're famous, or private, or very rich," Cosima explained to her.

"He must be very rich. He paid a lot for it. Francesca said you were very lucky," she repeated. Cosima nodded, she'd had enough of the conversation. She thanked the girl for coming and they left.

The sisters were both quiet on the boat ride to where they could catch a cab to the airport a little while later. They had come to do what they said they would do, say goodbye to their family's palazzo and all the history that went with it. Cosima thought of what Gian Battista had said. He didn't need to see it again. He had his memories. That seemed to be true about a lot of things in life. She thought about him too on the flight back to Rome. She was seeing him the next day for lunch.

When Gian Battista walked into the restaurant the next day, he looked as tall and handsome and strong as ever. She thought he looked thinner, and she noticed that he looked older. Time was catching up with him. But he was still a remarkable man. He kissed her on the cheek and sat down across from her. They were at one of their favorite little tucked-away restaurants that he loved, and he held hands with her all through lunch. He was in good spirits, and asked her about the palazzo.

"So did you kiss it goodbye?" he asked her with a smile.

"I did. But you're right. I have all the memories."

"That's all that matters. If you have the memories, you have them forever. They never leave you. People leave, the memories don't. You can't lose them."

"I always thought of my mother coming down the grand staircase in an evening gown, with my father in a dinner jacket or white tie and tails next to her."

"So did I," he admitted, and looked nostalgic for a moment.

He asked if she had heard from Luca and she said she hadn't, but he had signed the consent to sell the palazzo. He was going to make a lot of money from his share of the sale.

"Maybe he'll wake up and finally grow up in prison. It's a shame it had to come to that," Gian Battista said, and changed the subject.

She had been surprised to find that she didn't miss her brother. It was a relief not to have to worry about him and what he was up to. His lawyer had told her that Luca was selling his house on the Via Appia Antica. He had never liked it anyway, and he wanted a fresh start when he came out. She hoped it was a good sign. Or maybe he just wanted the money, but he would have plenty now with the sale of the palazzo. It had been insane of him to attempt the insurance scam. He had more than enough with the sale of the house, but he'd been greedy and always wanted more. Dishonest schemes always came to mind easily for him, more than honest ones. He didn't know how to be an honest man, and didn't want to.

They talked about a number of subjects during lunch and stayed at the table longer than usual. Gian Battista told Cosima openly that he loved her, which he hadn't done in a while, and she told him she loved him too. That had never changed, and she knew it never would.

"How's your friend in Paris? The honorable one who wouldn't buy Luca's shares in the business?"

"He's fine. We're going to do a collaboration as an experiment, and he's helping Allegra try out a line of her own. She's over the moon about it, and she appears to be in love with his son."

"Not the one in prison, I hope."

"No, the other one. He's an artist and seems like a nice boy." They touched on every subject and at the end of lunch she thought he looked particularly tired. He wasn't very old, only seventy-two now, but she had thought he seemed tired for a while. She wondered if he had missed her as much as she missed him. She had never gotten over him and thought she never would. Their separation wasn't as painful now. She had gotten used to it, she still missed him, but she knew he was never far away if she needed him.

He held her in his arms for a long moment when

they left the restaurant, and he smiled as he looked into her eyes. Everything about him was so familiar. Being with him was like coming home.

"My beautiful girl," he said softly to her. "You always make me so happy and so proud of you. Your parents would have been too. I want you to be happy. Don't work too hard. You need to have fun too."

"It's never been as much fun as when I was with you."

"That's not right," he said, frowning. "I'm an old man, you're a child." But she didn't feel like a child. She always felt like a woman with him. His woman. He kissed her one last time and then put her in a cab to take her back to her office. They had lingered for a long time over lunch. She sent him a text from the cab, thanking him for lunch and telling him again that she loved him.

He waved as her cab drove away, and stood smiling on the sidewalk, and as soon as she was gone, he turned and walked down the street, with tears running down his cheeks.

Chapter 12

Cosima never read the newspaper in the morning. She hated to start the day off with bad news. Her secretary laid them out for her on the coffee table in her office, so she could choose which ones she wanted to read during the day, when she had time during a break. The international edition of *The New York Times, The Wall Street Journal, Corriere della Sera,* and the London *Financial Times.* She read *The Business of Fashion* and *Women's Wear Daily* online for news of the fashion world. Two days after she had lunch with Gian Battista, she was surprised to see *Corriere della Sera* neatly folded on her desk when she got to work. His photograph was on the front page. She was startled when she saw it, and then her heart skipped a beat. She sat down at her desk, quickly unfolded the paper, and read the news. He had died at seven the night before, at his home, the newspaper said. He had died the day after she saw him. She realized instantly that he had known. He had been saying goodbye to her and she didn't suspect it, when he told her he loved her and kissed her on the sidewalk and told her memories were all that mattered. He had known it was coming when he invited her to lunch, and had lived long enough to see her. She got up and locked the door to her office, and sobbed as she read the article, as though it was a message to her.

The headline read, "Gian Battista di San Martino, attorney, political influencer, advisor to presidents and popes for forty years." It listed his many accomplishments, the many heads of state he had counseled, the boards he had been on, the countless awards he had received. He had achieved so many things in his lifetime, there was barely room enough for it in the article. The photograph was fairly recent, and even in his seventies he had been a strikingly handsome man.

The article said that he was survived by his widow, Maria Grazia Sant'Angelo di San Martino, to whom he had been married for fifty-one years. It didn't say that she was a cold, unpleasant woman he had been bitterly unhappy with for the entire time, or that Cosima had been the joy and the hope in his life, as he had told her so often, but she knew it more than ever now.

The obituary said that he had lost a four-year battle with a rare form of stomach cancer, which explained everything to Cosima, why he had insisted on ending their affair three years before and told her she had to marry and have children and forget him, and why he had stuck to his position resolutely no matter how much pain it had caused them both. He knew he was dying and didn't want to hang on to her until the bitter end. He had wanted to free her, but they were bound to each other heart and soul. He had never stopped loving her, nor she him. She didn't have a moment of regret for the fifteen years she had loved him, or the nine years of their affair, no matter how great the difference in their ages, or the fact that he was married and she had known he could never get divorced.

The article went on to say that he was deeply embedded in the politics of the Church, with strong ties to the Vatican. It mentioned his uncle, who was a cardinal, and his brother, who was a bishop. He came from a long line of noblemen who had been involved in the politics of Italy for centuries. He was even related to a sixteenth-century pope. She knew most of it from him. There was to be a state funeral at the Basilica di Santa Maria Sopra Minerva, and burial would be private for family only. Both his brother and his uncle, although older than he was, had outlived him, and would officiate at his funeral.

Cosima had never felt a loss as acute since the death of her parents. She didn't regret a moment she had spent with Gian Battista and wished he had told her he was ill when he left her, but then she wouldn't have allowed him to leave her. He had staunchly refused to put her through it, and the article said he had survived longer than expected due to experimental treatments, which had stopped being effective three months earlier. It explained why she had found him so tired recently and looked thinner at lunch two days before. She sat at her desk feeling like a stone statue for an hour and didn't answer her phone. She couldn't. She could barely breathe, knowing he was gone.

The memories came rushing back, of all the years they had shared, the wonderful times they had had, and she knew how right he had been that the memories were all that mattered. She had them all, and he would never leave her. They lived a full lifetime together in a mere fifteen years.

An hour after she had read the article her secretary had left on her desk for her, she unlocked her office door. Allegra came through it a few minutes later and stared at her when she saw her. Cosima was as white as a sheet. She looked like a ghost.

"Are you okay?" Allegra was instantly worried. "You look sick."

"Gian Battista died last night, at home. He had cancer. I didn't know. I saw him for lunch two days ago." Allegra had always suspected that there was more between them but had never asked. If Cosima had wanted her to know, she would have told her, and she never had. Cosima had always been fiercely private. Allegra knew something had happened a few years ago. Cosima had looked devastated for months and Gian Battista had suddenly become much less present than he had been before, but he was always there, nearby, on the fringes of their lives, and available if they needed him, like a guardian angel.

"I'm so sorry," Allegra said, and hugged her. Cosima clung to her and was shaken by sobs, and then Cosima sat on the couch, holding Allegra's hands and not speaking. "Are you going to the funeral?" Allegra didn't know if his wife knew or not, and didn't want to ask that either. Allegra had never been completely certain until that moment, but now it all made sense, and it was also why there had never been another man in her sister's life. Gian Battista had been the love of her life, the only one.

"I guess so." Cosima couldn't imagine not going, and Gian Battista had been deeply religious, so it would be a high mass at the funeral.

"Can I come with you?" Allegra asked her, and Cosima nodded. She didn't want to go alone. Cosima intended to sit discreetly in a back row. She felt hypocritical going since she had no sympathy for his widow, but people would have been shocked if the Saverios weren't there, and Cosima needed to be there, out of love and respect for him.

She was even more surprised when Gian Battista's secretary called her later in the day and said that the countess di San Martino wished to invite her and her sister to sit in the pew with her. Cosima wasn't sure if she should, but she accepted. It was a place of honor in a ritual that was important to him and would be to Cosima too.

"I have nothing to wear," Cosima told Allegra when she came to check on her after lunch, which she hadn't eaten. She had hated black suits ever since her parents' funeral. She had worn a black suit to that.

"I'll get you something," Allegra promised.

"I'll come with you," Cosima said. She wanted to look perfect for him, for this final appearance to honor him. They had gone out socially discreetly for nine years. He had always portrayed their relationship as her being his deceased closest friend's daughter, and very few people had ever suspected, if any. And no one knew for sure. He was always careful of her reputation and appearances, and when they went away together, they traveled separately, and met in faraway places. She always pretended to others that she traveled alone. They had met in Bali, Burma, Vietnam, Mauritius, Tahiti, the wilds of Provence or remote corners of Brittany, or the Dordogne. They had had so many good times together, shared so many important moments. She couldn't imagine her life without him now, but he had been preparing her for this for the past three years. She understood it all now. He had been teaching her to go on with her life and be happy without him. He had even said it the other day after lunch. He had been giving her his instructions for the future. "Be happy, don't work too hard, have fun." He had told her how proud he was of her, and called her "My beautiful girl," which was what he had always called her when they were alone. They had been madly in love for a long time, until the end. And he had been what was stopping her from getting more deeply involved with Olivier, whom he had called her "honorable friend" at lunch. It was his stamp of approval, his permission to go on and live, even with Olivier if she chose to.

Cosima didn't want to talk to Olivier now, or to anyone. She had her secretary take messages all day and say she was out of the office at a conference where she couldn't be reached.

She wondered if Luca read the newspaper in prison, and if he knew. Gian Battista had been there for Luca too, although he hadn't approved of Luca's behavior for the past several years and had given up on him. She knew that Luca would be shaken too. They all were, anyone who knew him. And he had been like a father to Allegra and Luca, and a husband to her.

The days before his funeral were a blur Cosima couldn't even remember afterwards and didn't want to. Allegra had clothes brought to the store for her to choose from. She picked a plain black wool dress, a very chic black Dior coat, and a gorgeous black hat she knew he would have loved. He loved it when she looked glamorous, and she wanted to for him. Allegra picked a simple black Chanel suit with black satin lapels to wear, of the kind Cosima hated, but it looked well on her, and was suitably funereal.

The two sisters went to the funeral together in a black Bentley, and Maria Grazia had sent them cards to present at the church, which would allow them to be led to the front to sit with her. Gian Battista had had countless cousins and great-nieces and nephews, but he wasn't close to any of them. The Saverios were the only children he was ever close to. Maria Grazia looked like a scarecrow in a black silk dress that hung on her, plain black suede shoes, an old black coat, and a hat that was long out of date.

She had never made an effort about how she looked and hated her role as an important man's wife. She had spent most of her time riding horses when she was young, gave it up after a hunting accident, and after that spent her time in church and on charity committees.

Maria Grazia and Gian Battista had spent as little time together as possible for fifty years. They had discovered within months of their marriage that they were ill suited, but a divorce was unthinkable at the time, nearly impossible to obtain in Italy, and unimaginable given his connections to the Vatican. He would have been satisfied with an annulment and had asked her for one within six months of their marriage, but she wouldn't agree to it. They had stopped sleeping together within a few months of their wedding, by her choice, and had separate bedrooms after their first year of marriage and from then on. She wanted the appearance of being his wife, but not the fact. Cosima had had the reality, but not the name.

Maria Grazia hugged both girls stiffly when they arrived. Allegra maneuvered her wheelchair as close as she could to the end of the pew, and Cosima sat between her and Maria Grazia, feeling uncomfortable but honored. The widow was wearing black suede gloves and patted Cosima's hand. "He loved you very much," she said in a voice no one else could hear. "Always. And your whole family." Cosima wondered if she knew, but Gian Battista always insisted that she didn't, and was careful not to cause her pain or embarrassment. He had been loyal to her for half a century, but hadn't loved her.

Maria Grazia had always said that she regretted not going into religious orders, and Cosima wondered if she would enter one now. She had wasted all the years as Gian Battista's wife, which Cosima would have cherished. She would have gladly been his wife and given him ten children. She had even considered having a child by him, unmarried, and was sorry now she hadn't. But he was afraid of the scandal for both of them and didn't want to compromise Cosima's reputation. They had been more than married in many ways, and she was more his widow than the woman sitting next to her in the ugly black hat with a widow's veil. Her face was

heavily lined and her features sharp beneath the
veil.

The high mass took two hours, the music was
beautiful, and he would have liked it. A choir of
Dominican nuns sang. There were many tributes
and readings, and a homily about a man of great
wisdom, wit, and humility, which almost did him
justice but not quite, and at the end of the mass,
Allegra and Cosima followed Maria Grazia out,
down the main aisle. She had honored Cosima in a
deeply respectful way Gian Battista would have
wanted and approved of. Cosima pushed Allegra's
wheelchair to steady herself and so she had something to hang on to. Allegra understood and didn't
object.

There was a reception at Gian Battista and Maria
Grazia's home afterwards, but the two sisters didn't
go. The hypocrisy was too much for Cosima, and
she avoided the reception out of respect for his wife
in case anyone did know about her and Gian Battista. They thanked Maria Grazia before they left,
and then they went home.

Cosima sat for hours alone on her terrace, surrounded by memories of him, just as he had said.
He had been teaching her how to live with what
had just happened, and the pain was very fresh. If
he hadn't been sick, he would never have left her
three years before. She knew that now and it was a
comfort to her.

She was somber and serious at the office afterwards for several days. The sale of the palazzo had gone through and she didn't notice or care. She didn't take a call from Olivier until the end of the week.

"Are you all right?" He was worried by her silence, but he knew why. She didn't need to tell him. He had guessed.

"Yes, I'm fine. I've had a long week."

"I read about your friend Gian Battista in *Le Figaro*. I'm so sorry. Did you go to the funeral?"

"Yes, with Allegra. We sat with his wife, she invited us." That surprised him, given what he suspected, but he didn't comment. He didn't want to intrude on her grief.

"It may be too soon, and you may not be in the mood, but I have meetings in Rome tomorrow. Do you want to have dinner?" She hesitated as she thought about it, and remembered what Gian Battista had told her after lunch . . . be happy . . . have fun . . . But how could she now?

"I'd like that." He was pleased and surprised by her answer, and so was she. She sounded very serious and somewhat shell-shocked. "Let's go somewhere easy, not fancy. Like Trastevere," the bohemian part of town across the river.

"That sounds perfect."

"Why don't you come at eight?" She liked eating late, after she had unwound from the office. He wasn't sure she was up to it, but he was glad she was willing to see him. He could only imagine what an immense loss it was for her.

"Can I do anything for you, Cosima?" She sounded so sad it pained him to hear it.

"You're doing it," she said gently. "I'll be happy to see you. I'm sorry I've been out of touch all week."

"I knew why as soon as I saw the article."

"He was an amazing person. I saw him for lunch the day before he died, and he called you my 'honorable friend,' because you didn't buy Luca's shares. That always impressed him, and me too." She smiled for the first time in days as she talked to Olivier, and some of the tension in her body eased. Every inch of her had been braced as though for an attack or a blow. She ached all over, and mostly deep inside.

"We'll have a nice quiet time tomorrow," he promised. "Do you want anything from Paris?"

"Just you. See you tomorrow night." They hung up then, and she thought about Olivier that night. He was a kind man, and had the same principled values as Gian Battista, which meant everything to her.

The next day she worked until seven, and then went to her apartment and changed. She had worn black all week, and decided not to for dinner. She needed to lighten her mood, and wearing black depressed her. She wore a soft white sweater instead, gray flannel slacks, and deep red suede shoes. She looked casual and chic, with one of her signature alligator bags in the same deep red.

Olivier smiled as soon as he saw her. She had champagne chilled for him and had ordered caviar. It seemed very festive considering how he knew she was feeling, and he was touched that she had made the effort for him. They both relaxed as they sat on the terrace under the heater. She enjoyed the terrace even in winter. And it was warmer in Rome than it had been in Paris.

They kept the conversation light and then left for dinner. The restaurant they chose across the river was noisy and crowded and jubilant, and it cheered her to see people having fun and enjoying each other. It was just what she needed. The noise level kept the conversation from getting too serious, and afterwards they strolled along the river, and Olivier could feel Cosima relax as though she was melting, as she leaned closer to him as they walked. They sat down on a bench and looked at the river, and Cosima seemed a million miles away. And out of the blue, she started talking.

"He was what has always been between us," she said in a soft voice.

"I guessed that," he said simply.

She was surprised. "When?"

"Right in the beginning. I didn't know who, but I knew there was someone. And then later I guessed it was him. You always sounded different when you talked to him, like a wife."

"He ended it with me three years ago. I didn't know until this week, but he was already sick then. He never told me he was sick. He must have decided to end it with me when he thought he wasn't going to make it. I was heartbroken, and I never stopped loving him. We were together, that way, for nine years. I was twenty-six when it started. But I loved him before that. He had an odd arrangement with his wife."

"Did she know?"

"He said no, but at the funeral I wasn't so sure. She invited us to sit with her, me and Allegra. Anyway, it's over now. For the last three years I've been in limbo, always waiting for him to come back. I've been thinking of it all this week, and I thought you should know. I didn't realize that you'd guessed." She smiled at him and he didn't dare kiss her, not tonight. They walked back to her apartment then, and he went back to his hotel. He had the weekend free to be with her, so he stayed in Rome.

On Saturday, they drove out to the country, and Cosima relaxed as she and Olivier talked, enjoyed the countryside, had lunch, and he told her funny stories. On Saturday night, they ordered food in and watched a movie together, sprawled out on her couch. He had built a fire in the fireplace, and they stood on the terrace afterwards to get some air. It was getting chilly recently. And then, with all the gentleness he could muster, he held her in his arms and kissed her. She didn't resist him or pull away or stop him. She wanted him. She was finally free of the love that had devoured her for fifteen years. Gian Battista was finally at peace, and so was she, and she could open her heart to Olivier now. She had the memories of Gian Battista in her heart and her mind forever, just as he had said.

They wandered slowly back inside, to her bedroom, and he ever so gently took off her clothes, and they lay on her bed, and they discovered each other little by little. She had known him for four months, and it had been long enough. Everything they did together felt natural, and as their desire heightened, he couldn't control his hunger for her any longer. He had waited a long time for her, and the man she had loved for so long had finally released her. They soared into the future together like two souls that had found each other at last. She didn't know it, but she had been looking for him for a long time, and finally found him, as Gian Battista retreated slowly into the past and Olivier became her present, and maybe one day her future. Their coming together was gentle and loving, and she knew that Gian Battista had approved. Olivier truly was her honorable friend, just as Gian Battista had said.

Chapter 13

As fall eased slowly into winter, Olivier and Cosima were both busy. Business was good for both of
them. Allegra was traveling to Paris regularly, and
Olivier tried to get to Rome every weekend. He and
Cosima were enjoying each other, and everything
was going smoothly between them. She mentioned
Gian Battista occasionally, but not often. She was
healing from the loss. A month after the subject of
the collaboration had come up, Olivier came to
Rome for the weekend a day early with two large
suitcases he had checked on the plane. He normally
only traveled with carry-on, and he had left clothes
at Cosima's apartment. Sometimes they went away
for the weekend, but there was so much to do in
Rome that they both enjoyed.

He brought the two big valises to her office on
Friday afternoon, and had asked Allegra to be there
too. Basile was coming in that night, and he and
Allegra were going to a gallery opening.

The two suitcases looked mysterious as Allegra rolled in. Olivier hadn't told either of the sisters what he was bringing, and he hoped they liked what he'd brought. He was very pleased. The factory he used in Santa Croce sull'Arno was considered the finest. Santa Croce was known as the "leather capital of the world." They had followed his instructions to the letter, but there were still some minor changes he wanted to make and he was eager for Allegra's and Cosima's comments.

"Are you moving in?" Allegra teased him as she rolled in. She was prettier than ever and thriving in her relationship with Basile. They were always talking about new projects, places they wanted to see together, and meeting new people. Their world expanded every day, and Basile was working on a gallery show for the spring.

Olivier started with the suitcase he had prepared for Cosima. There were six prototypes for their collaboration. He could hardly wait to show them to her. One was in shiny black alligator, another was a creamy matte beige. He thought both were very chic. They were a slightly pared-down, less intricate version of her famous signature bag. His were a little bit bigger, which made them seem younger. And Cosima had suggested three other styles to him for the factory to work on. Just as hers were, his designs were very pure. The craftsmanship was not as expert, but the workmanship was excellent. There was a bright red shoulder bag in beautiful leather, a smaller version in bottle green, a big black bag, and a tiny, very chic black suede for evening. He unwrapped them and set them on her desk as they watched him intently, and Cosima studied each one as he set it down. It really was just what it was meant to be, a collaboration of her exquisite styles and his slightly newer, more modern take on them, while fully respecting her original designs. It had been a labor of love to get them this far, and now he needed her input, even if critical, to tell him what they should change and where he had gone wrong, if he had. She didn't say a word as she examined each one, and he held his breath, waiting for her reaction, and then she turned and looked at him with the biggest smile he had ever seen. He nearly cried with relief.

"You are an absolute miracle worker," she said. "They're fantastic. At first glance they look like ours, and then you realize they're not, they're newer and just different enough to be exciting while remaining completely faithful to our designs." The word she thought of immediately was "respectful." They weren't knockoffs, they were evolution, and the quality of the materials he had used was every bit as fine as hers. His craftsmen were just younger and less experienced than hers.

"Do you like them?" He was still holding his breath, but he was smiling too. He had loved them when he saw them for the first time.

"I *love* them. They're exquisite!" She put her

arms around his neck and kissed him, while Allegra studied the bags carefully.

"They're incredibly well made, almost as good as ours, and you did them in a month. Ours take a year to make, and our production is so slow, it drives me crazy." But the Saverio bags were in great part handmade, and the price reflected that.

Cosima was curious about the price point.

"They won't be inexpensive," Olivier said. "These would be the absolute top of our line, for each store's very special customers. They're almost double what we've charged so far, but the cost of the material will demand it, and I don't want to go lower. We wouldn't expect big orders for them, but it gives the store a step up to offer their clients, without charging Hermès or Saverio prices. They're a middle ground between what you do and what we do now, without sacrificing quality." His own design team was thrilled with what they'd been allowed to do for the first time. "We can try it for one season, and just treat it as a special event, and see what happens, or we can add a whole new dimension to our line, for our elite clients." The bags looked even more expensive than they were, and all three agreed that the subtle changes made them more attractive to a younger customer than Saverio usually appealed to, although young people with the means had taken to Hermès in the past decade. Before that, Saverio bags had been designed for an older customer too.

"I just *love* them," Cosima said again, and tried each one herself in front of the mirror. They looked stunningly chic, and Allegra held each of them up too. She was crazy about the large red one.

"We can do them in any color you want, of course. We did some research, and we worked in the three colors that are your biggest sellers, and three of ours. I really tried to marry our two brands without upsetting anyone. The interiors aren't as finely finished as yours, but doing that increases the cost by a lot." The Saverio bags were as beautiful and finely worked inside as out. The Bayard bags were simpler inside, with fewer pockets, which was more cost-effective.

Olivier turned to Allegra then, and unzipped the second suitcase. "Now for our 'Allegra' bags," he said to her with a big smile, while they waited to see what treasures he would unveil. "We went in a whole different direction on these. We *didn't* want to shock with the collaboration, on the contrary, we wanted all the changes to be very subtle. With Allegra's bags, we want to wake people up, shake them up, jump in with both feet." And it was precisely what they'd done, as he unwrapped each one and set them on the low table in front of the couch, where Allegra could examine them closely. "We tried all kinds of materials, and some wild colors. We can do them in any colorway and basic material you want. I was trying to keep the price point down since you're aiming for a much younger customer, and you don't want a bag they can wear till they're ninety. You want them to buy a whole new wardrobe of them next season." Allegra nodded, he had captured exactly what she had described to him a month earlier.

Within minutes there was a rainbow of colors on the table, jewel tones, plaids, interesting fabrics, heavy wools, velvets, corduroy, leather, some with leather accents, a big bright gold bag that both women were drawn to the minute they saw it. He had produced twelve of her designs. Allegra's eyes were wide as she saw what he'd done. She'd given him her sketches, which were just rough, and he had transformed them, polished them, and really made them work, in all sizes, shapes, and colors. They were all her designs, but with a kick and a twist. He wasn't sure how she would react to them, or if his production team had interpreted them right. They had loved working on them, and Allegra looked bowled over. She screamed when he unwrapped the gold bag. She examined each one and sat beaming in her chair. "Oh my God, I *love* them!"

"So do I," Cosima agreed. The bags suddenly made her realize that she should have been more open to Allegra's ideas, but she wasn't sure how the Saverio customers would react or if they'd approve. But these were for Allegra's own line, if she decided to go forward with it.

"We kept the price points as low as we could on these without sacrificing quality, but it's why we went with fabrics in some cases, with leather trim. I think your designs are sensational, Allegra, and the production team says they're so clear that they're easy to work with. And none of the designs are tricky." Allegra had learned everything about construction working for her sister for seven years. With the very set, staid Saverio designs, her job had been tedious, but it had taught her a great deal.

Allegra was ecstatic, and Cosima was thrilled for her, and with their collaboration. They all sat around the low table then, and Olivier and Cosima sat on the couch.

"Are we happy?" he asked them, but he could see that they were. "I could hardly wait to get here today, and I was terrified the airline would lose one of the bags. I didn't want to disappoint either one of you, and my teams in Paris and at the factory are dying to hear what you think. Remember that these are just prototypes and the workmanship on the final products will be finer. Some of these are still a little rough."

"I think you're a genius." Cosima beamed at him, and she was excited for Allegra too. She was on the phone with Basile at that exact moment, telling him how gorgeous the bags were and how well the designs worked. She couldn't wait to show them to him that night when he arrived.

"I want to take them home so I can show him," Allegra said, looking like an excited child.

Olivier turned to Cosima then. "I want you to

study them carefully and tell me anything you want to change. I don't want to screw this up, even if it's only a one-time thing, if that's what you decide. I want to get it just right."

"You already did." She smiled and leaned over and kissed him. He had opened a whole new horizon to her and she loved it.

"You too, Allegra. We can do anything you want, change anything, size, hardware, color, fabric, leather grain. We're working for you here. You're the designer, we're your production team on this. And I have a proposal I want to make you. I'd like to back you in this venture. You're a talented young designer, and I think you're going to have a huge hit with these designs." He loved encouraging young talent, and hers was enormous. If Cosima let Allegra establish her own bag company, he thought she was going to be a gigantic success in a few years. "I'd like to help you get started. We could produce them at our factories in Santa Croce sull'Arno, which would give you quality control. You can bring the cost way down and position them at a lower price point if you use factories in China, for instance, but you won't get the same result, and then you're aiming for a different customer."

"I want to keep the quality high, like these," Allegra said, "without making them too expensive for young women like me. I don't want to buy a bag I'll be stuck with forever or feel I *have* to keep because it was so expensive or I can't afford a new one. I like buying new things," which was age-appropriate for her. The Saverio customer wanted a bag that was classic and would last a lifetime, that she would still be wearing in forty years. At twenty-nine, Allegra didn't think that way. And Olivier's usual customer, for his own line, wanted the Saverio look, but at a more attractive price, and was willing to sacrifice some of the quality, but not the style. He was going to step up in both look and price with his Saverio collaboration, and was excited about it himself. They each knew their customer well, which was essential, and what was expected of them. And there was a place in the market for all of their customers.

"Are you serious that you'd back me?" Allegra asked him, breathless with excitement and stunned by the offer.

"I am. And we can handle the wholesale orders for you. But I have another idea, as an experiment. We own several buildings in the Eighth Arrondissement. One of them has a store that's about to become vacant in January on the rue Francois Premier just off the Avenue Montaigne, across from Dior. I'd like to use it as a concept store for the collaboration for Fashion Week, and we could sell your bags too, in a limited amount, like what we have here. And after that, if the numbers look promising, you could open a store there of your own." What he was talking about took money, and Allegra was willing to put what she'd made on the house sale into it. "We can talk about it later." He had another idea too, which he shared with Cosima that night. He didn't know if she'd be open to it, and it had been counter to their policy until then, he knew.

"I think you should open a store in Paris," he suggested to her after dinner at one of their favorite restaurants. They'd been talking about the venture he wanted to help Allegra launch. He had already told Cosima what a huge success he thought Allegra was going to be, and now that she'd seen her designs come to life, she agreed. It was a double-edged sword for her, because she didn't want to lose Allegra from her business. She worked hard, and she was family, which was sacred to Cosima, but she didn't think she could hold Allegra back for much longer. If she and Basile stayed together, she would want to move to Paris, and had already alluded to it a few times. Cosima could see what was coming and didn't want to stop her. Allegra was turning thirty and wanted her own full life, with the man she loved, and to grow as a designer. She was ready. Cosima wasn't, but she knew she'd have to face it, and it wouldn't be fair to stop her, or force her to stay in Rome.

"I'm serious," Olivier said about a Saverio store in Paris. "I know it's against your policy, but that was in your grandfather's day. Italy was the hub of his world then. The world is a bigger place now, and Saverio belongs in Paris to give Hermès a run for their money." He smiled at her. Hermès was their biggest competitor, and the only store like Saverio, on a much larger, worldwide scale. "I've had my eye on a store for you on the Faubourg Saint-Honoré. I could negotiate it for you if you let me."

"I don't know if I'm ready for that," she said, taken aback by his suggestion. "Having two stores is already a lot to deal with. Three would keep me running all the time." It was true, but feasible, and a possibility she hadn't even considered.

"You'd have to hire good people to run it," he advanced cautiously then, "and I'd love to have you with me in Paris, at least some of the time." He was commuting to Rome almost every weekend to see her. She hardly had time to travel, so much rested on her with the stores in Rome and Venice. Adding Paris to them would be huge.

She smiled then. "My grandfather always forbade my father from opening another store. He waited until my grandfather died to move to Rome and launch the store there, and it was much bigger than the original. It was his dream. My grandfather always told him what a mistake it would be, and of course it wasn't. It grew the business exponentially and made us what we are today."

"Paris would too, and take you to another level. And I'm not just saying that so you come to Paris for me. You need to do that for the business. Your brand is too important to confine it to just Italy." When he said it, she wished that she could ask Gian Battista what he thought. He had rarely made mistakes with his advice to her in business, and Olivier wasn't entirely objective, since he wanted her with him, and she never based her business decisions on her personal life. She was a smart businesswoman. Commercially, she suspected he was right, but opening a store in Paris would be a huge undertaking, though maybe a wise one in the long run.

"I'll think about it," was all she would commit to at the moment, but she was trying to be open to new ideas, like the pop-up stores, and her collaboration with him.

"I'll show you the store I have in mind on the Faubourg when you come to Paris." He hoped she could see the merits of it. "It's not enormous, but I think it's the right size for you. It's on two levels. And this isn't for you right now with your customer, but Allegra should sell online too. That's a huge market for her, especially at her price point, and the age of her clients. They do everything online."

With the exciting prototypes he had brought with him, they had a lot to talk about that night, and so did Allegra and Basile.

"Did you tell her?" Basile asked Allegra as soon as he arrived. He was excited to see the prototypes of her bags, but even more so about the plans they had been discussing recently. He wanted her to move to Paris.

"I didn't want to bring it up with your father there, and we were talking about the bags. And she's with him tonight, and will be all weekend." Allegra wanted to move to Paris too, but she knew Cosima would be upset. Cosima wanted Allegra to work for Saverio with her, and she worried about her being able to manage physically. She did fine in Rome, and was independent there, but she lived a floor away from her sister, and had any assistance she could need near at hand. "She worries about me."

"I can take good care of you," Basile said. He was twenty-seven years old, two years younger than Allegra. "And you'd be living with me. You'd be even safer than you are now." She had a tendency to get into a jam occasionally, trying to reach for something, or doing things she shouldn't alone in her apartment at night. Nothing stopped her, and she was very brave.

"I'll talk to her about it when your father leaves, I promise." But Allegra knew that leaving the family business and moving away would be a huge blow to her sister, and Allegra felt guilty about it.

"My father wants her to spend more time in Paris too. He thinks she should open a store there."

"I don't think she'll do that," Allegra said. "We've always been completely based in Italy. My grandfather thought it would keep us more exclusive." But spreading their wings internationally would have made them more profitable. Allegra believed that too.

They enjoyed the weekend together and went to several art shows. Father and son left together on Sunday night, and after they left, Allegra called her sister and invited her down for a glass of wine. Cosima was happy to visit her. She was always sad when Olivier left on Sunday nights, and she missed him. During the week she was so busy she hardly noticed, but Sunday nights were lonely.

They talked about how terrific the prototypes were. Cosima had only made a few minor suggestions, and Allegra loved all the bags based on her designs. Olivier's production people had interpreted them masterfully. Allegra took a breath then and set down her glass of wine. She couldn't put it off any longer, and didn't want to.

"Basile wants me to move to Paris," she said in a cautious voice, watching her sister's face closely. She could see the sadness in her eyes instantly.

"And what do you want?" But the fact that Allegra was telling her told Cosima all she needed to know.

"I love him. I want to be with him," Allegra said, unhappy at the pain she knew it would cause her sister. Cosima had dedicated herself to the business for so long and so completely that she had little else in her life. She rarely even saw friends. For years, she had led a hidden life with Gian Battista, which Allegra could only guess at. She had been available to him at all times, whenever he could get free, and for the past three years she hadn't even had that.

And now she had Olivier with her on weekends, but he lived in another city.

"You're both so young," Cosima said.

"I'm almost thirty, and he's almost twenty-eight. And he's very responsible." Cosima had observed that too, and had no objections to Basile, but she didn't want to lose her sister to him, no matter how sweet he was, or how much Allegra loved him. Allegra's healthy, open, enthusiastic attitude had kept her in the mainstream of life, and Cosima had wanted that for her. But she had always feared that this could happen one day, that some man would carry Allegra off to a life somewhere else, and she had always sensed that Allegra would be open to it, just as she apparently was now. Allegra was fearless and Cosima had helped her to be that way. And their fluency in French made doing business in France an obvious option for both of them.

"It's a big thing to leave your home, your country, your family, and your job for love of a man," Cosima tried to warn her. "What happens if it doesn't work out and you break up in a few months or a year? You're both young to settle down forever."

"Not that young," Allegra said realistically. "Some people get married younger than that. And we're not rushing into marriage. We want to live together and see how that feels. He doesn't care about my legs. He's in love with me, not my legs. Paris isn't very far away. I could still do design work for you. I change so little on our classics, and I can send you everything I do by computer."

"Won't you be too busy, if Olivier helps you start your own brand?"

"Never too busy for you," Allegra said lovingly. "You're my sister and I love you. I can easily do both. I really don't do much for Saverio," in fact so much less than she wanted to do and was capable of. She was aching to exercise her talent, and her own company would allow her to do that. "I hate leaving you. We can wait a couple of months if you want. I could move after Christmas, which would give me time to train someone to do some of what I do. I'd do the rest from Paris. And if you open a store in Paris, we'd see each other all the time," she said, and Cosima smiled. It was an incentive.

There was no way Cosima could seriously object. Basile was a lovely young man, he had a blossoming career he worked hard at, and a nice father and good values, and he loved her sister deeply and was protective of her and completely undisturbed by her disability. They had already agreed that they wanted three or four children, which the doctors had always said would be possible in spite of her spinal cord injury. Basile was what every mother wanted for her daughter and more.

"Thank you for asking me," Cosima said, feeling deeply emotional about it. She felt like she was losing the baby sister she had loved and protected like a mother for more than half her life. She had done it so well that Allegra was ready to fly on her own wings now. Cosima was almost sorry that she had helped Allegra to become so independent, but she knew that was selfish of her, and she was better than that. "I want you to be safe and happy and living the best life you can, and I think you'll be all those things with Basile, so I give you my blessing," she said, and hugged her sister. They drank another glass of wine, and then Cosima went back upstairs. Change was in the air. It would be very different with Allegra living in Paris and not just a few steps away down a short flight of stairs, where Cosima could see her all the time. She would feel lost without her. Mothering Allegra had given meaning to her life. And with Luca in prison, Cosima would have no family left near at hand.

She called Olivier as soon as he got home in Paris.

"I thought she would tell you tonight," he said. "Basile talked to me about it on the plane. Do you object?" He hoped not, for their sake. Basile was madly in love with Allegra, in a serious, mature way that impressed his father but didn't surprise him. Basile was such a good man, and Olivier was proud of him.

"How can I object?" Cosima said honestly. "He's what every mother would want for her daughter. I'm just sad she'll be leaving, but it's the right thing for her. I gave her my blessing. She said she'd move after Christmas, which gives me two months to get used to the idea."

"I promise I'll keep an eye on them, and take good care of her for you," he said seriously.

"Thank you."

"Maybe that will motivate you to open a store in Paris," he said, and she laughed.

"Maybe you're right. Maybe it's time. I have to think about it."

"What are you doing this week?"

"I have to go to Venice tomorrow to check on things there."

"Problems?"

"No, it's running smoothly, but I like them to see my face regularly, so they remember who they work for." She was never an absentee boss in either store, and was hands-on, and would want to be with a Paris store too, which was why she was hesitating. In addition to the Saverio traditions and company policy, she didn't want to spread herself too thin and take on more than she could handle. But she agreed that they had to broaden their horizons too, in order to stay current and grow. And just as Allegra did, Cosima wanted the business to keep growing. In the era of the internet, the days of a small, elite local store were over, if they wanted to be viable among her competitors.

"Are you staying in Venice?" Olivier asked her.

"No, I'll be back tomorrow night." She was tired of staying at the hotel, and preferred to come home to her own bed, since the family no longer owned the palazzo.

"Call me when you come home, and try not to worry about Allegra. I think this will be good for her, for both of them. They're very mature and responsible. Basile is much more stable and sensible than I was at his age."

"Allegra said they're not rushing into marriage. People don't these days. And I certainly never did." She laughed. In love with a married man, she had missed the boat on that, but didn't regret it. A husband might have interfered with her running the family business, which she would have hated. Even Gian Battista had expressed opinions she didn't agree with at times. Married, he might have been more insistent about it, but he never had been, in the situation they were in. They were just grateful for the time they could spend together, and he respected her independence, since he couldn't offer her marriage or children. There were many women in her situation in a country that had forbidden divorce for so long and made it so difficult even once it was allowed. The Church was a powerful influence, as it was in many countries in Europe, and in Italy longer than in most, with the strong hand of the Vatican in the country's politics.

Cosima went to Venice the next day as planned, which was an easy trip. She changed some of the displays, and made some suggestions about the lighting. She watched several transactions and was satisfied by how the staff were handling them. And before she left for the airport, she took a walk, and without planning it she found herself standing outside the garden of the Palazzo Saverio, and was surprised to see that there was construction going on. Not a lot. The palazzo wasn't covered by scaffolding, but there were a handful of workmen going in and out, and she noticed a new young foreman. He looked familiar and she realized that he was the grandson of Tomaso, who had retired when she sold.

She greeted him, and he recognized her too. She asked for his grandfather, and the young man said he was happy in his sleepy little beach town and went fishing every day. She hadn't heard anything about Guillermo in Sicily.

"Is the new owner remodeling the palazzo?" she asked, curious, and it tugged at her heart a little to see it. The realtor had said he planned to do it over time, and wasn't in a hurry.

"Not yet. They're just repairing the fire damage. We had to replace the floors, they were raised and cracking all over the main floor and getting worse," he informed her. "And they're bringing the moldings back to the original. They've done a good job so far, and the electricity is being rewired, so it's safe now. They're doing it all pretty slowly," the young man commented.

"Have you met the new owner?" He shook his head.

"He never comes here. It all goes through a lawyer. I don't think he's planning to come anytime soon. There's no furniture, and everything needs to be repainted and cleaned up before he can come. It's only the fire damage for now, and whatever wasn't safe." So he was a responsible owner at least. Cosima wondered if he would ever come there, or just clean the palazzo up enough to sell it, which was a possibility too. She hated to think of it changing hands again, instead of being owned by a family who loved it, but she had no control of it now. But oddly, standing there talking to the new young caretaker, it still felt like home. The same roses were still in the garden, and she felt as though she could walk through the front door and find things as they were, although some of her things were in storage and the rest had been thrown away after the fire. "Do you want to come in?" he offered, and she shook her head. She felt like she would be trespassing, and she didn't want to see it empty now. She had her memories, as Gian Battista had said, and that was enough. She thanked the young man and left, and a few minutes later she took a water taxi on the canal, and watched the Palazzo Saverio disappear behind her, slipping back into the past. Her present and her future were now in Rome.

She mentioned seeing the house when she talked to Olivier that night.

"How did it feel?" he asked her gently. He was very sensitive about the things he knew were painful for her.

"Weirdly, it still felt like home, even though it belongs to someone else. My guardian's grandson is working for the new owner now. He says they're only repairing the fire damage, and doing it very slowly. I guess they're in no rush to use it. The Qatari probably has ten homes all over the world, and the palazzo isn't high on the list." And repairs took a long time in Venice. Workmen were often slow and unreliable, and there was no one to supervise, except her guardian's grandson, who was in his twenties, but seemed very efficient.

"Do you miss it?" he asked her.

"I try not to," she said. "As Gian Battista said, I have my memories, that's enough." It would have to be now, the Palazzo Saverio was out of her life forever. Her brother appeared to be too. She had heard nothing from him since his arrest and imprisonment. She wondered if she'd ever hear from him or see him again. And now Allegra was leaving. It was a time of change. She was grateful she had the business to keep her busy, and Olivier to keep her warm on weekends. She preferred to see the glass as half full rather than half empty, which was Olivier's philosophy about life too. He was coming back to Rome that weekend, as he did every week now.

Chapter 14

The time flew until Christmas with everything Cosima had to do. Allegra was busy too, training two assistants to do the more menial part of her job. She would do the rest from Paris, as she'd promised.

The prototypes of her bags that she had approved were being produced in Santa Croce sull'Arno. And she was getting organized to move to Paris after Christmas. Every weekend she went to Paris now and brought more of her things to leave at Basile's apartment. He couldn't wait for her to move in. His building had an elevator that made it easily accessible for her.

In January, they were going to start working on the pop-up store, where they would showcase the collaboration bags, and Allegra's new line, named after her. They were going to be dizzyingly busy after that until Fashion Week in Paris at the beginning of March. Allegra's line was going to be Paris-based, and the collaboration bags were being produced by Bayard in Santa Croce and their factory outside Paris, under Olivier's careful scrutiny, so it was appropriate to show the bags during Paris Fashion Week. And Cosima was doing another concept store in Milan for Saverio's line, for Fashion Week there before Paris. It was always a month of madness for anyone in fashion with Fashion Week in New York, London, Milan, and finally Paris, but they were used to it. Basile was working frantically, preparing paintings for his gallery show at the same time.

Olivier and Basile joined them in Rome for Christmas, since they had no other family either, and after Christmas, Allegra would fly to Paris with Basile, to move into his apartment officially. Olivier was staying to spend New Year's with Cosima in Rome, which was always fun and very festive.

Cosima sent a basket of food and all the things that were acceptable for Luca to receive at the prison for Christmas. She sent him a warm sweater, some books, cigarettes, and as much food as they would allow, including all his favorite things to eat. He didn't respond or acknowledge the gifts, but she wanted him to have as decent a Christmas as he could in prison. She signed it all from her and Allegra.

She gave Allegra a beautiful warm cashmere

coat for Christmas, and framed all the photographs she could find and duplicate of their parents, and herself, Allegra, and Luca when they were children, and some more recent ones. Allegra was thrilled when she opened them. She gave Cosima an antique gold heart-shaped locket, with a photograph of her and Cosima, and Cosima put it on immediately and swore she'd wear it every day. It was going to be hard for the two sisters to separate for the first time in their lives. Olivier was aware of how difficult it would be for Cosima, and Allegra tried to hide her elation to be moving in with Basile. Olivier was having some accommodations built for her in Basile's apartment, so it would be easier for her.

When Allegra and Basile left two days after Christmas, Olivier surprised Cosima with a three-day trip to London to distract her. They stayed at Claridge's, went to the theater, ate at fancy restaurants, visited museums, and went shopping. It was the perfect boost to her spirits, and he had given her a pair of wide gold cuffs with sapphires and diamonds on them, which were antique Cartier and as chic as she was. He had impeccable taste and knew what she liked.

"You made all my dreams come true this year," he said. "I never thought a year ago that I'd be doing a collaboration with Saverio, or would ever meet you." He was making her dreams come true and had turned her gently from the past toward the future. She was excited about everything they were going to be doing in Paris during Fashion Week, only two months away.

Cosima went to Paris two weeks before Fashion Week started to get the pop-up store ready. She was amazed at how much Allegra had already done with Basile's help. There was a crew painting Cosima's side of the store in a pale blush pink that Allegra had selected. And on the wall behind Allegra's side, Basile was going to paint a mural of his street art. Allegra had her own logo by then, and the bags were ready. And Cosima had shipped what she would be selling from Rome. She had chosen everything carefully.

Olivier insisted on showing her the shop on the Faubourg Saint-Honoré that he thought would be perfect for her if she decided to open a Saverio store in Paris. She still hadn't made up her mind. It was a beautiful store in the perfect location, with wood-paneled walls and an elegant staircase, nestled between the best jewelers in Paris, with Chanel, Givenchy, Saint-Laurent, and even Hermès right down the street. If she was going to open in Paris, it would be the ideal place. Olivier was right. He didn't tell her, but he had put down a deposit to hold it until she made up her mind. A store like that would be snapped up immediately by one of the luxury brands. As a wholesaler, he didn't have a street-level store, but his ultramodern showroom was one of the most impressive in Paris.

Cosima was happy to see Sally Johnson in Paris. She was there with her stores' chief buyers. Sally had always been very involved in the Johnson and Dean stores, and was even more so now since Bill's death. She had lost some weight and looked well. She had heard that the palazzo had been sold and said that it would break her heart to see it again.

"I have such happy memories of it," she said warmly to Cosima.

"So do I. Sometimes I still forget that we don't own it anymore. The last I heard, the new owner was repairing the fire damage, but he wasn't doing anything else."

Sally was impressed that Saverio was doing a collaboration with Bayard, and had already told her buyers that she wanted them to buy the entire line. It made an exclusive, elite brand available at a price point they could carry in their stores. She was as thrilled about it as Cosima was herself.

Once Fashion Week got started, it was a whirl-wind of parties, dinners, extravagant displays, pre-sentations, and fashion shows. Cosima went to see the shows of all the designers she loved, while Al-legra ran their concept store very efficiently, with two young women to help her.

Fashion Week in Paris was a star-studded event, even more than in Milan. Movie stars and celebri-ties of all kinds attended from every country. Allegra was elated when Cosima went to the store to check on her. Her three favorite rock stars had showed up in the last hour and bought nine of her bags and two Saverios. They were doing a booming business at the pop-up, the fashion press had discovered Allegra's bags and gave them rave reviews, and the bloggers loved them. They were all over Instagram, and the talk of the fashion world. Olivier had taken several very large orders for their collaboration. Cosima was excited to hear it.

On the second day of Fashion Week, Olivier, Cosima, and Allegra went to the opening of Basile's gallery show. The work he had chosen to exhibit was perfect for the audience with his bold artistic taste, and he had done a few pieces that were fashion-oriented, which already had red dots on them, indicating that they were sold, when Cosima and the group arrived half an hour after the show opened. Basile was the hot young star of the art world, and his dealer was thrilled.

It was a whirlwind week and a huge success for all four of them. Olivier said he hadn't had as many orders as he had for their collaboration since he opened the business.

He took Cosima to Alain Ducasse for dinner to celebrate, and she looked nervous when she told him her decision.

"I'm going to do it," she said, and he wasn't sure what she meant. "I'm going to open a store in Paris, in the location you showed me on the Faubourg. My father and my grandfather would have killed me for it, but I think it's the right decision in today's world. These are modern times, the world is bigger and broader than in their day, and I have to be modern with it. I'd like to be open by Fashion Week at the end of September or early October, whenever it is. That gives me seven months to do it. I should be able to pull it off. The store looked in good shape when we saw it. So here we go. I hope it's the right decision. And I made another one. Before I start expanding, I want to buy Luca's share of the business. I don't know if he'll be willing, but he'd probably like to have the money to add to what he made on the sale of the palazzo. He'll have plenty of money when he comes out of prison." He had another year and a half to serve on his sentence, and for Cosima at least, the time was moving quickly. Olivier's son was due out in six months, and his father was exploring opportunities for him in the States. Olivier thought Max needed a fresh start, where everyone wouldn't know he'd spent a year in prison. People would find out eventually in the States too when they checked him out, but he would be the object of constant gossip in France from now on. Just as Luca would be in Italy when he got out. As far as Olivier knew, from what Max told him, the two men hadn't seen each other in prison. The prison authorities kept them apart so they couldn't get up to mischief again together.

Cosima was excited about her decisions. Allegra

had already decided to rent the store from Olivier that they were using for their concept store. Basile was going to decorate it with his art, which was perfect with her ultramodern, trendy designs and bright colors. He was already doing sketches for the murals he was going to paint, and Allegra had told Cosima and Olivier she wanted to open in June. Cosima would open Saverio on the Faubourg Saint-Honoré at the beginning of October. They all had plans.

Olivier loved the fact that Cosima would be spending a lot more time in Paris now, getting the store ready, and that she'd come regularly once it was open. She would be moving at jet speed from now on, even more so than she had been.

"Do we have time for a vacation this summer in the midst of all that?" he asked her as they ate the delicious dinner at Ducasse.

"Probably not. I'll be spending it with painters and lighting people at the store in Paris."

"No one works here in August, so I'm taking you away," he said firmly, and she laughed. "How does the South of France sound?"

"Delightful for a lady of leisure." She grinned. "I have three stores to run now, and you can't complain because you talked me into the third one." They both looked happy at what lay ahead, although they knew it would be an enormous challenge for her, and she liked keeping her hand in everything they did at Saverio. She couldn't rely on

Allegra anymore to keep an eye on things for her, now that she was in Paris and would have a store of her own. Allegra planned to hire a woman to run it, and she would spend time there herself at first. She was going to put a design studio in the store, so she could work there and be close at hand for special orders or questions. She wanted to develop a strong sense of who her customers were, and the Bayard staff would be handling her wholesale orders.

All during Fashion Week, Allegra had gotten requests for press interviews and meetings with bloggers. *Vogue* wanted to do a photo shoot of her with Basile once it became known they were together.

"Our children are stars, or my son and your sister," Olivier said, looking pleased. "Do you suppose they'll get married soon?" he asked her over coffee and dessert, with a tray of delicious chocolates.

"They don't have time to get married," Cosima said practically. "We're all workaholics, and in love with what we do." She didn't want Allegra to wind up like her, opting for her work instead of marriage and a family, but it wasn't likely to happen to Allegra and Basile. "They're young. They don't need to think about that yet. There's no hurry." She wasn't ready to see her baby sister get married yet.

"I was too young, and blew it," Olivier said.

"And I chose a different path and missed the boat," Cosima said matter-of-factly, but she had no regrets.

"You didn't miss the boat," he said gently.

"Yes, I did. Can you see me opening a store in Paris now, with a baby carrier in my hand, or a two-year-old?" He grinned at the image. "Work has always excited me more than kids," she said, although she had wanted to have Gian Battista's children, even if illegitimate, and he wouldn't let her. Olivier smiled.

"You could probably manage it, if you wanted to." She didn't answer, thinking about it, and didn't look convinced. She didn't want a different life than she had now.

"Allegra is all the child I ever needed. I might have felt differently if my parents had lived and I hadn't been responsible for her." But destiny had given her Allegra to mother and Gian Battista to love, in lieu of a child and husband of her own, and she was satisfied with that.

"You did a fabulous job with her. She's oblivious to her disability. Nothing stops her and she has a positive outlook about life." Olivier was in awe of both sisters, more so each day.

"That's just who she is. I didn't create her. And I was just as present in Luca's life, and look what a mess he is. They're like black and white. I wonder what he'll say when I try to buy him out of the business."

"I hope he's decent about it and doesn't try to hold you up for a fortune." They both knew he was capable of it. But she didn't want to share the profits of a third store with him, particularly if the Paris store became a great success. He didn't deserve it.

"I'm not sure if I should try to see him in person, to reason with him, or just do it all through attorneys."

"I don't know. You know him better than I do," Olivier said.

"It's hard to guess with him. It's all about money." Olivier did know that about him. Max was the same way, but not as daring as Luca, who was three years older, and more skilled at coming up with some terrible plans and luring people into following him. He'd been a rotten influence on Max, but Olivier didn't blame him for it. Max was bad enough on his own and could have refused to follow Luca, but didn't.

They talked about more pleasant subjects after that, and went to have a drink at the cozy, lively Hemingway Bar at the Ritz. There was so much for them to do in Paris. Olivier loved having her there, and she enjoyed it with him. She went out much more in Paris than she did in Rome. Rome was a smaller city, and she worked late almost every night. She ended work earlier in Paris and she and Olivier went out a lot. Olivier enjoyed taking her out, introducing her to people he knew, and showing her off.

They had much to talk about now with the new store she was going to open, and she wanted to hire the right people to run it. Her manager in Venice had just quit a few days before, which was one of the hazards of owning a store, and she had to start interviewing for the position now, a headache she didn't look forward to.

Before she left Paris, Cosima met with an architect Olivier recommended. She walked the store with him, and told him what she had in mind, and the look she wanted. She wanted him to go to Venice and Rome so he could see the atmosphere they tried to create in their stores, combining history and tradition with enough modern beauty to appeal to new generations of customers.

Olivier was flying back to Rome with her. It was always hard for her to leave Allegra in Paris. Cosima hugged her tight and kissed her and Basile.

"Take good care of her," she admonished him with a lump in her throat.

"I promise," he said solemnly, and there were tears in Cosima's eyes on the way to the airport. Olivier put an arm around her and pulled her close. She had made some big decisions while she was in Paris, and her most recent ones had proven to be the right ones. Now she had to convince her derelict brother to sell his shares to her, at a decent price, get a new store in another city ready in seven months, and run her business as usual.

She tried to read a magazine and fell asleep on the plane. Paris had been tiring, but fun too. Now she had to get back to the grind of daily life and running a business. Olivier would be back the following weekend. They had fallen into a comfortable routine, and he liked the idea that she would be spending more time in Paris now.

He brought up the subject of their summer vacation that night again, and Cosima looked blank.

"I have no idea what I'll be doing, if I'm trying to open the Paris store at the end of September."

Allegra and Basile were planning to rent a farmhouse in Tuscany with friends.

"I like the beach," Cosima said vaguely.

"Me too. I'll figure something out and see what appeals to you."

"Allegra and I always like Sardinia. My parents used to have a house there. Capri is fun, but it's so overrun now. All the cruise ships stop there."

"Do you like boats?" he asked her. There were things about her he still didn't know.

"I love them."

"Maybe we should just charter a sailboat and float around."

"I just want to lie in the sun, swim, and not answer an email for two weeks. And Saint-Tropez is insane in the summer, so not there. Other than that, you're in charge." He smiled and wondered if that was true. Knowing her as he did now, his being in charge seemed unlikely.

Cosima tried reaching out to Luca and suggested a face-to-face meeting, and he didn't respond. So she eventually contacted a lawyer she used for the business, outlined what she had in mind, and wrote Luca a letter, saying she hoped he was well. After his silence at Christmas, it was obvious that he still blamed her, Max Bayard, and everyone involved for his time in prison, even though she'd been the victim of his dishonesty. He thought she should have moved heaven and earth, and used all of Gian Battista's influence, to get him off completely or at least reduce his prison sentence further. Gian Battista had said that no one could have, and Cosima believed him. Luca had to face the music and pay the penalty for what he'd done. She wondered if he would punish her for it now that she wanted something from him. His silence seemed to indicate that, but she had to wait and see what his response to the lawyer would be.

She didn't have long to wait. He answered the lawyer's letter in a week, and told Cosima via her lawyer how much money he wanted to relinquish his shares in the business. He said he had no emotional attachment to it, which she believed, it was strictly a question of money and what the business was worth. He overestimated it dramatically, and asked for an insane amount, which she couldn't pay him, and wouldn't have anyway. She thanked him and let it go.

She didn't tell him she was opening a Paris store, but he would receive his share of the profits at the end of the year, so he would know. He was lucky she worked as hard as she did, and he reaped the benefits of it every year, without lifting a finger. It was the story of his life so far, benefiting from other people's work, spending whatever he got, and being dishonest so he could get more. It was one way to make a living and had wound him up in prison for setting the palazzo on fire so he could get his share of the insurance money. And now she knew he hadn't changed. She told Olivier about it when he came for the weekend. He was disappointed for her that Luca hadn't been more reasonable, but not surprised.

"Max isn't much better. He doesn't like anything I lined up for him in the States. He wants fast turnover, big profits, and minimal work. As a convicted felon, he'd be lucky if they gave him a job washing dishes, let alone some highly paid hotshot job. He says he's looking into some opportunities in Asia. I'm just going to step aside and let him figure it out for himself. It's the only way he'll learn, if he ever does. He tried to get some money from Basile, and Basile wouldn't give it to him, at my request. They're really both rotten apples, the two of them," Olivier said, discouraged, referring to Max and Luca. But it was less embarrassing for both of them, since they were in the same boat. Someone else might not have been as understanding about the baggage she brought with her.

Cosima went to Paris in June for the opening of Allegra's store. She was amazed by how great it looked with Basile's exciting street art murals, with Allegra's logo, which she had designed herself, integrated into them. The store had an upbeat, youthful feel to it, and the display cases Allegra and Basile had designed showed all the styles available to their advantage and made the bags part of the décor.

Cosima sipped pink champagne at the opening and was proud of her little sister. The shop had opened right on time, and had all the summer styles exhibited, and some advance samples for winter that wholesale customers could preorder for the fall. The fashion press had come and several bloggers were there, taking pictures of everything for social media. Allegra had established a totally modern brand, and already had advance orders for fall/winter. Cosima knew, looking around, that this was what Allegra had been meant to do. Her alliance with Olivier's company was going to be immensely profitable for both of them. And he'd had the foresight to recognize it.

It was exciting for Cosima to know she'd have her own store there soon, in three months, and she'd see more of Allegra again. She missed her terribly in Rome, but she'd been busy.

Cosima flew to Venice on the way home from Paris. She wanted to see her new store manager there in action, interfacing with customers. She had come to them from Hermès in Portofino, but Venice was a bigger store with more merchandise and serious buyers. Olivier went with her, so he could visit Max in prison in Padua. He hadn't seen him in two months. Max had three months left of his sentence to serve, and said he was taking a job in Bangkok when he got out. Olivier just hoped it was a legitimate job and he wouldn't be dealing drugs or something just as bad. He was still talking about get-rich-quick schemes, and the job in Thailand was one of them.

Cosima went straight to the store after they landed in Venice. Olivier went to see Max in prison in Padua. They were going to meet at the Piazza San Marco at six o'clock after he got back, have a drink, and go back to the airport to fly to Rome.

He kissed her hurriedly when she got into the water taxi, and a minute later she took off, and he took a cab by land to see his son.

Everything seemed peaceful at the store. The new manager was a little shy, but seemed like a nice woman. The summer merchandise was well displayed in light colors, and Cosima was satisfied and decided to wander for a while when she left the store. She had three hours before she had to meet Olivier. It was a warm day, and she always loved walking around Venice. It brought back so many memories for her, of her parents, and her youth, their visits there. It was still a magical city for her. And inevitably, she walked past the Palazzo Saverio to see if there were any obvious changes, and wondered if her old guardian's grandson was still working there.

She didn't see him at first, and the front door was open. Her mother's rose garden was in full bloom. She had planted it during their vacations there. The sun was warm on Cosima's face as she looked around. The grounds were clean and well tended, and then she saw the young guardian appear and waved to him. He smiled when he saw her and came out of the garden shed, carrying some tools. He came to say hello, and she asked him what he was working on.

"The moldings are good now. We're going to start painting this summer." She had an urge to peek inside, but didn't want to appear curious, even though she was, and as she glanced at the front door she saw Olivier appear. He had a tool kit in his hands too, and looked shocked when he saw her. They stared at each other and Cosima didn't understand what was going on as he walked toward her.

"What are you doing here?" she asked him, as the young guardian disappeared into the house. "Do you know the new owner?" It was the only explanation she could think of for his being there, and his face broke into a slow smile.

"Yes, I do," Olivier said, and offered no further explanation, and she continued to stare at him as he took her by the hand and led her toward the front door.

"What are you doing? Are you crazy?" He nodded and pushed the door open wider so she could see inside. Everything was clean now, and there was no sign of the fire, or smell of smoke. The floors were smooth and even and laid in the original pattern, with big black-and-white marble squares in the front hall. The tall windows were bare. The burned curtains were gone. She could smell fresh paint, and he gently pushed her inside so she could see the grand staircase, and the ballroom in the distance at the other end of the house. Everything about it was familiar and it still felt like home, except that it was fresh and new and clean. The chandelier that had come crashing down in the fire had been replaced with a similar one.

"Olivier, what are you doing here?" Cosima asked him again, and then slowly she understood and remembered what the realtor's assistant had said, that a Frenchman had bought it, and Cosima had insisted she was wrong. "Did you . . . ? Are you . . . ?" Tears filled her eyes as she looked at him, and he nodded.

"I thought you might want it back one day. It belongs to you, it's part of you, it's your history. And if you don't want it, I can sell it, probably for a profit."

"Oh my God . . . Olivier, you're crazy. What are you going to do with it?"

"Clean it up slowly. We've been working on it

since I bought it. And give it back to you one day. That's why I bought it."

"You can't just *give* it back to me," she said, looking around at all the things he had cleaned up and repaired and replaced, some of which had been damaged and old and broken before the fire.

"Yes, I can," he said simply. "We're putting in a new kitchen this summer." The old one hadn't been replaced since the 1940s, because her grandparents had liked it and didn't want a new one. He took the keys out of his pocket then and handed them to her, as she stared at him. "I love you, Cosima, just as you are. You work too hard, you worry too much, you take care of everyone except yourself. You're the woman I've dreamt of all my life and never found until I met you. It's an anniversary present," he said, smiling at her. She had never known anyone like him either, he was the most generous, kind, loving man she had ever met.

"What anniversary?" She looked puzzled as well as shocked.

"I met you a year ago today, at that silly party the Johnsons gave, with their awful décor with all the turquoise and coral and crystals and pearls. No one but a Saverio should live here, and your children one day, and Allegra's. This is your legacy, from your parents and grandparents, and to your own children. But I'd prefer to leave your brother out of it, if that's okay with you, so he doesn't set fire to it again." He put his arms around her as he said it.

"That's fine with me," she whispered, and he kissed her. "I can't believe you did this. When were you going to tell me?"

"When I got it cleaned up. We're almost there. We've been moving slowly. You can take over and do the decorating."

"I still have a lot of things in storage that need to be re-covered, but they're fine. And all the crystal and original china and silver." Her eyes were full of tears as she clung to him. He was crazy, but the best kind of crazy, and there was no question in her mind that he loved her and she loved him.

"When we get it all put back together, it will be nice for you to stay here when you come to Venice. It's not far from Paris or Rome by plane. We could come here on weekends."

"I want to work on it with you," she said, looking around, and they walked through the main floor holding hands. She was excited looking at it. It was as though the palazzo had been reborn and had come back to her with the memories and a whole new lease on life, thanks to him. There wasn't even a minute sign of the fire anywhere. "Did Francesca Viti know you bought it?" she asked, amazed.

"Not at first, but I had to tell her eventually. It got too complicated otherwise. I was afraid she'd tell you."

"She didn't. No one did."

"No one else knew. I figured that was the best way to keep a secret." He walked her into the ballroom, and spun her around, the way her father had done with her mother. She could almost hear the music, and she could feel them all smiling at her, her parents, their friends, even Gian Battista. Olivier really was her honorable friend, her amazing friend, her beloved friend.

"Did you visit Max today?" she asked him.

"No, he texted me this morning that one of his friends showed up for a visit and he told me not to come. So I decided to lend a hand here instead."

They spent two hours walking around the palazzo that was hers again, or theirs, and still got to San Marco in time to have a glass of wine to celebrate before they left for the airport and flew back to Rome for the weekend. She was sorry not to stay and work on the house with him, but she had a lot to do.

She called Allegra when she got home and told her all about it, and Allegra was as stunned as she was, and then she whispered something to Basile and giggled, and came back on the phone to talk to her sister.

"We want to get married in Venice," she said, and startled Cosima all over again.

"You do? When?" And when was she going to plan a wedding in the midst of everything else? Their plans came as a surprise.

"A year from now. Basile asked me last night. I was going to tell you. We thought next June. We have a lot to do until then. And now, can we have the reception at the palazzo?"

"I'll ask Olivier. It's his now. That's fantastic news. Next June. And congratulations to both of you." She was delighted and couldn't think of a better match for either of them.

She went to find Olivier on the terrace after she hung up. He was enjoying the moon over Rome. Cosima was beaming and looked full of mischief.

"Now I have a surprise for you," she said, mysteriously.

"What's that?" He patted the seat next to him on a little outdoor settee. She sat down and he kissed her.

"I just spoke to Allegra and told her about the palazzo. She and Basile want to get married in Venice next summer, a year from now. She'd love to have the reception at the palazzo. I said I'd ask you." She beamed. "A wedding brings the house good luck, as long as it's the right people getting married," she added, "and they are. Basile proposed to her last night."

Olivier grinned broadly. "He didn't tell me he was going to ask her." He looked very pleased.

"I guess they have their secrets too." She snuggled up next to him in the moonlight, and he looked serious.

"That's what the palazzo is for now. It's why I

bought it back for you. Of course she can have her wedding there. Is there a list one has to get on? Who books the weddings around here?"

"I have no idea," she said primly. "You own the palazzo now, so I guess you do."

"I'll put you in charge of that. I think that boat you say you missed just pulled up to the dock again. You'd better get your name on the list fast so you don't miss it again."

"Is that right?" She laughed at him. "I'm thirty-nine years old. I'll be forty next year. That's too old to get married." She sounded definite about it.

"Really? Who made that rule? I would marry you if you were a hundred years old."

"That gives me another sixty-one years to plan it, so I guess there's no rush."

He got down on one knee then, in front of her. "Sixty-one years from now, I won't be able to get up again, so I'd better do this now. Cosima Saverio, will you marry me?"

"Yes, I will," she said in a small voice. She had long since given up the idea of marriage. He sat down next to her then and kissed her and took her breath away. It had been a day of monumental surprises, and the Palazzo Saverio was theirs again, with countless delights and blessings in store in the coming years.

Chapter 15

Cosima and Olivier spent a week in Saint-Jean-Cap-Ferrat in August, and the second week working on the palazzo together. They went through her enormous storage unit just north of Venice and picked out the furniture they wanted to restore and use again. There was more than even Cosima had remembered. And she was going to use Venetian fabrics to re-cover them.

They picked fabric for curtains, and she insisted she was going to pay for all of it, since it was his money anyway, from the sale. She was going to use her share of what he had paid for the house for all the decorating.

They bought new beds and dressers, some antique mirrors, rugs at some of the rug merchants in Venice, and by the end of August, the house was livable again. The furnace was being worked on so they could use the palazzo in winter. It was going to be more comfortable than ever before.

Basile and Allegra came to see it and marveled at the condition it was in now. They ate at the big table in the kitchen that had been replaced after the fire, and Olivier had replaced the ramps with better-looking, more efficient, newer ones. The entire palazzo was accessible to Allegra now.

They all went back to Paris together to get ready for Fashion Week and the opening of the Saverio store on the Faubourg Saint-Honoré. The store looked elegant and dignified and exactly the way Cosima had envisioned it. It was in sharp contrast to the wild modernity of Allegra's store in the 8th Arrondissement, which was doing a booming business, mainly on the internet. Allegra had found her niche, and her man, and they were excited about their wedding, still nine months away. Basile had sold all the paintings from his last show. He had bought Allegra a rubellite engagement ring from what he'd made on his paintings, and it suited her perfectly.

Cosima's office and the PR firm they hired sent out invitations to the opening party at the Saverio store on the second night of Fashion Week. The champagne flowed, they had a caviar bar, several of their best customers were there, and there was a section in the store for their collaboration bags with Bayard.

Cosima floated through the evening wearing a pale silver dress that molded her figure, with high-heeled silver sandals, and her blond hair in a sleek

French twist. Olivier was beaming with pride. The store was truly beautiful and Cosima told everyone it had been Olivier's idea.

It was a glamorous, fun, profitable week. The week after, Max was released from prison, and flew home to Paris. Much to his father's relief, the job in Thailand had fallen through. He had decided to accept a job he considered beneath him in Oklahoma. It didn't sound glorious to Olivier either, but it was the best Max could do for now, as a convicted felon. Only his father's connections had gotten him the job. There was a small manufacturer of handbags there, and they'd offered him a position in marketing. It was a start on the long road back to a clean life. The owner's son had had trouble with the law, and had gone to prison too, for dealing drugs, so the owner was sympathetic and offered Max the job, with the proviso that if he screwed up or did anything shady, he'd be fired immediately. Max had no other options, and his father was no longer willing to hire, house, or support him, so he had no other choice.

Olivier put him on the plane to Tulsa, and hoped for the best, well aware that Max's success and staying on the straight and narrow was by no means a sure thing. And he had burned his last bridge with his father, who wouldn't rescue him again.

Three days after Max left for Oklahoma, Luca contacted Cosima and asked her to come and see him, which was a surprise. She hadn't seen or heard from him in a year, and she had turned his demand down flat, for what he wanted for his third of the business.

She agreed to meet with him, and went with her lawyer so there would be a witness to whatever he said. He wasn't pleased when he saw them arrive at the prison visiting area, but he had requested the meeting.

She greeted him stiffly, not sure what to expect, and he kissed her cheek and said he was happy to see her. He didn't look it, but she let it go at that.

"Are you all right in here? Is it dangerous?" she asked him, still concerned. He would always be her little brother, no matter how badly he behaved.

"It's what you make of it," he said philosophically, which she suspected was true. He seemed older, and subdued. He was still working in the prison kitchen and said he had become a pretty good cook.

"I've been thinking about your offer and was wondering if you'd reconsidered," he said hopefully.

"No, I haven't. What I offered you is a fair price for what the business is worth, for your third of it. You cost us a lot of money, Luca. I had to sell the palazzo to cover your gambling debt, and after the fire, I decided to sell it anyway. We couldn't afford to repair the damage. Because of what you did, we could collect no insurance to pay for it. And I still gave you your third of the sale price when we sold it. I've been fair with you. You haven't been fair with us."

"What part of this do you call fair?" he said angrily to her. "Two years in prison for setting a small fire in my own house?"

"It's not your house, it was *our* house, and it wasn't a small fire. You did up to two million euros' worth of damage."

"You could have withdrawn the charges, and fought for me, and I wouldn't be here."

"That's not true. The police would have prosecuted you for arson no matter what we did. And you were going to try to collect the insurance money, which was fraud."

"I did you a favor. You would have gotten part of that insurance money. You could have made a profit on it if you did the repairs cheaply or let the buyers pay for it. Then we could have kept the insurance money. It would have been a bonus for us, free money in addition to the sale. That was the whole idea. We could have sold the place *and* collected the insurance money, and let the buyers pay for the repairs." Listening to him depressed her, and made it clear how twisted his mind was. He always had an angle, and a scheme to make "easy" money, even illegally.

"It was all dishonest," she said, he still didn't get it, and didn't want to. "And you would be serving a longer sentence if Gian Battista hadn't intervened for you."

"Agh, Gian Battista and all his holier-than-thou bullshit. He was a pompous ass and he didn't do a damn thing for me. With his connections he could have gotten me off if he wanted to."

"He said he couldn't," she defended Gian Battista. "Your reputation all over Venice was too bad. You even bragged at the casino about setting the fire. At least you'll have money now from the sale of the palazzo, when you come out," she said, wondering if he still had it a year later or was spending it from prison, making bad deals.

"Life in here isn't cheap, if you want to live comfortably and be safe. I pay other inmates to protect me." She knew he had to be behaving badly if he needed protection from other criminals like him.

"So, what do you want for your third of the business?" she asked him directly while the attorney listened to the exchange. He felt bad for her as he did. He thought Luca was rotten to the core and he was sorry she had to pay him anything. So was she. Luca gave her the same number he had before, which was about four times what it was worth. She stood up when he said it. "Fine. Then we're done. It's not worth that, and you know it." Maybe it would be one day, but it wasn't yet. And he could decide to wait until then, but she suspected he wanted money now, probably for crooked deals he was making. She wondered if he was dealing drugs from inside. She knew that was common in prison.

"All right, all right, sit down. What are you offering me?" She repeated the number she had offered him in June, based on the appraisal of the business. "You cheap bitch. You can do better than that," he said angrily.

"Actually, no, I can't. We have heavy operating costs, to maintain the high quality of our product and pay our staff. What I offered you is all we can afford. If it's not good enough for you, then I'm sorry, and we're done." He was quiet for a moment and she didn't move, waiting to see what he would do. He spat at her feet, narrowly missing her shoe, and she didn't react. "Are we done?" she asked him. She didn't like being there with him, even with her lawyer present. She realized then that Luca seemed agitated and nervous, and she wondered if he was on drugs.

"Fine," he said fiercely, with a look of fury. "I'll take it. But don't expect me to thank you. You're a bitch, Cosima, you always were, acting as though you were some kind of angel sent by our parents. What did you ever do for me?"

"You mean other than support you for the last fifteen years, pay your bills, and cover your gambling debts? I tried to bring you up to be a decent human being and an honorable man. I failed abysmally. You're just a small-time crook, and you'll wind up in prison again if you don't wake up and straighten up."

"Oh, you mean like that little wimp who squealed on me? Your boyfriend's son," he said viciously.

"You turned him in first. You two deserve each other."

"How fast will I get my money?" he asked her, which made her think he really was up to no good and it was why he wanted the money now. He should have still been more than okay with his share of the money from the sale, if he hadn't spent it.

"You'll get your money as soon as I write the check." She would have preferred to give it to him in installments, but she guessed that he would prefer it in one lump sum, so she stuck with that.

"All right. Transfer it to my account today," he said nastily, as the attorney handed him the papers to sign and a pen, which Luca grabbed roughly from him. His manners, what was left of them, had vanished in jail. He had the same upbringing she and Allegra did, but one would never have known it, or even that they were related.

"There's no more money for you after this, Luca," she told him bluntly. "You're out of the business, and the palazzo. After this you're on your own."

"I am anyway," he said bitterly. "You and that pathetic cripple of a sister of ours have it all." What he said then was too much for her, and in one leap she got to her feet, crossed the small room, stared him in the eye, and slapped him as hard as she could. He didn't react, and didn't return the blow, and she wouldn't have cared if he had. The lawyer looked panicked.

"Don't you *ever, ever* speak about Allegra that way again. I don't care what you say about me, but she's a saint and an incredible, wonderful human being. *You* are dirt under her feet." She was shaking with rage and he looked mortified, which surprised the attorney. "Now sign the damn paper and we're done." He hastily scrawled his signature and handed all three copies back to her. Her slap had woken him up, she really had been like a mother to him for fifteen years, and he knew it.

He touched her arm as she turned her back to him and waited to be let out of the small room they visited him in. The lawyer had rung the buzzer, twice, for a guard, anxious to leave. "I'm sorry, Cosi," Luca muttered. He hadn't called her that since he was a child, and it touched her heart for an instant.

"So am I," she said sadly, "that it has to be like this. I hope you find your way back from all this one day." He shook his head as though even he knew it was hopeless, as the guards opened the door and he disappeared back into the bowels of the hell he lived in, without looking back at her. She walked out with her back straight and her eyes looking ahead. She thanked the attorney and took a water taxi to the station where she could get a cab to the airport and fly back to Rome.

As the plane took off over the city, she saw Venice below her, a city of dreams and mysteries, magic, hope and despair, and mourned the brother she had lost and feared she would never see again. She prayed that somewhere deep within him, there was a shred of a human being left that would surface again one day. Long ago, he had been a child loved by his parents and his sisters, before he turned into a monster. She remembered the moment he had told her he was sorry. It was a final flicker of hope that had gone out just as quickly. And now it felt like he was dead.

Chapter 16

Allegra and Basile were married at the Chiesa di San Moisè near the Piazza San Marco on a brilliantly sunny day in June. It was the second anniversary of the day Cosima and Olivier had met. Cosima walked beside her sister as she rolled down the aisle in her grandmother's exquisite antique lace dress with the train behind her, draped over the back of her wheelchair. And she wore a nineteenth-century pearl tiara on her dark hair. As the head of the family, Cosima gave her away, and then took her place next to Olivier in the front pew. The church was filled with lily of the valley. Allegra and Basile had chosen San Moisè because there were no stairs for Allegra to negotiate in her chair. The ceremony was solemn as they sat beside each other in two huge chairs at the altar, and the music they had chosen was beautiful. After he kissed the bride, Basile stood up, swept her into his arms, light as a feather, and walked down the aisle triumphantly carrying her, with the train of her gown trailing behind them and Allegra laughing. One of the ushers folded her chair and took it away, as everyone marveled at how perfect they were together.

All two hundred guests, mostly from Rome, many from Paris, and a few from Venice, rode to the Palazzo Saverio in gondolas decorated with white flowers. The bridal boat was covered by a canopy of white orchids and lily of the valley.

It was a spectacular wedding, and a jubilant celebration. The guests danced until five in the morning to an orchestra Cosima had had sent from Rome. Basile held Allegra in his arms and spun her around the dance floor. And there was a wedding breakfast at six in the morning, which lasted until seven. When the sun was well up in the sky, the guests repaired to their various hotels and yachts to recover from the celebration. The wedding feast had been one of the best Cosima had ever tasted, and the wedding cake a white spun-sugar fantasy flecked with gold. There was caviar in abundant quantities at the wedding breakfast. Olivier had selected all the best French wines.

Every moment of the wedding was perfection, and best of all was the obvious love between Basile and Allegra. They stayed at the palazzo that night and left on their honeymoon the next morning, with Olivier and Cosima and a few lingering friends who had stayed at the palazzo throwing rose petals at them. It was everything Allegra had said she wanted and that Cosima had hoped it would be. It was yet another memory for all of them to cherish forever. The sacred union of Allegra and Basile.

On New Year's Day, a hundred of the same people came together again. The ceremony was at Santa Maria dei Miracoli Church near the Rialto Bridge. Its interior and exterior were decorated with magnificent colored marble, with a gilded ceiling. The church was filled with light. Olivier and Cosima wanted a smaller wedding, but it was just as beautiful as Allegra's and more intimate. The choir sang, and they both cried when they exchanged their vows. The gondolas took them all from the church on the "Rio dei Miracoli" canal to the Grand Canal and to the Palazzo Saverio with the bridal gondola leading. Cosima was wearing her mother's wedding gown, which they had found in a trunk in storage, perfectly preserved, with the original lace veil, and the pearl tiara Allegra had worn, and generations of Saverio women before her. Even her mother's embroidered handmade white satin shoes in a Renaissance style fit her.

When they joined their guests, Cosima and Olivier came down the grand staircase arm in arm just as Cosima's parents had at their wedding. The wedding dinner was sumptuous, the wines perfect again. They danced all night, and the wedding ended at four in the morning. It was snowing as the guests left, light flurries like tiny angels blessing them. Every moment of the night had been perfect and exactly what Cosima and Olivier wanted. The people they loved most had come. Allegra was six months pregnant, with a son. Cosima and Olivier had agreed to see what would happen without trying, after they married, and would be fine either way.

When the last guest had left, they stood together in the immense doorway of the palazzo, watching the snow. It was the perfect beginning to a new day, a new year, a new life. Olivier handed Cosima a small, neat box wrapped in silver paper.

"What's that?" she asked him. He had given her a diamond bracelet as a wedding present, which she had worn to the wedding. She unwrapped the box carefully, and there was a large heavy metal key in it, ornate and partially rusted. She looked at him, puzzled, and then realized what it was. It was the original key to the palazzo. He had found it when he was renovating the house after he bought it. And folded into the box was the deed to the palazzo. It was hers now. He was returning it to her. It was her history and her heritage.

"It was always meant to be yours," he said simply. "I just borrowed it for a while as gatekeeper to return it to you in good order." He kissed her and she smiled up at him, and together they closed the heavy door of the palazzo and walked up the grand staircase to their bedroom, with the train of her wedding dress trailing behind her down the stairs.

They had made memories that night, and history in the life of Palazzo Saverio as six centuries of her ancestors blessed them. As man and wife, they were the guardians of the palazzo now, and its history. They were part of Venice, with all its magic and mystery, as he kissed her. Their adventure together, their own history, and the memories they would share, had only just begun.

About the Author

DANIELLE STEEL has been hailed as one of the world's bestselling authors, with a billion copies of her novels sold. Her many international bestsellers include *Never Too Late, Upside Down, The Ball at Versailles, Second Act, Happiness, Palazzo, The Wedding Planner, Worthy Opponents,* and other highly acclaimed novels. She is also the author of *His Bright Light,* the story of her son Nick Traina's life and death; *A Gift of Hope,* a memoir of her work with the homeless; *Expect a Miracle,* a book of her favorite quotations for inspiration and comfort; *Pure Joy,* about the dogs she and her family have loved; and the children's books *Pretty Minnie in Paris* and *Pretty Minnie in Hollywood.*

daniellesteel.com
Facebook.com/DanielleSteelOfficial
Twitter: @daniellesteel
Instagram: @officialdaniellesteel

Look for

Only the Brave

Coming soon in hardcover

Chapter 1

Even at eighteen, in 1937, Sophia Alexander knew that things in Germany had changed in the past four years since the Nazis had come to power. There had been many changes in her life too, although her family was not Jewish. They were defined now as "Aryan." These days, with even one Jewish grandparent, whether by faith or origin, a person was considered non-Aryan.

Sophia's life in Berlin had altered dramatically ever since her mother fell ill with tuberculosis when she was sixteen, two years earlier. She had been cared for at home for the first year of her illness and was now in a sanatorium for people with tuberculosis. Sophia visited her several times a week. Her younger sister Theresa, sixteen now, went to see her less often, and her father was so busy he hardly had time to visit. Sophia was the family member who went the most frequently. She was a serious student, but always made time to see her mother, as often as she could. Sophia and Theresa went to the same school. Sophia was in the final months of high school, and Theresa had two more years after this one and hated every moment she spent in class. Sophia was a star student.

Their mother, Monika Alexander, was a gentle person, and had always had fragile health. She was a delicate beauty, and adored her daughters. Sophia had long, serious talks with her, and often read to her, as her mother lay in her bed with her eyes closed until she fell asleep, and then Sophia would leave. As soon as her mother was taken to the sanatorium, Sophia had promised her that she would take care of her sister and father, and she had kept her promise and grown up quickly. When she turned eighteen, she had learned to drive. Her father let her use the car, which made Sophia's visits easier, since the sanatorium was outside the city.

Sophia's father, Thomas Alexander, was a famous surgeon, and had his own private hospital. People came to see him for complicated procedures from all over Europe. He practiced general surgery and was highly skilled. It frustrated him that he couldn't cure his wife, but with rest and the medicines available to them, he was hoping she would have a full recovery. Sophia was worried about her. Her mother seemed so frail. She slept a great deal but awoke with delight when her oldest daughter was visiting her, which she did faithfully.

At home, Sophia had taken full charge of her

sister, who needed a strong hand to manage her. Theresa took full advantage of how busy their father was and her mother's absence to flirt with every man who crossed her path. Men seemed to fall at her feet like ripe apples, much to her older sister's amazement. Sophia had always been shy, like her mother. She was a dark-haired beauty with huge green eyes, and always looked serious. The men who pursued Theresa didn't notice Sophia, and she wasn't a flirt. If one looked closely, Sophia was in fact more beautiful. She had perfect aristocratic features, a long, graceful neck, and elegant posture. Theresa's looks were showier and caught one's attention faster. She had almost white blond hair like their mother, translucent porcelain-white skin, which she dusted with powder, full red lips, and brilliant blue eyes the color of a summer sky. She had a wide, instant smile, perfect teeth, and a sensuous figure. She always looked like she was about to laugh. She teased the boys she knew relentlessly. Her long blond hair fell in thick waves. Sophia's shining dark hair fell straight past her shoulders. She had a slim build like her father, and she kept a stern eye on her sister, as she had promised their mother. She kept her on a short leash and Theresa complained about it constantly.

Theresa meant no harm with her flirting and enticing laughter, and she had little awareness that her natural sexiness was an aphrodisiac to the men who wanted her. Her father assumed it was all harmless and would come to nothing. Sophia wasn't as sure. Their mother thought that Theresa should marry early before she got into more mischief than she could handle. She would need a strong husband to control her. But at sixteen she was still too young to be considered marriage material, and had to finish school. So Sophia played watchdog at the palace gates, waiting for their mother's return, and she hoped it would be soon.

It had been a long year for all of them without Monika, particularly for Sophia. Theresa was enjoying it, although she missed her mother too. She loved to go dancing, and to parties, but her opportunities were limited due to her age. Their parents had stopped entertaining when Monika got sick. Before that, there had been many elegant dinner parties at their home, filled with women in beautiful evening gowns. Theresa crept into her mother's dressing room sometimes and tried on her mother's gowns. When Sophia found her doing it, she scolded her soundly.

"That's Mama's! Take it off immediately! You'll tear it." Several of their mother's most beautiful dresses had been made for her in Paris, others by dressmakers in Berlin. As the wife of the most important surgeon in Berlin, they were invited everywhere, to the most dazzling events. Thomas Alexander was greatly respected. Sophia had loved watching her parents dance with each other, when they gave formal dinner parties at home for important guests.

She knew her father loved his wife very much, but his work kept him from visiting her as often as he wished. Sophia wanted to help him too, and aside from running the house for him now, she worked as a volunteer in his hospital after school and on weekends, after she finished her studies. Her father marveled at how efficient she was, how bright and how dedicated. She had a talent for nursing. Sophia said she would become a nurse one day and work for him in the operating theater. Theresa just wanted to get married and have babies. She hadn't met her future husband yet, but she enjoyed all the attention men lavished on her, as they flew around her like bees approaching a beautiful flower. No one could resist her, and she loved it.

Theresa had no real interest in the boys in school, but flirted with them too. She had an easy way with men, which they found enchanting. Sophia was harder to talk to. She was serious, and spoke to them of important subjects which required them to think rather than just admire her. She spoke of recent medical discoveries, her father's flawless surgical techniques, books she had read on many topics, which usually didn't interest most men, or she spoke of the political unrest in Germany for the past few years. Her father had cautioned her several times not to engage in discussions about politics. It was a sensitive subject in Germany now, with the strengthening of the Nazi party in the last four years. Adolf Hitler had become Führer three years before, in 1934. Privately, Thomas didn't admire his zeal, but he kept his opinions to himself, and was busy with his private clinic. He had operated on several members of the Nazi High Command and had met the Führer himself, but what interested Thomas Alexander was medicine, not politics.

The changes in Germany had troubled Sophia for several years, even before her mother got sick. People with even partial Jewish origins had been singled out and discriminated against. In the beginning, in 1933, when Sophia was fourteen, Jews were suddenly barred from being teachers, professors, judges, or civil servants, and many had lost their jobs. Several of the teachers at her school had quietly disappeared without saying goodbye, which made her suddenly aware of what was going on. Months later, people of Jewish faith or origin were excluded from the arts, then from owning land, and were forbidden from being journalists or newspaper editors. All within a year. And by the end of 1933, homeless and unemployed people were sent to concentration camps that were being opened near Munich. Dachau had opened in 1933, Sachsenhausen, close to Berlin in 1936, and Buchenwald a year later in 1937. No one spoke of it openly, but one heard about it in whispers. A girl in her class had told her. She had heard her journalist uncle talking about it with her father, and they thought the camps were a good idea to get undesirable elements of the population off the streets, which was the Nazis' intention.

By the following year, in 1934, when Sophia was fifteen, she learned that Jews were denied health insurance, and prohibited from becoming lawyers. And the year after Hitler became Führer in 1934, when Sophia was sixteen, Jews were banned from the military. They lost their citizenship and could no longer marry Aryans. A few months before, they had been forbidden to work as accountants or dentists. The list of professions they were not allowed to engage in grew longer every day. Sophia's father had to find the family a new dentist when theirs left Germany, saying that this was only the beginning of worse things to come, which her father thought was an extreme point of view.

Sophia talked to her mother about it at times, and removed from the world, Monika found it shocking. Some of the physicians they knew were Jewish, but Sophia's father said nothing would happen to them, they were respected important men, as he was. In his opinion, doctors would always be exempt from political actions because they were so highly educated, honored, and desperately needed for their skills. Thomas had warned Sophia repeatedly not to talk about such things outside the family, and he scolded her for thinking about it at all. Her mother never scolded her. She shared Sophia's concerns about the ruling party taking such harsh positions.

"How far do you think it will go?" Sophia asked her one day, since they were alone and could talk freely.

"I suppose it's gone as far as it can by now, but I do feel sorry for those people who have lost their jobs and their livelihoods and have families to take care of. The Nazis just want to show people how powerful they are. I'm sure they'll relax the rules in time." Sophia was never as sure, but she didn't want to frighten her mother. She had seen people rounded up in Berlin, and dragged away for deportation, with their children crying and police beating them.

Every year, more people Sophia knew had disappeared, all Jews, and some of her friends' fathers had lost jobs. A dentist, an accountant, a well-known journalist—none of them were dangerous, but all were Jewish. Even some of her classmates said nasty things about the Jews now, when they had been friends before. It seemed so wrong to her, and so hypocritical. How could their friends become their enemies overnight?

"Don't talk to Papa about it," Monika warned Sophia again, and she promised not to. Her father didn't care about anything but his hospital anyway. Medicine was all that interested him. He lived in a rarefied, isolated world, in his operating theater, saving people's lives with surgery. He didn't care what religion they were. If they were sick, he helped them heal. If they needed surgery, he operated on them. Illness was the great equalizer, just as it was for her mother with TB. Sophia's father was a scientist above all, and cared deeply about his patients. Government policies were of no interest to him.

Sophia had always been profoundly disturbed by all forms of injustice, and had compassion for those less fortunate, almost as though she felt guilty for how well she and her family lived and what they had. Theresa thought it was ridiculous and made fun of her for it. "Why don't you give them your clothes then?" she teased her. "They probably wouldn't want them anyway." Sophia dressed in somber colors and simple clothes not to show off. Theresa longed for her mother's Paris gowns and snuck them into her own closets whenever she could, now that her mother was gone. She planned to put them back when her mother returned. Sophia got angry at her sister whenever she caught her wearing something of their mother's. She recognized the items immediately, beautiful alligator handbags, or exquisite French kid gloves, delicately beaded sweaters, or a well-cut coat, which Theresa was too young to wear. But she was dying to be fashionable and grown-up. Their father paid no attention to things like that, and often Theresa got away with it, if Sophia was working at the hospital, visiting their mother, or out, when Theresa raided her mother's closets.

They lived in an extremely comfortable, luxurious home, which Monika had decorated beautifully, with art that she and Thomas had inherited from their families, and things they bought. They had built the house when he had built his hospital many years before. It was large and handsome, and suited his respected position in the community. Sophia was embarrassed by how well they lived, which Theresa thought was ridiculous. Sophia thought the trappings of wealth, which were second nature to them, set them apart from others in a negative way. She had always been drawn to religion even as a child, and this too made her different from her family. Her father openly admitted that he did not believe in God. He believed in science and medicine, and a surgeon's skill, not a higher power. Theresa said that church bored her, and avoided it whenever possible, and only since she had been ill had Monika's beliefs grown stronger. She and Sophia talked about it at times. Sophia had a faith which nothing could shake. Her father blamed it on a nanny they had had when Sophia was very young. He had eventually fired her for filling Sophia's head with ideas that he considered nonsense and beliefs he didn't share and thought were dangerous. Sophia had been sad when she left, but her beliefs remained the same. If anything, they grew stronger. She never spoke of them in the presence of her father and kept them to herself, but they were there, a powerful, comforting force in her life. Sometimes she went to church on her own and prayed for her mother. Monika always seemed better to her after she did. But in spite of occasional brief respites, Monika's health had deteriorated in the last year. Sophia was terrified that she would die. Monika was

peaceful and philosophical about it, and always reassured her. Sophia wanted to believe that she
would come home soon. Her father said so too,
and he never lied. He was an honest man, even if
he didn't believe in God.